DEATH AT CHATEAU PEVERIL

RUSSELL WATE

CRANTHORPE
—MILLNER—
PUBLISHERS

Copyright © Russell Wate (2023)

The right of Russell Wate to be identified as author of this work has been asserted by them in accordance with section 77 and 78 of the Copyright, Designs and Patents Act 1988.

All rights reserved. No part of this publication may be reproduced, stored in a retrieval system, or transmitted in any form or by any means, electronic, mechanical, photocopying, recording, or otherwise, without the prior permission of the publishers.

Any person who commits any unauthorised act in relation to this publication may be liable to criminal prosecution and civil claims for damages.

This book is a work of fiction. Names, characters, places and incidents are either products of the author's imagination or are used fictitiously. Any resemblance to actual events or locales or persons, living or dead, is entirely coincidental.

First published by Cranthorpe Millner Publishers (2023)

ISBN 978-1-80378-165-5 (Paperback)

www.cranthorpemillner.com

Cranthorpe Millner Publishers

This book is dedicated to my wife
Deborah

Foreword

This is a story about a detective, his skills and the process involved to investigate homicide. It shows us that detective as a man, his family and his life. The book is also a travelogue as seen through his eyes.

∞

The investigation branch within the Foreign, Commonwealth and Development Office described in this novel is fictional and is not currently or will ever be real in the format I have described within the story. They do have very gifted police superintendents who work there on a seconded basis as liaison officers and they do all they can to support families and police forces. They work with a murder and manslaughter team within the FCDO.

∞

My absolute thoughts and wishes go to all those families who have lost loved ones abroad and the nightmare they face in trying to come to terms with and understand it, as well as having to plan for their loved ones to be returned to the UK.

Chapter One

There was a lot of moaning and groaning as Alexander (Sandy) McFarlane eased himself into a seat on the train that he was taking from Ely to London, where he worked. Everybody sitting nearby that Monday morning would have had no doubt that the man moaning and groaning was in a high level of physical discomfort. Sandy's father, Gregor, who was sitting opposite to him and who also worked in London, while trying his best not to laugh, just smiled and said, 'Sandy, you really are feeling the effects of your triathlon yesterday, aren't you?' Even though Gregor had tried to say this to his son in a sympathetic way, unfortunately, it had not sounded like that at all.

'Actually, Dad, for your information,' an indignant Sandy said, 'it is not from the triathlon, it is from playing a full eighty minutes of rugby on Saturday.' Sandy played rugby for the Ely Tigers second team if they had a game when he was at home in Ely. 'The pain from completing the triathlon is probably not going to kick in until tomorrow,' he said while grimacing and shaking his head.

Now, not concealing his laughter at all, Gregor said, 'Well, you and Hannah did a fantastic job completing the triathlon in a very good time and for such a good cause. Your mum, sisters and I loved watching and cheering you both on and we especially enjoyed celebrating afterwards at the Cutter Inn.'

Sandy and his girlfriend, Hannah Tobias, had taken part

in a triathlon on the Sunday on behalf of a charity set up in the name of a police officer who had been killed in the line of duty. The police officer had formerly been a Grenadier Guard so the charity was to raise money to support veterans from the various guard regiments. The Ely Tri Club had helped to set up their sub-event with the main triathlon happening in Derby, where the police officer that had been killed had lived and worked.

'Have you got much work on this week?' Gregor asked. 'Let's hope not as you look like you are probably going to physically suffer the whole week through,' he said, unable to stop laughing again.

'No, not really,' Sandy said, wincing as he tried to stretch his legs out under the table. 'Just paperwork and several meetings.' Sandy was a detective chief inspector based in London and he worked for the Foreign, Commonwealth and Development Office in their consulate investigation team.

As the train pulled into Cambridge railway station it became a lot busier, and much to Sandy's evident upset, an extremely large man almost fell into the seat next to him. As the man pushed along the seat, he banged into the stiffness in Sandy's legs and arms, who, after being barged into, made a yelping sound in pain. It was at this point that the phone in Sandy's pocket started to buzz extremely loudly. The large man sitting next to him – in fact by this stage practically sitting all over him – looked pointedly at Sandy as he could also hear the phone buzzing. It was as if he was saying, 'Are you going to answer your phone or not?' Sandy had decided to ignore his phone and took a large sip of his tea instead. He had a feeling that today wasn't going to go too well for him at all, which made him almost gulp down his by now only warm cup of tea, looking for some comfort from it.

When his phone went off again almost immediately, Sandy, with a huge amount of effort, managed to make a little bit of room for himself by pushing hard away from the large man and extracted the phone from his trouser pocket and answered it. 'Sandy, it's me, Arabella Montague.' Sandy didn't need telling who it was as he recognised the voice immediately. 'I wondered if you are going to be in London today?' Arabella said. 'I want to talk to you about the death of my father.' Arabella's father was the late Viscount Peveril who had died three weeks ago at Chateau Peveril near Bordeaux in France.

'I was so sorry to hear about your father's sudden death.' Sandy had sent a text message offering his sincere condolences to both Arabella and her brother, James, who was an MP but also now the new Viscount Peveril. 'I am just on my way into London and should be available late morning, but can you come to me please as I have some afternoon meetings I really can't get out of,' Sandy replied.

'How about coffee at St James's Café near to the FCDO building in St James's Park at eleven a.m., would that be OK for you?' Arabella asked.

'Yes, that will be fine, and I know it's a nice day but please don't go up onto the rooftop terrace of the café as I am not sure steps and me are going to get on too well for a few days I am afraid,' Sandy said, as he carefully stretched his aching legs out again underneath the table, this time knocking into his dad's feet as he did so.

∞

St James's Park is one of a number of London's Royal Parks and covers almost fifty-seven acres. Places such as the Mall and Buckingham Palace are all part of the area around St James's Park, which is often full of tourists and Londoners going about their daily business, whether this is for their work or leisure. As Sandy walked across Horse Guards Road, having just passed the statue of Clive of India in Great Charles Street, he looked across at the park and could see what an incredible and wonderful space it was, situated right in the heart of London and so close to where he was based in the FCDO main building. If people thought he was a very lucky man, well he most certainly was.

While he was walking, Sandy seemed to be moving a lot more freely; it was just the sitting or staying still for long periods of time that was making him painfully stiffen up. He had led the Monday morning team meeting, which had gone smoothly, and he had managed to sign off all the cases the team had of the British people who had died abroad that needed to be filed as needing no further investigation. This was something that the consulate investigation team did on behalf of police forces in Britain, where one of their residents had died abroad and their families wanted further investigations into the circumstances of their loved one's death. Sandy was actually quite free of work at the moment, except for a couple of meetings to be held later that day that he had to attend on behalf of his boss, Detective Superintendent Jane Watson, as she was on leave.

As he neared St James's Café, he could see ahead that Arabella was about to sit down at a table outside the café and she was carrying two large coffee cups. Sandy had got to know Arabella and her family really well when her brother James's young adult son, George, had gone missing, and Sandy had tried on their behalf to find him. As he got closer, he saw that Arabella was dressed in what was best described as a pink tweed jacket, and she was wearing a pink scarf and had on a pink hairband over her dyed streaked blonde hair. He felt pleased he had put on a pink tie himself that morning to go with a fairly boring grey suit. It would appear that he was matching the uniform required for the meeting.

After saying hello to each other and Arabella telling Sandy that her husband, Charles (Monty) Montague, was at home at Peveril Farm in Norfolk, Sandy asked her, 'What did you want to talk to me about in relation to your father?'

Arabella was the CEO of Peveril's, a multi-million-pound company that grew and sold on an industrial scale linseed, and, of course, wine from the vineyard in Bordeaux, as well as a number of other business interests. She started to cry, not sobbing, but tears were clearly running down her face. Her extremely professional veneer had cracked in an instant and she said, 'I know I can rationalise how I am feeling by acknowledging that I have lost my father suddenly, so I am grieving, and I need to accept it only happened so recently. So, I must give it time.' Arabella took the tissues that Sandy was offering her and after dabbing her eyes and wiping her cheeks, she very quickly regained her composure. 'I just feel that there is something not right about it. My gut feeling is telling me that something happened to him that caused him to die so suddenly.'

'Gut feeling is actually really important and something that we shouldn't ignore in detective work,' Sandy interjected, trying to reassure Arabella. 'It normally comes about after years of experience where your brain has processed similar information hundreds of times before that gives you that feeling. Some people define it as judgement. There is even a number of research papers that have been published to back it up as being a legitimate feeling. It is not just a bad feeling in your stomach.' This comment brought a smile to Arabella's face. 'We just need to back it up with evidence though,' Sandy said.

'I have no evidence for you, Sandy, just the feeling something is not right about his death. My father's wife, Monica, has shown no emotion whenever I have seen her since my father died,' Arabella said, smiling sheepishly. 'In fact, I now feel somewhat foolish for mentioning it to you, but Monty and James, both told me that I needed to talk to someone about it and we all simultaneously thought that someone had to be you.'

Sandy took a large sip of the coffee that Arabella had bought him. He actually preferred tea but was enjoying the coffee in the very pleasant surroundings of St James's Park on a bright, but not too cold, late March morning. He took a pen out of his pocket in an almost flourishing movement and opened his new, fresh notebook where he had already written on the front: 'The death of Viscount William Harrison Peveril.'

∞

Looking straight at Arabella and leaving her in no doubt they were now moving into a detective and witness phase of their conversation, Sandy said, 'I am sorry, there is no strict set of rules on how people will react when a loved one dies.' Arabella nodded, accepting what he had just said.

'Let's go through some facts that you do know. When was the last time you saw your father?'

'What, alive or dead?' Arabella said, looking a little startled as a bad memory and experience crossed her mind. 'I saw him in a chapel of rest twice, once at the undertakers in Bordeaux and then in Derbyshire shortly before he was buried.'

'OK,' Sandy said, realising that he had worded the first question badly and the emotion of talking about the death of her father was clearly going to affect Arabella. Sandy was experienced in talking to family members of loved ones who had died, but he realised that he was mixing up his relationship with a friend and trying to be a detective in the case. He now needed to be more detective and less friend and asked, 'Sorry, when was the last time you saw him alive, please?'

'It was at Peveril House in Eaton Square in London before he went to France with Monica. Probably the twenty-first or the twenty-second of February. James and his family were there as well as it had been half- term that week for his two girls.'

That helps with when James would have last seen him as well, thought Sandy. 'How did your father seem to you?'

'He was fine, complaining about a bad back and worried about driving down to France with his back hurting him. Monica was agreeing to do some of the driving, which was strange as she never drove anywhere, but she seemed happy to do it,' Arabella replied, while at the same time putting on a pair of sunglasses as the late March sunlight had turned quite bright.

'Did you speak to him in France at all?'

'I did, but James unfortunately didn't. He had meant to

call to ensure they had got there safely but got busy and didn't get round to it and now regrets it.'

Not knowing for sure, as he couldn't remember when he had seen it reported in the press that Viscount Peveril had died, Sandy asked, 'Sorry to ask two things together but when was the phone call and when did your father die?'

'I spoke to him on the evening of the twenty-sixth of February and he seemed to be fine, enjoying the food and wine. His back had got worse and Monica, who was making visits to the nearby town of Saint-Émilion, had got him some strong painkillers, which I think were helping him.' Arabella had forgotten the second part to the question and when she saw Sandy waiting, suddenly remembered and said, 'He died on Monday the first of March.'

'Arabella, how did you find out that he had died?'

'I received a lot of phone calls on that day, but the first one telling me my father had died was from Antoine Chevalier.'

Sandy glanced at his watch, and then on looking round to see that there were only two people in the queue at the café counter, decided that it would be best to get something to eat now before he would have to rush to his first afternoon meeting. 'Arabella, do you want a sandwich or a piece of cake and another drink at all?' Sandy had stood up quite gingerly as he had now stiffened up again. He bought a sandwich, a cup of tea and the requested chocolate cake and coffee for Arabella.

Munching on his food but still able to speak, Sandy asked, 'Who is Antoine then, is he one of the gendarmes from Saint-Émilion?'

'Monsieur Chevalier has been with us for twenty-five years. He is an incredible combination of house manager, caretaker and butler, all rolled into one, for the house in France. His wife Claudette is the cook, and in essence, our housekeeper. They have nothing to do with the winery though. We have another manager for that part of the business.'

'What did he tell you had happened?'

'In-between his tears – he was very upset as he regards all of us as his family – he told me that my father had died of a heart attack.'

'Who told him that, was it a doctor or the local gendarme?'

'I think it must have been a combination of all of them that said it was a heart attack, and of course Monica told him this too, then she told me that this is what had happened.'

Sandy was not sure, having heard that the late Viscount Peveril had died of a heart attack, that there was much more he needed to know. It seemed pretty straightforward that Arabella's father had died of a natural cause and there were no suspicious circumstances involved. He did ask though, 'Did you see the post-mortem report, is that what it said in it?'

'I never saw it, but it must have said that.' Arabella watched as Sandy put his pen away and closed his notebook, and could see by his body language that their conversation and the result of her gut feeling was coming to an end. She said in closing, 'His death certificate had written on it "cardiac arrest".'

Chapter Two

Taking a slightly longer route back to the FCDO offices, Sandy walked through Horse Guards Parade, which is a ceremonial parade ground on the outside edge of St James's Park and the place where a huge traditional pageant called 'Trooping the Colour' takes place every June, to mark the queen's official birthday.

Horse Guards dates from the eighteenth century. Sandy had always felt that the architecture of the buildings of Horse Guards was magnificent, and he particularly liked the large clock tower over the archway, which he looked up at as he walked towards Whitehall. Sandy paused as he walked into Whitehall so that he could join all of the other tourists, who were stopping to look at the incredibly smartly dressed two mounted cavalry troopers of The Queen's Life Guard. They were sitting on two equally magnificent horses, who were posted there to guard the entrance. He walked past the entrance to Downing Street, where the Prime Minister resided, and around into the FCDO.

After he had finished his meetings, Sandy walked into the open-plan offices that housed, as well as other teams, the consulate investigation team. Sitting at a desk was DS Juliet Ashton, who was the DS that Sandy normally worked with. Juliet asked, 'How did you get on with Arabella Montague?' Juliet had known about the meeting as Sandy had mentioned it to her at that morning's team meeting and she knew Arabella from when they were trying to find her nephew, George. 'Have we got a trip to the chateau in Bordeaux for ourselves?'

'No trip, I am afraid. Viscount Peveril died of a heart attack.'

'Is that what it said on the post-mortem report then, that he had a bad heart?'

'No one has seen the report as far as I can make out.'

'Well, I think we should go to France for a couple of days to find out,' Juliet said, smiling. It was clear she was desperate for a trip. 'You are in charge this week while the superintendent is on leave, you could just authorise it.'

Smiling back at Juliet and really tempted, Sandy said, 'So, when teacher is out of the classroom the children play, is that it?'

'Yes, exactly!'

'I am sorry, I just can't justify it.'

'But you could if Viscount James Peveril MP asked you to look into his father's death. You know how Jane Watson likes to keep MPs on side and especially important ones like James,' Juliet said, looking at Sandy imploringly with her big brown eyes.

Sandy had no alternative but to give in. Juliet, as well as being an experienced detective, was also an extremely persuasive one. Not that he really needed much persuasion to have a trip to France, especially as it was so quiet in the office that week. Sandy rang James straight away.

'My Lord, it is DCI McFarlane,' Sandy said when the phone was answered. 'Have you got a few moments to talk through the circumstances of your father's death please?'

'Sandy, good to hear from you. Please call me James, and I heard from my sister Arabella this afternoon that you think the matter of his death is closed.'

'I do think so, but there a few unanswered questions in our mind. Seeing the post-mortem report or speaking to the pathologist would answer them.'

'Any autopsy would have taken place in France, not here. It would be in Bordeaux, as that is where his body first went. We never knew he had any heart problems so it was a surprise to us. He had a full medical check-up only a couple of years ago and he was deemed physically sound.'

'That was actually going to be my next question. Do you know what tablets he was taking for his bad back?' Sandy asked, hoping that the remainders of these had come back with the late Viscount's property from France.

'No, they were apparently bought in Saint-Émilion, not sure from where, but there are only one or two chemists there.' James paused for a few moments as he could pick up some hesitancy in Sandy's voice, then said, 'You couldn't go to France to iron out some of these queries, could you?'

This had turned out easier than Sandy thought, but he realised what a perceptive man James Peveril was, so just maybe he sussed what Sandy was alluding to. In order to ease his own conscious of not being used by the Peveril family, Sandy asked, 'James, is this concern about your father's death all about not letting Monica have shares in the Peveril family business?'

'Fair question.' Good, so he isn't offended then, Sandy thought. 'No, Monica will get no shares. It is all tied up in the family – Arabella and I now increase our stake to being equal partners.'

'So, Monica won't get anything then?' That rules out a motive, thought Sandy, that's if it was, by any chance, a suspicious death.

'She will, though,' James said, 'get several hundred thousand pounds of my father's personal money, but has to share it with my father's second wife. I don't know the details of his will at the moment.'

∞

The Eurostar to Paris departed from St Pancras International railway station. The trains were extremely modern and after travelling through the Channel Tunnel, they can travel at speeds of up to two hundred miles per hour. The early morning train was exceptionally busy and the waiting area and platform was very crowded with families who had lots of excited children, helping to raise the noise levels. The Easter holidays had arrived early and from the conversations overheard on the platform, the destination for the families was Disneyland Paris. How exciting for those children and their families!

The standard premier carriage was a lot quieter than the platform had been, and the breakfast was very welcome as Sandy hadn't had the time that morning to have breakfast. The train time from London to Paris was only two hours and twenty minutes. Sandy was regretting that he hadn't been able to pop into his favourite bookshop, Heffers, in Cambridge, to pick up a couple of guidebooks for the Bordeaux region of France. Juliet had her laptop open and was busy working to clear some outstanding emails and reports. Sandy busied himself messaging his girlfriend, Hannah, who was a barrister and was at court in Nottingham. She was complaining about her stiffness following Sunday's triathlon. Sandy was pretending to her that he wasn't struggling with any stiffness himself.

When they got to Paris, they needed to change stations. The train to Bordeaux went from Paris Montparnasse rather than Gare du Nord, which was the station at which they had arrived. Sandy felt if they walked really quickly, they would also get a chance to experience a small bit of Paris, but Juliet was having none of it. Not wanting to try and negotiate the Metro, they took a taxi, which, due to the heavy traffic that morning, only made their journey a slow trip to their new station.

As they approached the entrance to the station, there was a young lady standing there grinning at them. She had on bright red, round rimmed glasses and had black, very curly hair. How she was dressed though was what stood out the most. The green and red check skirt suit looked good, but the green tights made the whole outfit stand out. She walked straight up to Sandy and said, 'Good morning, DCI McFarlane, it is going to be great to work with you.' Sandy had no idea who she was, although he thought she was vaguely familiar. Juliet, extending her hand to the young lady for a handshake, said, 'I presume you are Miss Saffron Dupont?'

Sandy was looking very bemused and unsure who Saffron was, how she knew him, and even more importantly, why she thought she was working with them. 'Please call me Saffy. Shall we go through to catch our train?'

As they followed Saffy into the station, Sandy mouthed to Juliet, 'Who is she?' Juliet didn't get a chance to answer as they had to run and get onto their train that was about to leave.

Saffy sat opposite Sandy so he asked her directly,

'Saffy, how do you know me?'

A doe-eyed Saffy, which made Juliet smile knowingly, replied, 'I work for the FCDO based in the British Consulate here in Paris, but before January this year I was based in London and I used to see you there.'

Even though he was oblivious, Juliet knew that Sandy, who was just over six foot tall and very athletic, with strawberry blond hair, was very popular with a lot of the young, and not so young, female civil servants. Juliet said to Saffy, 'I am sorry to say he has a girlfriend,' then said to Sandy, 'I thought we would need some help as neither of us speak French, nor do we understand French processes, hence we have Saffy with us.'

Sandy straight away gave an appreciative nod to Juliet; he knew what a good decision this was by her. He remembered his maternal grandfather, a retired detective inspector, telling him of a murder enquiry he knew about where two senior detectives went to France to follow a key lead on the main suspect. However, neither of them spoke a word of French and they lost crucial time on the investigation, which the suspect could have taken advantage of, and no doubt did take advantage of. 'How long have you worked for the FCDO then, Saffy?' Sandy asked, thinking that she only looked eighteen years old at the most, but knew she must be older.

'I am on the civil service fast-track graduate scheme and on the FCO, as it was when I joined, graduate stream. It will be two years this summer. I know I have done really well to get a posting to a major consulate this early in my career, but I have a French father and being able to speak fluent French definitely helped.'

'Where did you go to university?' Juliet asked.

'My college was St John's at Cambridge.'

Sandy nearly fell off his seat as that was his college at Cambridge, which, when he told Saffy, made her even more doe-eyed at Sandy. Juliet couldn't help herself and laughed aloud at how uncomfortable Sandy was looking.

∞

Saffy told them that Bordeaux had parts of it that were the world's largest UNESCO urban heritage site, and after Paris, it had more listed buildings than any other French city. The architecture in some of the districts originated from the eighteenth century. Saffy had clearly completed some research and was demonstrating what a smart young lady she was. It turned out that she had a serious boyfriend and she was teasing Sandy a little bit with her approach to him.

The journey from Paris to Bordeaux only took just over two hours and the train was aptly named the 'bullet train' as it hurtled through the French countryside. The main train station in Bordeaux, Gare Saint-Jean, was itself a magnificent building and retained a lot of its grandeur from when it had been originally built in 1855.

They only had time to book into their hotel rooms and drop off their bags, to make sure that they made their first appointment at the hospital mortuary. The FCDO business admin had done well by putting them in a hotel just off the Place de la Bourse, which was meant to be Bordeaux's most elegant square. Sandy insisted that they walked to the hospital, although there was no time to marvel at the buildings or fountains, or to walk down to the River Garonne; that would have to wait until later.

As with all hospital mortuaries, this one was no different and was located by going around the back of the hospital. There was a non-descript entrance that looked grubby and finding a bell was a challenge, as was Juliet pressing the bell three times before a bemused man in his late fifties wearing green scrubs opened the door. He didn't speak a word of English so Saffy took charge and eventually managed to get the man to understand that they needed to ask some questions about a body that had been brought there a month ago.

The office they were taken into was in the bowels of the hospital and had a young woman in it, sitting at a desk in the middle of the room. She was no more than thirty years old. She, like the man, was also dressed in green scrubs. Both of them had green clogs on their feet. She spoke a small amount of English, but Sandy decided that it was best for Saffy to translate the whole conversation. The people they were talking to were not pathologists but mortuary technicians.

'Please can you tell us about a post-mortem, or what you might call an autopsy, which took place here four weeks ago? The man's name was William Harrison Peveril, he was seventy-three years old.'

A large bound book was taken out of a drawer by the man – still pen and paper here. The office itself had no windows and the lighting was poor, but the man had no trouble finding the entry he was looking for. 'Mr Peveril...' Sandy didn't feel the need to correct the man, who, having put on some glasses and talking in French, was speaking directly to Saffy, who was translating what he said. '... was brought here by the Pompes Funèbres Gerard. We placed the body in one of our freezers and they came the next day and collected the body. They have a smaller freezer themselves at their offices.'

'When did the post-mortem take place?' In Sandy's experience, this seemed fast for this to have happened.

The man and woman looked at each other quizzically and the woman replied, 'No post-mortem took place here.'

'So, could one have taken place elsewhere then?' Juliet asked, trying to understand what could have happened.

'Possibly, but probably not,' the woman replied. 'In France, a post-mortem is usually carried out at a legal medical institute. We have one here in the excellent medical school of Bordeaux university. We do carry them out here sometimes but we didn't in this case and as far as we are aware, one wasn't planned.'

Sandy and Juliet looked at each other. This complicated things and added another place for them to visit. Juliet looked at her watch and saw that it was clearly too late to get to the university now. They would have to go tomorrow or first thing on Friday before they left France.

Saffy, who showed again that she had clearly prepared for this assignment, told them that post-mortems are extremely rare in France and only take place in a small percentage of cases, compared with the UK where there had been nearly eighty thousand the previous year.

Chapter Three

The next morning as Sandy entered the dining room of the hotel, Saffy was just leaving to collect the car that they had hired for the day, in order to get them to Saint-Émilion to visit Chateau Peveril. Sandy had wanted to get up an hour earlier so that he could have a walk and take in some of the sights of Bordeaux; however, maybe because the time in France was an hour later, he had slept in compared with what he would usually do.

As he ate his warm croissants and sipped his strong coffee, he was pleased that yesterday evening, on the way back to the hotel from the hospital, they had walked down to and along the River Garonne and into the Place de la Bourse, where they had looked at how the building's beautiful horseshoe shape was positioned to face the river. The Fontaine des Trois Graces in the centre of the square was well worth their time to see and they all took a few pictures of the fountain on their phones.

As soon as they had returned to the hotel that previous evening, Sandy, who had not unpacked – not that he had brought much with him – threw himself in and out of the shower, changed and headed to the Place du Parlement. At a café in the square, he sat outside, glad that he had put on a jumper and a coat. He treated himself to people watching, but also to an aperitif – a glass of the local Lillet Rosé. At dinner that night, both Juliet and Sandy had had snails in garlic butter followed by beef bourguignon, much to

Saffy's distaste as she didn't eat meat.

The car that Saffy had hired was a Fiat 500 and as she sat smiling in the driver's seat, her face was in contrast to the expressions on the faces of the rather large Juliet and the six-foot-plus-tall Sandy. They squeezed into the car and set off on the twenty-five-mile drive to Saint-Émilion. The car sped along too quickly from Sandy's point of view, especially for the type of car that Saffy was driving. The great plus side was that there was no other way to describe the countryside of rolling vineyards other than picture-postcard perfect, albeit in a few months when the vines were in full leaf, it would have been even more intoxicating.

They reached the limestone plateau that the village of Saint-Émilion was situated on. The village, Saffy told them, was also a UNESCO world heritage site. They passed the entrance to Chateau Peveril but they couldn't see the grand main house from the road. The fields of vines, although still rolling, were now gentler.

The office for Gendarmerie Nationale was situated just outside the centre of the village. The gendarme on the front desk seemed very confused by what they were asking him, despite Saffy's excellent French. He kept repeating, to their disbelief, that they had not attended any death at Chateau Peveril. '*Non, non,*' he kept saying. It was thought best by him that they saw his boss and the man in charge of the police in Saint-Émilion, Lieutenant Marius Legard.

The lieutenant's office was extremely small. Juliet and Saffy took the two seats in front of the desk that dominated the room. Sandy hovered at the back in the doorway, keeping the door open due to the extremely strong smell of cigarette smoke that was permeating the room. Marius was a much younger man than the gendarme on the front desk – in his mid-thirties – and was smartly dressed in his uniform. He had impeccable English and a very welcoming, affable smile. He asked, 'How can I help the English police such a long way from home?'

Sandy took the hidden meaning to say, 'with no authority to be here asking questions'. Juliet, less sensitive than Sandy, replied, 'The family of Viscount William Peveril has asked us to look at the circumstances of his death that took place at his chateau here near the village of Saint-Émilion. Please can we ask what happened when one of your officers attended after he died?'

'We did not attend any death,' Marius replied, looking quizzically at them all. 'There might be a culture difference in policing here. We do not attend all deaths. I think in the UK the police attend all unexpected deaths, is that right?'

Juliet responded, 'Yes, we naturally presumed that one of your officers must have attended the death and commenced an investigation. So, is it right that no one attended and no investigation into the death has taken place?'

'Madam, can I correct just one aspect of what you have just said?' Marius said, looking not just at Juliet, but all of them in the room. 'We were not called to attend, that is why we didn't attend, rather than we just didn't attend.'

There was no point taking up any more of Marius's time, even though he was very affable and wanted to be helpful. He was already lighting up his next cigarette as they left his office.

∞

They left the Fiat 500 in the Gendarmerie car park and split up. Saffy suggested that she could go and check out any pharmacies that might have dispensed the painkillers for Monica to give to Viscount Peveril.

Juliet and Sandy went to the Hotel de Ville (town hall-Marie), which was a stone-built building that looked centuries old. They went into a large office space. Standing at the window that looked out onto the street was a slim and very elegantly dressed woman, in her late fifties, but she looked younger. She was wearing a green, flower-patterned woollen dress that looked very expensive, and she had on a string of white pearls. Sandy asked by whispering to Juliet if she thought the pearls were real. 'Oh yes,' was Juliet's reply.

Sandy asked, 'Excuse me, we are British detectives and are trying to find out information relating to the death of a British citizen, called Viscount William Peveril. Do you know if someone here can help us, please?'

'I can. My name is Suzanne Valadon, I am in charge of the Marie, or town hall, as you would call it.' Suzanne's English was immaculate. 'I knew William extremely well, for probably the last forty years or more, since when I was still a girl. I was incredibly sad to find out that he had died.'

'We are presuming his death was registered here in this town hall,' Sandy said. 'If so, is it possible please to see the death registration?'

'You are a very polite young Englishman,' Suzanne said, and flashed a provocative smile at Sandy. He wondered whether she was flirting with him. She moved to an old oak side cabinet and took out from one of the drawers a large bound book. While she put it on the table in the room, she put on a pair of tortoiseshell glasses that had 'Dior' written on the arms. 'I registered the death myself the very next morning.' She pointed to and showed them the relevant entry.

'So, it was Lady Monica Peveril who registered the death?' Juliet asked, looking at the entry with Suzanne. 'And you took the details of her and William Peveril's passports?'

'Yes, that is the law here, the person registering the death and the deceased identity documents must be seen.'

'Did Lady Peveril come into this office by herself?' Sandy asked, not really sure why, and added, 'Or did anyone accompany her?'

'Into the office here itself?' Suzanne asked, and hesitated while waiting for a reply.

'Yes, to register the death.'

'She was on her own in here. There is also the letter she brought from the doctor who declared the death the previous evening.' Suzanne removed the letter from another drawer. The letter was written in French, and on seeing the concerned looks on Juliet and Sandy's faces, she smiled and said, 'Let me translate. The letter outlines the doctor attending at nine thirty p.m. and states that William Peveril, who was seventy-three years old, was sitting in a chair in his bedroom. He was deceased and had died of a cardiac arrest, most commonly called a heart attack.'

Juliet and Sandy looked at each other as this news was most probably the end of their enquiries. They were both disappointed because for them, as detectives, they loved to investigate, and for them on this occasion there might not be anything worth investigating any further.

Suzanne, on seeing their disappointed faces, told them that the doctor, Francois Aubery, was only five buildings away and they could speak to him in person.

Suzanne copied the entry in the death registration book and copied the letter. She then personally walked them to the doctor's surgery, announcing to the receptionist that the two people with her needed an urgent conversation with the doctor. When they were shown in to see the doctor, she waved at them sweetly and left, heading back to the town hall.

Dr Aubery spoke a lot less English than Suzanne and unfortunately there was no sign of Saffy as yet. Juliet showed him the copy of his letter and asked, 'Please can you describe what you saw and how you knew it was a heart attack that William Peveril died of?'

'Antoine Chevalier called me. I am the doctor for all who live at the chateau, including the English family when they are there.' Francois looked at them both to make sure they understood what he was saying. He was in his late sixties, so had been a doctor for the chateau for a long time. 'I knew William very well. He was sitting in a chair in his bedroom, deceased. I checked that he had no life, then left after writing this letter,' he said, pointing to the letter Juliet was holding, 'for his wife.'

'Was Monica, his wife, present in the bedroom when you examined him?'

'Yes. I didn't examine him as such, just checked there was no heartbeat or breathing.'

'How did you come to the conclusion then that he died of a heart attack?' Both Juliet and Sandy wanted to ask at the same time, but Sandy just beat Juliet to ask it.

'Antoine told me that on the phone. He was very upset.'

There was nothing else that the doctor could help them with and there were now more questions that needed answering. Antoine Chevalier was next on their list of people to see.

∞

Just as they got back to the car, Saffy came running into the car park. 'Sorry I'm late,' an out-of-breath Saffy muttered. 'There is only one pharmacy in the village, and they didn't dispense any drugs to the Peveril's. I tried everywhere else that might have sold any drugs but couldn't find anywhere, but there are more wine shops than in the whole of London put together here in this one village.' Saffy kept talking and neither Juliet nor Sandy could get a word in edgeways, not that they tried as it was clear Saffy had more to tell them. She had opened the car and they got into their seats. 'I wanted,' she continued, 'to go up the bell tower of the monolithic church, but it was one hundred and ninety-six steps to the top and if I had done that who knows when I would have got back here, but the three-hundred-and-sixty-degree views would have been spectacular.'

'Breathe, and keep your eyes on the road, not us,' Juliet shouted. 'Please take us to Chateau Peveril, we passed the entrance to it on the way into the village.'

They drove through the entrance way to the chateau. They hadn't driven far before they saw an imposing house in front of them. It was three stories high but must have cellars as well. It was a rectangular shape with matching wings on either side. There was a sign pointing to the winery, which must have been right round the back of the house as there was no signs of a winery to the front of the house. They pulled up and no sooner had they started to get out of the car when a small man came out of the front door.

He was dressed in a three-piece suit with the buttons bulging on his waistcoat. This must be Antoine Chevalier.

It was, as he proudly announced himself. He walked straight up to Sandy and started embracing him. Reaching up on his tiptoes, he kissed Sandy on each cheek and then again on his left cheek. 'DCI McFarlane, it is our honour for you to visit us.' Sandy had no idea why it was such an honour and he was even more embarrassed when Antoine kissed him on each cheek again. Sandy swiftly took a step backwards as Antoine continued speaking. 'Thank you so much for what you have done for Master George.' So that was it. He had looked for George Peveril when he had gone missing. Juliet and Saffy were only honoured with a handshake.

The front door opened into an extremely large and high-vaulted hall. The exposed oak beams were spectacular. Sandy was trying to look around when a small woman of a similar age to Antoine appeared. She walked straight up to Sandy, embraced him and started the ritual cheek kissing. Sandy stepped quickly away before it was repeated.

They were shown into the large kitchen area that had a long, wooden table, which had on it cheeses, cured meats, pâté and French baguettes. The table was only set for four and the woman who had told them she was Claudette, while getting out another plate, knife and fork, said, 'Suzanne only told us there was two of you, so sorry.' So that was how Antoine came to be waiting for them to arrive: Suzanne Valadon had phoned ahead.

As they ate and sampled a glass of wine from the Peveril winery, it was possible to see through the windows of the kitchen the numerous buildings that housed the winery. There was no sign though of any vines. Antoine told them that they had twenty-seven hectares of vineyards, almost entirely the merlot grape, but also cabernet franc and, to a lesser extent, cabernet sauvignon. If they wanted, he could get the winemaker to give them a tour.

'How old is the house?' Juliet asked.

Antoine, who was doing all the talking while his wife busied herself, hardly eating and making sure everyone had a hot drink as well as the wine, replied, 'Built in 1861.'

'The Peverils have owned it all that time?' Sandy asked.

'No, they bought it in 1922,' Antoine proudly announced. 'One hundred years next year. They renamed it straight away. There had been a house here before this one though.'

Chapter Four

The meal came to an end and Claudette started clearing the remaining food and plates away with Saffy's help. Sandy said to Antoine, 'I am going to try and carry out a technique detectives use called a "cognitive interview" with you. I am afraid that this might stir up and remind you of still fresh emotions. Will this be OK to try an interview like this?'

'Absolutely OK,' Antoine said, who looked anything but convinced. He looked to his wife for reassurance and as she was smiling and nodding at him, he said, 'Yes, let's do this, anything to help the Peveril family.'

'Where were you when you heard that William Peveril had died?'

'Just in here, in fact I was sitting at the very same seat then as I am now.' With Sandy's bidding, he went and sat down in his seat. 'The door to the kitchen opened and in walked Lady Peveril. She told us that Viscount Peveril had died of a heart attack.' So, that was where the mention of a heart attack had begun and who it had come from. 'She asked me to phone for a doctor to attend and to confirm death.'

'That woman showed no emotion,' Claudette shouted, wanting to give her seemingly low opinion of Monica.

Antoine, looking straight at her but talking to all of them, said, 'In the three or four years we have known Lady Peveril, she has never shown any emotion. Rarely talks to us at all.'

Antoine continued speaking and thinking through his actions by saying, 'I didn't call a doctor but went straight upstairs to their suite on the first floor. It is the one on the right.' He gestured with both hands then pointed right.

Antoine stood up. Sandy and Juliet followed him through the door and up the oak staircase to the first floor, then turning right they entered a large room. The room had at the front a large sitting area with chairs and a sofa, with a low, dark-wood table between them. At the back was a king-sized bed and through the window at the back they could see a balcony, and beyond this rows and rows of vines. There was a door directly opposite where they were standing that they presumed was the ensuite bathroom. Antoine told them there were four of these identical suites: two on the upper floors – they had one themselves, directly above this one – and the other two were the ones that James and Arabella used.

'Please enter again and try and do everything that you did at the time,' Sandy said to Antoine, as he and Juliet stood to one side to give Antoine some freedom of movement.

After going out and coming back in, Antoine said, 'I led the way and Lady Peveril followed me. Viscount Peveril was sat in the chair there.' He pointed to a high-backed chair towards which he was walking. 'He was wearing check pyjamas and looked quite peaceful. I could see that he was dead. I then went to the phone there.' He walked to the phone and picked it up as if to make a call. He then said, 'I called Dr Aubrey.'

'What did you tell him?'

'That Viscount Peveril had died of a heart attack and to please come quickly. I was very upset and went down to see Claudette in the kitchen and wait to open the door for Dr Aubrey. I let him in and he went upstairs. He stayed no more than two minutes and then left. Lady Peveril asked me to phone a funeral director to take his lordship to Bordeaux.'

'OK,' Sandy said. 'Let's try some of your different senses. When you were in this room, what did you smell?'

Antoine looked at Sandy as if he were mad, but he did think about it. 'Nothing.'

'Did you hear anything?'

After a slight pause, 'No, nothing. Am I doing this correctly,' asked Antoine, 'as I don't seem to be helping?'

'What did you touch?'

'I touched his lordship. Is that what you mean? I touched the phone.'

'What did his body feel like?'

'Now you mention it, he was warm when I touched him. I thought dead bodies are cold.'

Juliet explained, 'Depends how long after death you touch them. You told us you had only seen him half an hour before so he should still have been warm.'

'OK, please come and stand with us Antoine.' He walked across the room to stand with Sandy and Juliet. 'I now want you to look at what happened, but from this different angle. Do you see anything additional?'

Antoine shut his eyes and after a few moments said, 'Yes, Lady Peveril was very close to me throughout and followed me to the chair and then to the phone. I also remember that there was a half empty glass of water on the table next to his lordship and a brandy glass with liquid still in it.' Antoine smiled at them both, proud with what he had remembered.

∞

As they left the chateau, Antoine and Claudette, waved goodbye to them from the front door. They were holding each other closely and visibly crying. Sandy sent a message to Arabella to please contact the Chevaliers as understandably they were now upset after their visit.

The Gerard family funeral director's building took some finding. Saffy got lost driving around some of the backstreets of Bordeaux and had concerned both Juliet and Sandy as she was driving exceptionally quickly through some very small and narrow streets. In fact, hurtling along was the best way to describe her driving. When they entered the front office of the funeral directors, they saw a young woman no older than Sandy, so around thirty, dressed smartly in a suit. She welcomed them inside.

As the young woman only spoke a limited amount of English, Saffy translated. The young woman was Isabelle Gerard, the youngest in a long line of Gerard funeral directors. She told them that her elder brother and her had a call from a Monsieur Chevalier, from Chateau Peveril near Saint-Émilion, to collect a man called Viscount William Peveril.

'What did you find when you went into the house?' Sandy asked.

'My brother and I were shown in, by we presume Monsieur Chevalier. We went into a large bedroom suite on the first floor and placed the man who had died into a body bag. We took him to the hospital morgue, as they have more freezer space then we have here, as we thought that it would be sometime before anything was decided about the body.'

'Who was in the bedroom suite when you went in?'

'A woman who didn't speak to us or acknowledge us. I think she might have been on her phone, but I didn't take any notice.'

'What happened that caused you to collect the body the next day, if you thought it would be sometime before anything was decided?'

'I received a phone call from…' Isabelle looked at some notes in a book that she had on her desk in front of her. 'A James Peveril, who spoke very good French. He told me that he had organised for his father's body to be repatriated at the end of the week, and could I get the body ready for him and his sister to visit and for the repatriation. We went and collected the body from the hospital and brought him here.'

'What does getting ready for repatriation mean?' Juliet asked.

'Three people arrived to view and spend time with the body in our chapel of rest.' Isabelle again looked at her notes. 'Sorry, I didn't take their names but it was James and his sister, and I think her husband.' Isabelle looked at them, but at Saffy in particular, waiting for their next question, then realised she hadn't fully answered the previous one about repatriation. 'Sorry, that same day, after they had visited, I embalmed the body ready for being collected.'

'Did you do this yourself?' Sandy asked. 'Did you see any marks or bruises, or any injuries to the body at all?'

'No, there was nothing of note. If there had been I would have been in touch with the authorities straight away.'

So, no sign of external trauma. What Isabelle was in essence telling them was that there were no overt signs of why Viscount Peveril had died.

The car was almost overdue to be returned so Saffy had driven off at speed, convinced that she was going to get lost, which she probably was, and then be too late for the car hire office. Saffy had also been clearly a little troubled by all the talk of bodies, morgues and embalming, so Sandy and Juliet had told her they would talk it all through with her over dinner that night. As detectives, they were used to dealing with dead bodies but their twenty-four-year-old FCDO civil servant was not.

∞

On the way back to the hotel, Juliet and Sandy, while walking nearby to the Palais de la Bourse, saw the Miroir d'Eau, which is the world's largest reflecting pool. They were attracted to it by the dense water vapour mist that occurred when the fountain regularly sprayed water jets into the air. The black granite slabs of the vast fountain helped the remaining streams of water to become the reason it was reflective. This was, of course, before the water jets started again and the dense mist appeared. On a hot day it might have been good to walk through the water mist, but not that cool March evening.

Juliet and Saffy were keen to join Sandy for an aperitif. They went to the same café that he had visited the previous evening and sat outside. Juliet and Saffy had the rosé, while Sandy tried the Crémant de Bordeaux. After they had talked through with Saffy the blasé way that they, and Isabelle, had talked about William Peveril's body, and had ordered another drink, Sandy informed Juliet, 'I think we have now done everything that we can do and seen everyone we needed to, but I do feel we have taken one step forward only to take two steps backwards.'

'Yes, I agree, it's all a bit inconclusive. The only thing left to do is to talk to Monica Peveril back in London.'

This was something Sandy had been thinking about, but he was loathe to do this just yet because what would he say to her: 'You say your husband died of a heart attack, but how do you know that?' Juliet agreed but told him if he were going to investigate the death any further, it was inevitable that he would need to speak to her at some stage.

When they went for dinner, Saffy, as a vegetarian, wasn't convinced with Juliet and Sandy's choice of dinner – at least they hadn't had snails, but they had a local Bordeaux dish of beef steak in a red wine sauce. Sandy wondered how Saffy survived outside Paris, as the French appeared to him to be great meat eaters.

There was just time the next morning for Sandy to visit Cathédrale Saint-André, a gothic-looking building dating back in places over a thousand years. It was well worth a visit and he was glad he had made the effort. The bell tower for the cathedral was, interestingly, free standing, and although Sandy would have liked to climb the two hundred and thirty-one steps to the top, which was more than Saffy had wanted to climb in Saint-Émilion the previous day, it was unfortunately still closed. He needed to get back quickly for their train to Paris, then onto the Eurostar for London. He got back to the hotel just in time to collect his bag as the taxi to the station pulled up outside to collect them.

The two hours to Paris went by quickly and as they said goodbye to Saffy in Paris, Sandy wondered if her hug with him had been longer than the one she had given to Juliet.

Saffy had been a great help, not just her language skills but also her company. She was undoubtably going to have a stellar career in the FCDO, and if he stayed as a detective working for them, there was no doubt that one day she could possibly be one of his senior bosses.

They arrived fairly late on the Friday evening at St Pancras International train station in London. Juliet was in a very happy mood as she now had two weeks' holiday. She passed over her notebook for the case to Sandy for him to make use of, and to copy, then hand back to her when she returned from holiday. One thing she wasn't going to do was think about work or William Harrison Peveril at all for the next two weeks.

Chapter Five

There was no trip home to Ely this weekend as Sandy had only arrived back in London late on the Friday evening. Hannah was busy anyway, working on briefs for a sentencing hearing on the Monday, at Leicester Crown Court, and then a plea and directions hearing at Cambridge Crown Court on the Tuesday. As a result of this, Sandy stayed in the flat that he and his father shared in the City of London. It was extremely rare for either of them to stay there at the weekend and Sandy wasn't feeling too comfortable about it.

After a reasonable amount of time allowing himself to have a lie-in, and after the completion of some domestic chores, Sandy was feeling bored. He had thought about meeting up with Arabella and James so that he could explain what had happened on his visit to Bordeaux. After sending a message to Arabella, enquiring about her and James's availability, he found out that she had gone straight home to her farm near Hunstanton in Norfolk after their meeting in St James's Park. James, due to the Easter parliamentary recess, was at his home in Hope, in Derbyshire. Neither of them was due back in London for at least a week or two, unless he urgently needed them to be, then they would return.

After dismissing the thought of going straight round to Peveril House in Eaton Square to interview Monica, a trip to the British Museum was the favoured option to occupy

Sandy's time on the Saturday afternoon. The British Museum, located in Bloomsbury, was in walking distance from the flat. Over the past two hundred and fifty years from when the first building had been erected, it was now a considerable-sized complex. The museum housed some incredible displays. There were over eight million works in the collection, an amazing depiction of human history through the artefacts on display in various rooms and exhibitions.

Sandy knew that any attempt to see everything was impossible. As he had visited the museum a few times in the past, albeit not for a number of years, he decided he would purchase the highlights tour audio guide, as he knew he would enjoy this. Some of the highlights that he looked at and listened to on his headset were the Egyptian section, the Rosetta Stone, the Parthenon gallery and the Elgin Marbles. Finally, he finished by looking at the Sutton Hoo helmet.

The next day, Sunday, was also too quiet for Sandy. He was used to being in company. A run in the morning helped a little bit, in particular as the effects of the previous weekend's rugby and triathlon had pretty much gone.

Getting out his and Juliet's notebooks in relation to the death of Viscount William Peveril, Sandy wrote in his book a number of standard questions in cases of unexpected deaths:

Where did William die? This he could answer easily: in his suite at Chateau Peveril in France.

When did William die? Again, fairly easy to answer from the evidence of Antoine and Claudette Chevalier: shortly before Monica came and told them that William had died.

How did William die? Sandy thought that this, in some respects, was also easy to answer. He died of a cardiac arrest. However, there was no medical proof that this actually was the case; it was all made up of assumptions that this was how he had died. So, as an alternative hypothesis to this one, he could have died of another natural cause or disease, or, of course, a third party may have killed him, most probably Monica. This would have been covert as Isabelle Gerard had told them there was no sign of any external trauma. There was no evidence that this was the case, but due to cardiac arrest not being confirmed, as a hypothesis, it couldn't be dismissed. A final hypothesis in these sorts of cases was the death was accidental. There was nothing that Sandy had found to show that this was the case and so this should not be worthy of further investigation.

Why did William die? Untreated heart disease or other untreated natural disease was the most probable answer. If the hypothesis was true that Monica killed him, although Sandy was not sure how – there were no reports of any domestic abuse between the couple – was it for his money? She was well looked after while he was alive but would be less so after he died, as the Peveril family kept all of his possessions.

∞

On the Monday morning, the consulate investigation section of the large, open-plan office in the FCDO was looking almost empty of people. A number of the team had taken two weeks off for the Easter holidays, which started that day. One person though, who had returned from two weeks' leave, was the other DCI in the team, DCI Phil

Harris. He was dressed that morning in a dark blue, three-piece pinstripe suit, with a red tie and matching red handkerchief that was flowing out of the top pocket of his suit. He looked like a senior barrister rather than a senior detective.

Sandy was always pleased to see his older, and much more experienced, colleague. He smiled as he walked up to Phil, who, on smiling back in return, said, 'The boss has told me she wants to see you as soon as you get to work this morning.'

Putting his backpack on the empty desk next to Phil, Sandy didn't sit down but went straight down the corridor and into a small office that was used by Superintendent Jane Watson. Sandy thought Jane was an excellent boss to work for. Jane, in her early forties with shoulder-length dyed blonde hair, was sitting at her desk wearing her gold-rimmed glasses, peering into her laptop and typing away hard at her keyboard. She also had just returned that day from a two-week holiday with her husband.

No sooner had Sandy sat down than Jane, while taking off her glasses and placing them on the desk, asked, 'Sandy, how do we get referrals to carry out or assist in investigations within the consulate investigation team?'

So, not a well done then, Sandy thought, for looking after the team for the last two weeks while Jane was away sunning herself on holiday, which was also at the same time as his fellow DCI. Sandy thought better of saying what he was thinking and said, 'Good morning, Jane.' There was no use of ranks and calling Jane 'Ma'am' in the FCDO, just first names. 'We get them from police forces,' he answered, 'or coroners around the country who ask for help with investigations of their residents that have died as a result of homicide or in suspicious circumstances abroad.' Sandy now knew where this conversation was heading.

'I see that you were in France last week. Were you asked to help a police force or a coroner with an investigation there?'

You know the answer to this already, thought Sandy, but he had to play along with the line of questioning that a not cross- but determined-looking Jane was leading him along. 'No, I wasn't.' Sandy thought, where is Juliet Ashton when I need her? It was Juliet, after all, who had convinced him that they should go and investigate, but he was the DCI not her, so he needed to take the can, so continued by saying, 'I was approached by Viscount James Peveril MP' – get the important name in first, he thought – 'and his sister, Arabella Montague, to investigate the suspicious death of their father in Bordeaux.'

'I know who approached you and I know of your close ties to this family, but whoever they are, we can't just go off and do this. You know how many hundreds of families would love for us to do what you have just done for this family. We just can't set a precedent like this. You know that, Sandy.'

Sandy knew that Jane was right, and he blushed slightly as he sat in his chair with his shoulders now drooping. All he could think to say at this moment was, 'I am sorry if I have caused us a problem.'

'No problem at the moment,' Jane said as she went to answer her phone that had started ringing, and Sandy, who knew this was usually the sign for him to leave, stood up. As he went to leave, Jane said, putting her hand over her phone receiver, 'You are to do nothing more on this investigation without an express request for assistance by either the police force or the coroner for the area that the late Viscount William Peveril was normally resident in. Am I clear?'

Sandy nodded in acknowledgement and got out of the office as fast as he could; staying in there any longer would not be good for his health.

∞

Following the team meeting, Phil said to Sandy, 'What have you done to upset the boss then?' Phil was smiling at Sandy as he could see how despondent he was looking.

After giving Phil a very brief summary of what had gone on, firstly with the meeting with Arabella and then the trip to France, Sandy said, 'What would you have done, Phil? Would you have gone to France?'

'Absolutely not!' Phil said, and then after a momentary pause, seeing Sandy look even more despondent, he smiled and said, 'Only joking! Of course I would have gone – any half chance to have a trip abroad I would have taken.' Phil could see that this had placated Sandy to a certain extent. 'However, Jane has a point. Let's be honest, William Peveril most probably died of a heart attack, which is the most likely explanation.'

'Yes, I know that that is the highly probable reason he died, but not conclusively.'

'Literally hundreds of people die abroad of suspected but not definitive heart attacks. We don't investigate any of those, do we?'

'No, I know you are right but something about the circumstances just doesn't sit right with me,' Sandy said. 'Mrs Montague feels the same and I trust her judgement.'

'Well, unless you get the police or the coroner from the area where he was resident to ask for our help, you are not going to get Jane's blessing to do any more work investigating this death.'

Although he fully understood what Jane and Phil had said to him, Sandy had a tenacious streak. He sent a message to James Peveril asking where his father had been resident and did he know the name of the coroner who had released his body to them for burial.

James didn't send a message back but rang instead. 'Hi, Sandy, why do you want to know? You have been to my father's home, it is Peveril Hall in Derbyshire. I suppose it will technically be my official home when Monica moves out, not that she ever goes there, she only stays in London now. Not that I am going to live there either, we shall stay here in Hope, and I'll mostly be in Eaton Square in London.'

'It is the Derbyshire Police Force then,' Sandy said smiling to himself, as he knew officers in Derbyshire very well. 'Do you know the coroner for the Peak District?'

'Yes, very well. Arthur Ramsbottom was a friend of my fathers and his wife was very friendly with my mother. Like all of us, she took it badly when my mother died.'

'I will be honest with you, James, I am not able to do anything more in relation to investigating your father's death unless I get a request from them to do so.'

'I don't think there is anything more you can do, is there? I will call Arthur myself. It will be nice to catch up with him anyway and I will let you know what he thinks.'

Likewise, Sandy thought to himself, as he made a call to DCI Rishabh (Rich) Singh, the head of CID for the Peak District in Derbyshire. It would be good to catch up.

'Sandy, how are you?' There was the noise of children in the background. 'I am looking after the children this week, as you can no doubt hear.' It was quiet; he was whispering to the children. 'Well done on completing the triathlon, albeit Lofty Dobson said you cheated.'

'I didn't cheat, I finished the same distance as he did.' Lofty and Sandy had had a wager that if Sandy didn't finish within thirty minutes of Lofty, he would have to double the sponsorship he had raised. 'I can't help it if the Fens are flat and Derbyshire has some rather large hills.' They both laughed together. Probably unknown to Rich but known to Lofty was that he had doubled the sponsorship anyway.

'He said you did the swim in a pool called The Hive, and you had pacesetters from your local Ely triathlon club throughout the whole of your triathlon.' Both very true statements, which caused them more laughter together. Rich put the television on for his children. 'That's better,' he said, now in relative quiet. 'Only the first day of the holidays and I am exhausted.'

They had worked together in Canada and had become good friends. Sandy said, 'Rich, I am investigating the death of the late Viscount William Peveril, he was a resident of yours in the Peak District at Peveril Hall, the natural heritage place.'

'I read about it in the newspaper, he died of natural causes though, didn't he?'

'Not conclusively though, that is why the family, his daughter and son, have asked me to look into it. But to do anything further I need your say so, just an email to me would suffice.'

Although they were good friends Rich still took his responsibilities seriously and said, 'Sandy, let me think about it, and if Mr Ramsbottom, the coroner, says yes when I ring him next week, I will let you have your email.'

Chapter Six

The conversation with Saffy about them both having attended St John's College in Cambridge had stirred up in Sandy the desire to show Hannah his old college. He contacted the deputy head porter at the college, who was honouring them with a private tour, led personally by him on Wednesday morning of this week. Sandy had taken the day off and Hannah was going to be on holiday from that day for ten days. She was going to spend her holiday with her father in Harrogate, in North Yorkshire, where he lived.

Tuesday was dragging in the office as he cleared through all of the files that Juliet and others had dumped on him as they left for their holidays, but also because Sandy was keen to get home and at least have a day with Hannah before she went away. And he wanted to have the long Easter weekend at home with his family.

Two things that happened on Tuesday that had pleased him though were that he had received an email (James must have given him Sandy's email address) from Mr Arthur Ramsbottom, the senior coroner for the Peak District, saying he was in agreement for the Derbyshire Police to enquire further into the circumstances of the death of Viscount William Harrison Peveril, with the assistance of the FCDO, if they felt they required it. The second one was from Rich, who was still clearly working while on leave, to say that the coroner and Derbyshire Police would welcome the FCDO support with any further investigation, as required, into the death.

On forwarding the emails to Jane Watson, she had replied, 'Very well, but make sure you do not go to France without you and I having a discussion first.'

Driving his 2011 red Morgan Roadster was one of the most pleasurable things that Sandy did. He loved his car, which was a graduation present from his paternal grandfather, now almost ten years ago. That Wednesday morning, he had a wide grin on his face as he drove to Cambridge to meet Hannah, not just because he was going to see her but because he was driving his car a little further than just around Ely. The only downside was that it was too cold to drive with the roof down, even though he was really tempted.

Hannah, who was twenty-seven years old, was ready and waiting outside her flat for him. She was wearing a very smart, grey check trouser suit and she had her long, dark hair neatly tied back and up on her head. 'You look really smart,' Sandy said, as he locked his car and kissed Hannah, at the same time considering that he might be underdressed in his jeans.

'I thought I needed to look smart to be visiting a Cambridge College, and especially your old college.' She smiled sweetly at Sandy as they walked along Regent Street heading to the college. As they were slightly early for their appointment, Sandy took them to visit the excellent Heffers bookshop near the college. He treated himself, from the crime section to the latest John Grisham novel to read over the Easter weekend. He stayed away from the travel section to avoid wanting to get a book about Bordeaux and then wanting to go back there. Jane had been very clear that this was not going to happen.

It appeared that Sandy's grandfather, John McFarlane, had gone with Hannah, as part of his mentoring of her, to Cambridge Crown Court the day before. Hannah didn't need mentoring any more but they both enjoyed each other's company so he had tagged along. Hannah remarked how pleased everyone at the court was to see him. He had been the Cambridge Family Court Designated Judge for a number of years. 'People matter to your grandfather and quite clearly he matters to people,' Hannah told Sandy.

As they stood outside the magnificent Great Gate to St John's waiting for the deputy head porter to arrive, Hannah glanced at the proud, smiling or, more to the point, beaming Sandy, and slipped her hand into his and gave him a kiss. The Great Gate looked, as it was of course, like a Tudor masterpiece of architecture, as were the college's Tudor quadrangles and their buildings called the first, second and third courts.

The college was founded in 1511 by Lady Margaret Beaufort, who was the mother of King Henry VII. Sandy, like most of the other undergraduates, lived in the college's accommodation for all of his three years at Cambridge. He had been back a few times in the almost ten years since he left, but having Hannah with him today made him feel really nostalgic.

The River Cam runs straight through the college with the absolutely magnificent Bridge of Sighs going across it. Anyone on the River Cam along the Backs would have seen the bridge and they would undoubtably all agree that the bridge is one of the most iconic Cambridge sights. The bridge led to New Court and its clock tower and the other courts and buildings built that side of the river, then on to the college's gardens and onwards to the college's extensive sports grounds.

Hannah was in awe with what she was seeing and hearing from the impressive and knowledgeable deputy head porter and was pleased that Sandy was not butting in with stories of his own, well not very often, as he couldn't resist it at times. One thing she found amazing and had never heard about before was that some of the fellows, who are worldwide renowned academics and teachers, actually lived in the college accommodation, some of them for decades.

A highlight for them both was when they climbed up the chapel tower and were taken up onto the roof of the chapel. They were said to be at the highest point in Cambridge, looking in one direction across Trinity College and to King's College Chapel and the other way at St John's clock tower and New Court.

On looking down at the master of St John's College's house, Sandy was so excited to see that outside was a Morgan sports car. It appeared that, like him, the master and her husband drove a Morgan. Hannah, on having him point it out to her, just rolled her eyes as cars were not something that excited her. Sandy thought the master must be by far the coolest master of all of the Cambridge colleges!

They had a late lunch, sitting outside in the front courtyard of Brown's restaurant, which had formally been an old nineteenth-century Cambridge hospital building but was now converted into a modern brasserie-type restaurant. As always, Sandy couldn't resist the fish pie that they served there.

As Sandy dropped Hannah off at Cambridge railway station, she told him that she would return a couple of days earlier the following week so that they could spend the weekend together, which, although this pleased him greatly, was still several days away.

∞

By the Thursday afternoon, the McFarlane house in Ely was starting to get very busy and to fill up with people. Sandy's youngest sister Isla, her husband and their dog had arrived. His other sister Aileen and her two children were at the house all of the time and his mother was totally focussed, requiring Sandy and his dad's help to cook for the whole family over the weekend, and in particular on Easter Sunday.

Attending the Maundy Thursday communion service in Ely Cathedral gave Sandy and his mum Katherine an hour of peace, well, slightly longer, as they walked there and back. The marina opposite their house had come to life over the last week or so and was now buzzing with people and boats on the move. The Cutter Inn had suddenly got much busier when Sandy and his father went in for their early evening drinks on the Friday. Unfortunately, his maternal grandfather, Tom Fisher, couldn't make it but he sent a message to Sandy telling him he was coming to watch him play rugby the next day.

The Ely Tigers second rugby team won their last game of the season quite comfortably. Sandy had managed to scramble the ball over and scored one of the tries, which pleased him and his watching grandfather. A drink and curry was planned by the team that evening but Sandy slid back home after having a couple of drinks, as he was enjoying his time with his youngest sister and her husband, who he didn't see very often.

The whole family, much to Katherine's delight, had attended the Easter morning service in Ely Cathedral. The cathedral had flowers everywhere; the women – and it was all women – had done the cathedral proud with their flower displays and everyone was given bunches of daffodils by the children at the end of the service. Sandy sat with his two nephews and his grandparents, Tom and Margaret. The only person missing was his paternal grandfather, John McFarlane, but his car was waiting outside the house when they got home.

Following the meal, the large family went for a walk through Jubilee Gardens, where the children had a play, then into Cherry Hill Park and round to the front of the cathedral, into the high street, along Fore Hill and Waterside and back home again. The high street had been fairly quiet, but all along the River Great Ouse the place was buzzing with people enjoying the spring weather.

Sandy went and sat outside his house with his two grandfathers: one, the retired senior detective, and the other – not yet retired despite his age – a former judge, but still a barrister and also a lecturer at the University of Cambridge.

As they all settled around the garden table with their cups of tea and coffee, Sandy said, 'I have a case.' He saw that he had immediately got the two old men's attention. There was nothing that they both, and Tom in particular, liked more than talking to their grandson about his cases, or to be fair, any case. Sandy continued, 'Where this person has died suddenly and everyone presumes that they died of a heart attack.'

'How old were they?' John asked, at the same time as Tom asked, 'Did they have heart disease or were they ill?'

'He was seventy-three.'

'Younger than us!' his Grandad Tom exclaimed. Both grandfathers were now seventy-six years old.

'I don't think he had any heart problems. His family didn't say he had, but I need to check with his family doctor. The only thing I know he had was a bad back.'

'Not surprised at his age, we both have bad knees,' John said, patting his right knee and then Tom's.

'This, Grandpa, is because you are playing too much golf, and you, Grandad,' Sandy said, patting Tom's stomach, 'is because you are carrying too much weight.'

'Don't you start! I have enough problems with your grandmother and your mother!' They all laughed heartily together. 'Do you think he was murdered then Sandy?' Tom asked.

'No, not really. At the moment there is nothing to suggest that he was murdered. I just don't like not knowing conclusively what has happened to him for his family's sake. There was no post-mortem done, you see.'

'If he hasn't been cremated you could think about an exhumation of the body and have a post-mortem, but if you don't think it is a homicide, you will have to get the family, in the first instance, to agree, and then try to get permissions and a licence,' Tom said, and then went into a fascinating story about an exhumation he had been involved in over thirty years ago, in the dead of night. There was little that remained of the body. The person had died twenty years or more before the exhumation. The post-mortem therefore didn't stand a chance to be helpful. 'How long ago did your person die then, Sandy?'

'Only five weeks ago.'

John said, 'I suggest the pathology in your case stands

a lot better chance than it did with the medieval remains Tom had dug up!' They laughed together and waved to Katherine to see if she could bring them out more tea and coffee and some of the cake that she was handing out as she walked around the house.

Sandy went in to help her, but at the same time he couldn't stop thinking about an exhumation in the case of William Peveril. It all seemed a bit bureaucratic and complicated, but if they wanted to try and get a definitive answer as to why he had died, surely this was something worth them considering. Rich would need some convincing, but less so James and Arabella.

Chapter Seven

It wasn't until the following Tuesday afternoon that Sandy had a chance to think about William Peveril. He had phoned the family doctor in Derbyshire and the only record of any contact they had for him over the last three years was him attending for his annual flu jab.

The police advice on exhumations talked about how emotive it was to do, in particular, for the family involved. Sandy acknowledged that it was likely to be a harrowing experience and most probably traumatic for all concerned, including the police officers. One of the first actions the advice outlined was for family liaison officers to be involved to work with the family. He supposed that must be him, so no need to look to appoint another person from the Derbyshire Police, albeit DC Lofty Dobson from Derbyshire knew the family well and was a trained family liaison officer.

Was it best to leave the death of William Peveril alone now and let his body rest in peace in his grave in the village churchyard in Derbyshire? However, that niggle that something was not right wouldn't go away from Sandy. He rang Arabella.

'Hello, it's Sandy. I don't want you to come to an immediate decision about what I am about to say and please take time to talk it over with Monty. We are unable to establish for sure that your father died of a heart attack but one way we could do it, if we get all of the permissions, is to exhume.' There was an audible gasp from Arabella, and she could be heard by Sandy to be moving a chair and sitting down on it. Sandy continued, 'Exhume his body and carry out a post-mortem by a forensic pathologist. What do you think and how do you feel about this?' After another pause, he said, 'I know it is a shock to you, give me a call back after you have had a chance to think about it.'

'I am not sure, Sandy. I know I am the one that started you investigating this, but exhumation and disturbing his grave... My mother is in the one next to him, my grandparents' and great grandparents' graves are also nearby and having my father cut up is quite a lot to take in.'

'I know, and I am so sorry to distress you even further in this way. I will give James a call now and if you both say no, this will be the end of it. I will not pursue it any further. I don't even know if we would get permission but I thought it might be worth a try.'

A cup of tea was what was needed for Sandy after the emotion of talking to Arabella, but he thought it best to make his phone calls first, and the next person that Sandy phoned was James, who was still at home in Derbyshire. 'Hello, James, did you enjoy the Easter holidays?'

'Yes, it was very nice thank you, Sandy, just the four of us.' His phone made a beeping sound. 'Sorry, Sandy, Arabella is ringing me, can I call you back after I see what she is after please?'

'I know what she wants to talk to you about as I have only just spoken to her.'

'Go on then, and I will ring her back after I hear what you have to say.'

'I mentioned to Arabella about the possibility of an exhumation of your father's body and us having a post-mortem. I don't know whether we will get permission for it, but I needed to talk to you both first before I looked into it further.'

'Yes,' James said straight away, which surprised Sandy. 'We have started on this investigation on questioning my father's death and we now need to know for sure.'

'OK, that was decisive of you.'

'Arabella may have a different view and I will respect that, but as far as I am concerned you have my permission to pursue this further. I will though insist he is reburied in exactly the same place, next to my mother.'

No sooner was Sandy back at his desk, after taking a bit of time out for a cup of tea, when he received a message from Arabella telling him that Monty told her unless she supported doing this now, it would always be a worry to her, and James was quite clear they should do it. As a result of their views, she was in agreement.

Although Sandy wanted to say, 'There is no rush, your father is not going anywhere and we can think about an exhumation in six months, a year or many years,' he didn't, and just replied, 'Thank you, I will keep you informed.'

∞

The next call should have been to Rich but Sandy felt he needed to know a bit more about the mechanics of how you got a licence for carrying out an exhumation. He printed off the Ministry of Justice application for a licence for the removal of buried human remains (including cremated remains) in England and Wales.

He got to question two, which asked, 'Is the spouse of the deceased still alive?' This troubled him as it looked like he might need to ask Monica's permission, which he was sure she wouldn't consent to.

He thought he might get away without telling her when at question seven it spoke about the nearest surviving relative, which surely must be James – he was, after all, William's heir. The next question asked, 'Have all the relevant relatives been informed?' and the following question asked for signatures from all relatives. Sandy threw the form down onto the desk in frustration, got up from his desk, and did a few laps walking around his office floor then up and around the next floor.

Sandy went back to his desk and picked the form up, convinced there was a solution. When he scanned through it again, he laughed at himself as he saw that because William was buried in a consecrated Church of England churchyard, they didn't need a Ministry of Justice licence, but one from the Church of England Diocese for the area where the body was buried. What a waste of the last hour or so of his life and such a waste of his emotions.

A phone call to Rich was what was needed now. 'Hello, Rich, you survived the week being in charge of the children then?'

'Yes, we had a great time together and although I tried to keep up to date with my emails and work, no chance. First day back today, still not got through answering all the emails!'

'What do you think about the exhumation of William's body?' Sandy said. 'He is in a grave in a churchyard in Derbyshire.' There was a pause the other end of the phone, presumably while Rich pondered this information. 'I have spoken to the family and they are in agreement.'

'This sounds very interesting. I have never been

involved with one of these before, so what does it entail? What do we have to do?'

'I hope you are not scared of churchyards in the middle of the night. My grandad told me he was involved in an exhumation that began at three thirty a.m.'

'I won't enjoy that bit, but the whole experience sounds, as I said, very interesting. What do you want me to do?'

'Are you happy we are investigating an unexpected death, and as a result of us not knowing how William died, is currently a suspicious death, where an autopsy would reveal a cause of death that might raise, or lower, our suspicions?'

'Yes, those are similar to the words I have used, to raise a non-crime incident on our computer system.'

'Please can you contact Mr Ramsbottom, the senior coroner for the Peak District, and explain that we would like his support for the exhumation, his permission to carry out a forensic post-mortem and his permission to take human tissue samples for examination, as felt necessary by the pathologist.'

'How much is this going to cost me out of my budget, Sandy?' They both laughed, but Rich was deadly serious as he no doubt had a budget to worry about.

'Let's get the permissions first. I will see if we can share the costs of the post-mortem and see if the Peveril's will pay the costs of the funeral directors for the exhumation and then the reburial, OK?'

'Yes, I will be able to do that. I will talk to the coroner, but it will have to be tomorrow now as I have meetings and more emails to attend to.'

On looking around the office, Sandy couldn't see Clare Symonds anywhere, who was the investigation team's lead

CSI. When he thought about it, he hadn't seen her all day. He presumed that she might be on holiday like a lot of the others until the end of the week. So he sent her an email outlining what he had planned, asking if we could share the cost of a forensic post-mortem.

∞

The next morning Sandy had already received a message from Clare, who was, as he suspected, on holiday. Clare had agreed to contribute half of the forensic costs from her budget. Clare did though have one condition, and that was that she must be involved in the actual exhumation and post-mortem herself! Sandy had laughed when he had read this. He had worked with Clare a few times in the last year, on a case in India and then in Canada, where she had also worked with Rich. They both knew that Clare was an outstanding CSI and any team would want her involved.

He had also received a message from Juliet asking to be involved. Clare and Juliet were great friends and had no doubt been messaging each other. Sandy would try and get Juliet involved if he could.

The Church of England petition for exhumation form had to be sent to the Worshipful Chancellor of the diocese. What a wonderful title that was! Sandy found out that this form was for the Diocese of Derby, which covered the parish that the church in Edensor was in. On researching further, he found out that the Worshipful Chancellor was a reverend, but a non-stipend one. He was also a practising barrister specialising in family law. A phone call to the diocesan main office in Derby revealed that Revd Paul Repton only worked occasionally in the office and that he would call him back.

A message he received later that morning from Rich was pleasing as the coroner had agreed to their requests. He stated within it that he would be pleased to find out how his friend of over forty years had died. Rich was equally pleased when Sandy let him know about the sharing of the forensic costs and the request from Clare and Juliet to be involved.

Early that afternoon, Sandy received a phone call. 'Hello, is that DCI Alexander McFarlane? I am Paul Repton.' It was the Worshipful Chancellor for the Derby diocese. 'You have been trying to get hold of me. How can I help you?'

'I would like to talk to you about giving consent for the exhumation of a body that is buried in St Peter's parish church in Edensor.'

'I need to stop you there. We are not too keen on exhumations. The disturbing of consecrated ground after the person's burial and where their earthly body remains are, following a Christian burial ceremony, should remain sacred.'

'I do understand your concerns,' Sandy said, trying to recover what seemed to suddenly be a hopeless situation. 'The coroner has agreed to an autopsy and the taking of tissue samples.'

'Oh, has he. What is the name of the person you want to exhume?'

'The late Viscount William Harrison Peveril.'

'Oh.' That seemed to be the favourite saying of the Worshipful Chancellor. 'That sounds even more problematic to me.'

'The family are also consenting,' Sandy said, trying

even harder to convince Revd Repton.

'Oh. So what you are telling me is that the police, coroner and the family want this to happen? I, though, on behalf of the church and the sacred remains of Viscount Peveril, am very hesitant to consent to this. Why do you and the family want to do this?'

'It is alleged that he died of a heart attack but there was no post-mortem so we are suspicious of the circumstances.' Sandy was feeling quite uncomfortable and he would have preferred to carry out this conversation in person, and rightly or wrongly, he needed to be totally honest, so said, 'I also need to tell you that one of the person's consent you won't see is William's spouse, Monica.'

'Well that makes it even more problematic,' Revd Repton said. Looks like he had now got an easy get out. 'Why didn't the coroner organise a post-mortem before he released the body to the family for burial?'

'William died in France and the authorities there accepted Monica's explanation that he died of a heart attack, and that assumption carried on throughout and to the burial. He had no known previous heart disease though.'

'Oh, I presume until you know otherwise that Monica Peveril is a suspect?'

Neither Sandy nor Rich had formally declared Monica as a suspect, but if this was what Revd Repton wanted to hear, Sandy said, 'Yes.'

'Fill the forms in and let me have time to consider it. Are you by any chance related to Judge John McFarlane?'

'Yes, he is my grandfather.'

'We are members of the same Inn of Court. I make sure I attend any lectures or after dinner speeches he makes. I have to go now but will give you a response in the next few days. I need to reiterate, though: a Christian burial assumes that the interment of the dead is permanent.'

Chapter Eight

Neither Sandy nor Rich, for the rest of that week, put any effort into organising the exhumation as it seemed that the Worshipful Chancellor wasn't likely to grant the necessary consent, or bishop's faculty, as he had called it.

As Hannah was coming back to Cambridge early, Sandy headed home on the Thursday. He got to Ely just as his mother was heading out for her book club meeting. 'What book are you reading, Mum?'

'*Hamnet* by Maggie O'Farrell,' she said. 'The language in the book is wonderful.'

'I am sure it is wonderful, but I prefer the John Grisham book I read over Easter.'

Sandy settled in his room after having had the pasta dinner his mother had left him. He looked at his notebook relating to the death of William Peveril. He started writing what actions he and Rich needed to complete to get themselves ready for an exhumation, which they hoped to carry out in a week to ten days' time.

Authorities and Permissions: they had this in hand with the coroner having given permission, and they awaited a response from the Derby diocese. The coroner could give them a warrant if they had a suspicion that a criminal offence had been committed, but they didn't really believe that at the moment.

Family liaison: this was being carried out by Sandy, but of course a key person that required family liaison – the spouse, Monica Peveril – hadn't had this supplied to her, or even offered to her. Reason, Sandy wrote: if it were established that a criminal offence may have taken place, the only suspect would be Monica.

Transport and Mortuary procedures: the same funeral directors that undertook the repatriation were contacted and would also assist with staff to help extract the coffin from the grave; they would also carry out the transport back for the reinterment.

Reinterment: James and Arabella had organised with the vicar to carry out a short service as their father was returned to his grave, with just them present.

Health and Safety: Rich had, as required by the guidance, contacted Derbyshire County Council, and DC Dobson had met the head of Environmental Health for the council at the graveyard in St Peter's Church. The environmental officer had told him that the police needed to ensure that no member of the public could view the exhumation and three thirty a.m. is the time it should take place. Luckily, due to its location, the hearse could get in position just next to the grave. He was happy with the soil sample he had taken and was sure that nothing from the exhumation would go into or disturb any of the surrounding graves.

Resources: these were all in place, including Dr Nicholas Stroud who would carry out the post-mortem. This would take place at a mortuary in Sheffield.

Sandy looked at all that he had covered. No doubt other detectives who were more experienced than him may have included anything he may have missed. However, between Rich and himself, they were, even if they hadn't realised it, all set to carry out the exhumation.

∞

Sandy spent the next afternoon wandering round Ely with Hannah, which included a nice walk along the River Great Ouse pathway. That evening, they visited the Cutter Inn with Sandy's father; his Grandad Tom was also there.

On the Saturday morning, Sandy planned to take Hannah back to her home in Cambridge. She had been away from there for ten days and was keen to get herself prepared for a court case she had starting on the Monday in Sheffield Crown Court. It was a rape case that Hannah was prosecuting, an area of the law that a number of CPS offices were now asking for her to prosecute on their behalf. Her empathy and fiery determination for her victims stood out for all to see.

Before they did, they took the short walk into Ely Market Place; it was buzzing with people everywhere. Saturday was market day, and on that morning, there were lots of stalls selling crafts and food and drink. Even though Sandy had just eaten one of his mother's large breakfasts, he was tempted by so many of the artisan foods on offer.

In the end all they bought was a coffee each, which they drank as they walked around looking at the stalls and talking to the large number of people that seemed to know Sandy and were keen to find out who the beautiful woman was that was with him. Sandy was so pleased that Hannah seemed to love Ely as much as he did.

Chapter Nine

Shortly after the Monday morning team meeting, an extremely pleasing email arrived. It was from the Worshipful Chancellor, saying that he had agreed to the request for a Diocese of Derby's Bishops Faculty for the exhumation of William Harrison Peveril. There was at the bottom of the permission form a number of conditions, but the main one was that the body must be reinterned in exactly the same grave, and for there to be a Christian reinterment service. This must take place as soon after the post-mortem as possible to ensure the body had not left the grave for too long a period.

'We have already organised to ensure that this condition is in place,' Sandy mumbled to himself, as he jumped up off his seat and shouted, 'Yes!' This brought a number of looks from those around him in the team and wider across the large open-plan office. Juliet, who had just returned from leave, looked at him quizzically.

'We have got permission for the exhumation,' Sandy mouthed to her across the room, which brought as large a smile to her face as there was to his.

When Sandy called Rich, he was equally pleased. The two of them provisionally discussed the exhumation, which they wanted to take place beginning in the very early hours of that Friday morning. Key people though needed to be available, one of which was, of course, the forensic pathologist Dr Nicholas Stroud, but also the head of environmental services for Derbyshire.

The next call that Sandy received, he was pleased to see, was from Arabella. 'Hello, Arabella, an opportune time for you to call.' Sandy didn't continue with what he was saying as he could hear that Arabella was crying. 'What is wrong?' he asked instead.

'Monica has gone crazy shouting at me,' Arabella sobbed. 'She has said she will fight me and James to stop William's body being exhumed.'

Sandy frantically tried to think how Monica knew about it. Who had told her about the exhumation? Was it Rich? No, it couldn't be, he would have said. It could only be one of two people: either the Worshipful Chancellor or the coroner. That's as long as James hadn't told her, but why would he?

'Can we stop making arrangements to have my father's body dug up and then cut up?'

Trying to remain very calm and not let it be heard in his voice, Sandy now had extreme nervousness that all of his and Rich's hard work to organise everything was going to fail, at almost the final hurdle, so he just said, 'Please don't cry, Arabella. Have you got someone with you?'

'Yes, there will be, as Monty is now on his way back to the farmhouse.'

'We have permission to carry out the exhumation. Hopefully it will take place this Friday morning.'

'I know. James had only just called me before Monica did, to say the vicar had asked for us all to be in the churchyard on Saturday morning for the reinterment.'

Got you, Sandy thought, it was the Worshipful Chancellor. 'What did you say to Monica when she was shouting at you?'

'I couldn't get a word in edgeways. She was going on about how James and I had never accepted her. How both of us, and even our father, had placed my mother on a pedestal. How could she ever have competed with this long-dead woman. She was really nasty and quite vile, which has surprised me.' Arabella started crying loudly again. Sandy was pleased to hear the kitchen door to the farmhouse open and close. Monty must have arrived home. 'In the four years or so since I have known Monica, I have never known her to display any emotion. There is another extremely frightening side to her as I have just found out.'

'I am not sure that we should stop the arrangements for the exhumation. It is the right thing to do now we have committed to it. Hopefully, we will find out why your father died. It may well be a heart attack, but at least we will know,' Sandy said, and he could hear Monty saying quietly in the background, 'Yes, sweetheart. It will be fine.'

'OK,' Arabella said. 'Please carry on with your arrangements, Sandy, and hope that Monica is not able to stop you.'

∞

After scrolling through his phone for a few moments, Sandy found the number that Revd Repton had previously called him on and rang it.

'Hello, this is Paul Repton, how can I help you?'

'This is DCI McFarlane.' Trying hard to be pleasant and not show how annoyed he was, Sandy said, 'Thank you for signing the Bishops Faculty to enable us to carry out the exhumation, which we hope to do this Friday morning.' Pausing for a moment to see if Paul Repton replied, which he didn't – Revd Repton was not a man for small talk – Sandy continued, 'Is it possible to please tell me who you discussed the exhumation with?'

'I'm not sure what you mean?'

'Did you tell anyone you were granting the Bishops Faculty?'

'Oh, yes, of course I did. I told the vicar of St Peter's Church in Edensor.'

The vicar was now another person who needed to be contacted to see if they had told Monica. It could quite possibly be the vicar as he had called both Arabella and James to organise the reinterment. 'Did you speak to any member of the family?'

'No, I didn't. I am sorry, but I have to go as I am due in court in ten minutes. Please say hello to your grandfather, Judge McFarlane, for me when you next see him.'

Who was it best to call next, the vicar or the coroner? As he had spoken to the coroner in the past, he thought it best to call him first before looking up the number of the vicar.

The phone call was answered straight away by the coroner's receptionist, who put Sandy through to the coroner.

'Hello, this is the senior coroner for the Peak District, Arthur Ramsbottom. How can I help you?' Mr Ramsbottom did sound extremely pompous, alerting Sandy to be aware that he needed to tread carefully.

'Hello, I am DCI McFarlane. I am working with DCI Singh from the Derbyshire Police looking into the death of the late Viscount Peveril.'

Before he could say any more, Mr Ramsbottom said, 'My dear friend William. Did you know we had been friends for over forty years.'

Yes, Sandy did know this as he had been told either by Rich or James Peveril – he couldn't remember which, nor did it matter now. He butted in to stop the reminiscing going back too far and said, 'Have you spoken to any member of the family about the exhumation?'

'Yes, of course. As a coroner it is my duty to work with families and ensure we treat their loved ones with the utmost respect. I had a case a few years ago...'

'Sorry to interrupt again,' Sandy said, breaking up the flow of Mr Ramsbottom's speech. 'In this case, who did you speak to?'

'Everyone involved.'

'Was Monica Peveril one of the family members you spoke to?'

'Yes, she was extremely cross. I would expect a phone call and complaint from her about DCI Singh, or you, or both of you.'

'Why did you call Monica?' Sandy asked, by now his extremely frustrated voice giving him away.

'Are you, young man, questioning me on who I should talk to?' The pompous voice had now turned into a very loud pompous voice. 'You have no right to do that. I am the coroner, not you, young man. So, I do not take kindly to you questioning me.'

Sandy was sure that Mr Ramsbottom was going to put the phone down on him, so quickly said, 'I am so sorry, but we were trying not to alert Monica Peveril in case at the post-mortem we find anything suspicious. We are still having a post-mortem, aren't we?'

'I wasn't asked not to contact family members. Of course we are still having a post-mortem. James is

William's next of kin. I originally released the body to him for burial. I will be honest with you; my wife and I have no time for Monica. We have only been out with them once and after that avoided her at any function we went to when they were present.'

Sandy breathed a long sigh of relief but it seemed he was going to be on the phone for a long while as Mr Ramsbottom went back to tell him the story that he had started earlier in the conversation.

∞

Everything had now been organised for the exhumation to take place in the early hours of Friday morning. Sandy, Juliet, Clare and Rich's team had a last-minute planning meeting via a video conference. Also present was the Environmental Health officer, who was nothing like as bureaucratic as Rich had portrayed to Sandy; they were just taking their responsibilities seriously. DC Lofty Dobson was not present but would be on Friday to help with exhibits. Rich had given the investigation an operational name and it was now called Operation Cornflower.

A phone call from Hannah on the Wednesday morning had caused Sandy to slightly change his plans for when he headed up to Derbyshire. It appeared that Hannah would not be required in court in Sheffield on the Thursday afternoon, but she had to be back there for Friday morning. They could spend the afternoon together in Derbyshire.

On Thursday morning, Sandy set off from home in his Morgan Roadster. He had made his way back to Ely the previous night. His trip to Sheffield was pretty uneventful. He was driving with the immense pleasure of having the roof of the car down, even though it was slightly overcast and a little bit too windy. Sandy made sure he had put the roof up as Hannah raced out of court at lunchtime, still dressed in her court suit but carrying a bag with, presumably, clothes for her to change into.

The journey to Chatsworth House, which was the place they had agreed would be brilliant to visit, took forty-five minutes. It flew by because they were so engrossed in conversation about Hannah's court case and Sandy's investigation.

As they drove up the driveway and over a magnificent stone bridge, the view across to the incredible house, which was nestled in the valley with the backdrop of wooded hillsides behind and water in the front of the house, was breath-taking. If there hadn't been a queue of cars behind him, Sandy would have stopped to appreciate this particular viewpoint for much longer. Hannah and Sandy glanced and smiled lovingly at each other, before looking back at the sight of the house and grounds.

While Sandy went and got tickets, Hannah went to the café toilet to get changed and also to buy Sandy and herself a sandwich each. She knew that keeping Sandy fed regularly kept him focussed. When Hannah returned to the car, she found that Sandy had wandered off and was looking across at the house from the front corner.

Chatsworth House is the home of the Duke and Duchess of Devonshire. Building for the house started at the end of the sixteenth century with another main construction phase in the early to mid-1800s. The house had been passed down through an unbelievable line of sixteen generations of the same family.

Within the house itself they were able to visit a number

of rooms with stunning art and architecture. Hannah couldn't help looking at Sandy and smiling to herself as she knew how much he loved this sort of visit, in particular the artworks. This beats sitting in a Crown Court in Sheffield, she thought.

Some of the highlights in the house for them were the painted hall that they went into soon after arrival and the chapel, which was very impressive, as was the state drawing room.

When Sandy eventually appeared, having early on dragged well behind Hannah, they went out into the beautiful gardens, which had water cascading down the hill and another body of water on the side of the house with a water fountain, which happened to be working that day as they walked around.

They didn't have much more time to look around, although it would have been fun to have a proper look at the grounds and enjoy a much longer walk in the vast estate. However, they needed to make their way to a hotel in a nearby village to meet up with Juliet and Clare. They were staying overnight ready for the exhumation, which was to take place very close to this hotel. Hannah was going to leave much later than them and get a taxi back to court in Sheffield.

Chapter Ten

By the time Sandy went out into the car park, Juliet and Clare were already in the car with the engine running and ready to go. Although they knew it was going to be dark, as it was only just after three o'clock in the morning, it was disappointing to see that the bright moonlight that they had seen when they had gone to bed had gone. The moon was now pretty much covered in clouds and there was a faint swirling mist all around them.

Even though he had made lots of noise while getting washed and dressed and packing his belongings away, Hannah had hardly stirred but had just roused enough to kiss him goodbye and wish him good luck before returning to her comatose sleep. Her taxi was not due until seven a.m., so she still had ample time to sleep. As they left the car park, Sandy glanced around to make sure his Morgan was still there. He planned to collect it much later that day.

St Peter's Church was a very short journey away and all of them were shocked by the amount of people milling around on their arrival. It looked like the exhumation had a cast of thousands. The first people they saw were a whole group of uniform officers lining the perimeter, one of whom had a clipboard and ticked off their names before letting them into the churchyard. Lofty, who was already there, came straight up to Sandy and gave him a smothering hug, which he then proceeded to do with Juliet and Clare, having also worked with them both before.

As soon as Sandy saw Rich, he said, 'I have just had a thought, that we need to make sure we have a media strategy in place. Even though it is the middle of the night, with this level of police activity, I am sure social media and then the press will get wind that something major is going on.'

'All in hand. I have put together a press response if we are asked, which says that we are investigating a suspicious death and need to exhume a body to clarify the reason someone died,' Rich replied, smiling. He looked wide awake and excited at the prospect of what they were about to do that day.

The swirling mist should have added greatly to an eerie feeling of being in a graveyard in the middle of the night. Sandy had thought that it might be a scary experience, but as he walked with Rich to the high wire-dense cloth-covered screens that had been placed all around the grave, he realised that with all of the activity going on, it was incidental that it was all taking place in a graveyard.

Another officer was standing by what was in essence an inner cordon and ticked off the names for Sandy and Rich to let them in. Inside the screens, William's grave was totally and powerfully illuminated by a series of lights that had been set in place. The lights were so bright that it could have been the middle of the day, not three thirty a.m. in the morning. The Environmental Health officer who was there told them that he was happy as the scans and tests they had taken of the grave showed there were no issues with the water table and the coffin would be dry. He had also checked the soil and there was no likelihood of contamination and no disturbance of any other body having moved into the grave, or William having moved elsewhere.

This presumably would have been a major problem in graves where people had been buried for a considerable amount of time.

It was now abundantly clear to see why Revd Repton felt that it was not respectful to disturb the remains of a body once they had had a Christian burial. He was right, there was nothing sacred in what they were doing to William Peveril's last resting place on the earth.

The grave diggers were in place. Three men were standing there with shovels; they, of everybody present, looked the most asleep and the most uninterested in what they were about to be doing. They, or at least two of them, had only a few weeks ago dug this grave and it probably seemed a bit crazy to them to be digging up the coffin again.

It was amazing how quickly the grave diggers worked once they were given the go-ahead by the environmental officer. The noise of the steady rhythm of them, digging and shovelling the soil into a pile at the side of the grave, reverberated throughout the graveyard. This noise brought everyone's minds abruptly back to what they were doing there and why they were doing it. All other noises, including any talking, had now stopped in recognition of the solemn activity now taking place.

Even with three men digging, it still took a considerable amount of time to dig down to the coffin. Although there was no set and fast rule, a coffin was normally buried at six feet below the ground. An hour or even more had passed by the time the men had got to this point, and the top of the coffin was now completely visible. They could see that the coffin was made of oak and still had a very shiny gold inscription plate on the coffin lid.

The next step for the men was getting down into the grave so they could move the earth from all around the coffin to enable them to get what looked like leather straps underneath it.

Two undertakers, Lofty – who had appeared from nowhere – and the grave diggers, extremely slowly but very carefully, lifted the coffin out of the grave and over to the pathway just next to the cloth-covered wire screens.

A car could then be heard to be reversing on the road directly outside the churchyard entrance. After a few moments, the six of them picked up the coffin by its gold-coloured handles and walked out of the churchyard.

Although not completely daylight as yet, the sky, in spite of the mist, had turned a lot lighter and the sound of birds in the trees in and around the churchyard was quite loud. How long the birds had been singing, Sandy had no idea, as all he had heard was the rhythmic noise of the spades.

They all left the churchyard together. Rich was going to travel with Juliet, Sandy and Clare, as Lofty was following the hearse to the hospital mortuary for continuity of the body purposes. The police officers around the churchyard were already packing up and getting into a police van, leaving one officer to act as security for the screened area around the grave itself until William returned to the grave the next day.

∞

On their way to the hospital in Sheffield they found a café that was open and they all had a very hearty breakfast. They were all talking incessantly about what they had just witnessed and how well it had been organised in such a short period of time. Sandy, feeling sorry for Lofty, had bought him coffee and a bacon bap takeaway.

The mortuary was like they all seemed to be, around the back of the hospital and almost in the basement. There was a man there waiting for them, who, it turned out, was someone Clare had used in the past to examine bodies using alternative light sources that would pick out bruising or other trauma not seen in normal lighting. It would probably be no use in this case due to a level of decomposition but Clare thought it was worth a try.

Dr Nicholas Stroud was there already, dressed in his blue scrubs, as were two mortuary assistants and also Lofty who was going to be taking any exhibits that Dr Stroud gave him. Clare went off to get herself in scrubs as she was going to be taking the photographs. The scrubs Lofty was wearing almost fitted his six-foot-six frame, but this didn't stop them all having banter and laughter with him about how it fitted.

Dr Stroud asked, 'Sandy, where is my coffee and breakfast?' as Sandy handed over the breakfast to Lofty. 'That meal you have promised for ages has just not materialised, has it?' They both laughed. The pair of them had promised each other months ago that they would meet up for a meal, either in London or Cambridge, but this hadn't happened as yet.

'William will be back with us in a moment as he has been taken for x-rays and a CT scan,' Dr Stroud said, which was a bit unnerving as he was talking as if William was still alive, but Sandy had heard him give evidence in court before and Dr Stroud had told the jury that a body was still a person to him and he always used their name.

After a short while, one of the mortuary technicians came through and told them that they had now placed William on a table ready for the examination. First to go into the room was Clare and the alternative imaging man to complete their examination.

Dr Stroud on looking at a computer screen said, 'That was quick.' The consultant radiologist had already sent an initial written report on her findings and would send through a formal report in the next few days. 'That's why he was in so much pain, he has a collapsed disc in some lower vertebrae. They have not ruptured, but he would have been suffering a high level of pain.' Dr Stroud looked around at Sandy and Rich and asked, 'Do you know what drugs he was on for the pain? That might end up being important, due to raising his blood pressure and putting pressure on his heart.'

'I am sorry, we don't, I am afraid. We checked in Saint-Émilion and Bordeaux, but nothing to help.' Saffy had got back to Sandy saying that she had rang every likely place in Bordeaux but she could find no one who had sold strong pain relief to anyone matching Monica's description.

'There is no sign of any broken bones or any trauma seen on the x-ray or CT scan that the radiologist can see,' Dr Stroud said, reading from his computer screen.

They all walked into a windowless room that had two stainless steel examination tables in the centre of it. The floor and walls were all tiled in what probably was best described as a cream colour. Juliet, Rich and Sandy went round to one side of the room and stood on the other side of a clear screen that looked over the table that William Peveril had been laid onto.

The first thing that Sandy noticed on entering was the

smell within the room. He had experienced this smell and the taste on a number of occasions before and it just didn't get any better. He got out one of the packets of extra strong mints that he had bought specially and passed them round.

Dr Stroud used the extremely strong lights that were over the table. He was able to pull down and move about these lights to assist him to examine the whole of the body. The body actually had little decomposition other than changes in colour to the skin.

'No sign of any external trauma. I think we would have presumed that anyway. Let me go to the area that we all want to know about.' One of the technicians had cracked open William's chest and Dr Stroud removed the heart, having had a good look at it before he did so. He went over to the other table with the heart in a stainless steel tray. This table was further away from them so they couldn't really see what he was doing.

After what appeared an inordinate length of time, Dr Stroud, looking over at Juliet, Rich and Sandy, said in a loud voice, 'Obviously very difficult to say without examining the heart microscopically, but it doesn't look like William died from a heart attack!'

Chapter Eleven

They all looked at each other in complete astonishment. Lofty and Clare moved forward to peer over Dr Stroud's shoulder, as if they would be able to see from the heart that he had been dissecting what he was talking about. All of them were struggling to understand what Dr Stroud meant, so he said, 'Don't get me wrong, this is not the heart of a young person, but there is little macroscopic evidence of any heart disease that is so bad to have killed him. I am almost certain, the failure of his heart is not why he died, but I will take samples of heart tissue to confirm my initial conclusions.'

'What could he have died of then?' Rich whispered to Sandy, not just a question but also a statement. Sandy shrugged his shoulders and Juliet had a look of concern on her face.

Sandy looked across at William Peveril lying naked on the examination table, or the slab as some people referred to it. He was lying there with his chest cracked open. Sandy had been to a number of forensic post-mortems during his detective career but none of them had been for someone who was a person he had known in real life. When he had first entered the mortuary examination room, he had felt more than a little bit unnerved when he had first seen the body. Seeing the very proud and charismatic William Peveril naked had added to the feeling of unease. The feeling had slowly subsided as they moved into a professional role as the post-mortem began. Sandy summoned back the thought that it was William lying there, not just a body that was being cut up, and he whispered under his breath to himself, promising William that, 'We will find out what happened to you.'

Dr Stroud walked back to the body and he moved methodically through each organ, firstly having it photographed by Clare, then examining that particular organ. He then took tissue samples, which Lofty then took and marked up as exhibits. He also took samples from a couple of muscles from which they would be able to extract blood as they were full of capillaries.

Samples were taken of cut and plucked hair from the scalp by Dr Stroud. After this had taken place, the sound of the mortuary technician opening up the skull to provide access to the brain was particularly unnerving to everyone but the pathologist and the two mortuary technicians.

When he had done all that he could and had been working for what felt like a number of hours, Dr Stroud came to a stop. He had finished his examination. He said to Sandy and Rich, not sure who might have the answer for him, 'I know that the coroner has authorised the taking of samples, but I presume the family have also authorised us to dispose of the samples when we have finished with them?' Everyone looked at Sandy as he was the person with the family contact. 'I only ask,' Dr Stroud continued, 'because I understand the reinterment of the body is happening tomorrow morning and the last thing the family will want is to have to then deal with the repatriation to the body of these human tissue samples at a later date.'

Sandy, who hadn't thought about this at all, now looked very sheepish and said, 'I will sort it out before tomorrow, in fact I'll ring the family after we have finished here.'

Looking very solemnly at them, Dr Stroud said, 'Well, the cause of death is, in my professional view, currently unascertained.'

'You must have your suspicion about what the cause of death could be though, haven't you, Dr Stroud?' Rich suggested. After watching over a number of hours almost every inch of the body being examined, he and the others thought there must surely be some clue.

'I am not one to speculate,' Dr Stroud said, very abruptly, but at the same time they could pick out the frustration in his voice. All of the detectives had to admit that he had done the most thorough and amazing examination.

'Have you please any suggestions for us on what we do now to further our investigation?' Rich asked, trying to regain the lost ground his last comment might have caused.

'Not too sure from a medical point of view what that could be. Of course, the key to this is sending off the samples to the right specialists to examine them for you. Another thing you could do is find out what painkillers he was taking, and then what happened in the moments before he died.'

The answer to these questions, unfortunately, were only known by Monica Peveril, and she was someone Sandy didn't want to talk to as yet because he wanted something definite to speak to her about. He still didn't know in his mind whether she was a significant witness or a suspect. Probably at the moment, a witness; no, not probably – definitely a witness.

There was nothing else that could be done. Dr Stroud had been talking into a Dictaphone throughout the examination and he promised Rich and Sandy that he would have an interim report for them in a couple of weeks at the most. However, there would be nothing new in there, unless by any chance the toxicology had returned and that cast any new light on the investigation. Clare, who had a contact in the Met Police lab, said to Rich that she should be able to fast-track them and she – well, the FCDO – would pay the premium payment bill.

Clare and Lofty went off to change out of the scrubs. Juliet was going to wait for them and go with them to a police station in Chesterfield to drop off the exhibits. Sandy, after taking a long last look at William, who now no longer looked like William, went off with Rich to travel back to Derbyshire. The incredibly skilled mortuary technicians had already begun their work by completely washing the body and then sewing and gluing William back together. They would also dress him back in his suit ready to be returned to his coffin and then back into the ground. Sandy and Rich, as they trudged back out of the hospital to their car, would have looked to anyone glancing at them like two very dejected men.

∞

Rich dropped Sandy off at the hotel that he had stayed in very briefly the previous night. It was only a few hours ago now that they had stood in the graveyard at Edensor's village parish church, so hopeful of having a definitive cause of death. However, they were now no further forward; in fact, they were possibly further back. If it had been a heart attack, the case would have been resolved. Now it was very much unresolved. What was the word Dr

Stroud had used… 'unascertained'.

After making a snap decision, as it wasn't too far away, Sandy drove to Losehill Farmhouse in Hope, the home address of James and his wife, Janice Peveril. As he drove up the driveway, he was pleased to see Arabella's large black Range Rover parked there. The house was in such a lovely location with the ridgeway that runs from Mam Tor to Losehill towering in the background behind the house.

Janice answered the doorbell when he rang it and was very surprised, but at the same time pleased to see him, showing this by embracing Sandy. She showed him into the large and spacious lounge. Sat there in a large armchair by an unlit stone fireplace was James. On the nearby settee were Arabella and Monty, who had come to stay at James's house ready for the reinterment at St Peter's the next morning. They all rose to greet Sandy.

Even before Sandy had sat down, Arabella looking at him very keenly, asked him, 'How did my father die? What have you found out?'

Sandy would have loved to be able to give Arabella, in fact all of them, an answer, but he of course was unable to and said, 'I am afraid we just don't know.' He looked around at the dejected faces in the room. 'Dr Stroud, the forensic pathologist, spent literally hours looking, but at the end of the post-mortem said the cause of death was currently unascertained. I am sorry I don't have any more conclusive news than that at the moment.'

'So, not even his heart,' James said, as he passed Sandy a cup of tea that Janice had made for him. This family knew him too well. James looked at Arabella while he said, 'I was sure it would turn out to actually be his heart.'

'Dr Stroud says it is unlikely that he died as a result of

heart disease, but more tests need to be done to confirm that,' Sandy said. He was starting to feel happier due to the large slice of chocolate cake that Janice had just given him to go with his cup of tea.

Looking very forlorn, Arabella said, 'I am so sorry that I have caused so much upset by wanting my father's death investigated.' She looked straight at James, started to cry and said, 'James, why didn't you say to me, don't go ahead with this, if you thought our father had died of a heart attack?'

'Sister, you know that I have and always will support you in everything, and in this you needed my support.' He would have gone to comfort her but Monty was already doing this.

Although Sandy felt now was the time to leave this family to their own private grief, he still had a couple of questions to ask. 'I know you have the reinterment in the morning but I need to ask you something. We have taken a number of tissue samples for further pathological investigation. These investigations may not be finished for several weeks at least. What would you like doing with them when we have finished with them?'

Monty asked Sandy, 'What do you mean? I am not sure that we have a say in this, do we?'

Before Sandy could answer, James – who, although an MP now, was a lawyer by trade – looking at Monty and the still crying Arabella, said, 'Monty, this is because the samples that Sandy is talking about come under the authority of the Human Tissue Act when all the tests have been completed. An option we have is for them to be reburied with our father.' He then looked at Sandy and said, 'I am the next of kin and I give the police and the hospital permission to dispose of them as they think fit. Can I sign something now?'

Sandy wrote out a couple of sentences in the notebook that he had for the investigation, and as James was signing the entry, Sandy asked them if they had heard anything else from Monica.

James said he had seen her a couple of times in the house in Eaton Square that week. They had exchanged pleasantries but Monica was showing no different emotions to what she had always done.

As Sandy got up to go, Arabella said, 'Sandy, can I go and see my father before we bury him again?'

Thinking about the extensive post-mortem and how much there remained of William, Sandy wanted to say, if not plead with Arabella, not to do it. He knew though that this wasn't his choice to make or influence. He didn't want Arabella to regret not doing it, if she really wanted to, even though it was not what he would advise. He said, 'It must be your choice, Arabella, not mine, and I am sure the hospital or the undertakers would facilitate it if you wanted.'

James said, 'Arabella, I am not going with you. I want to remember our father as that upright, strong willed and charismatic man we have known all our lives. We have seen him twice already while dead.'

Sandy quickly said goodbye and left the family to sort through their discussion on the viewing of the body. He was feeling very tired; it had been an incredibly long day. He was probably too tired to be driving back to Ely, so he drove to a friend's house, who also lived in the village of Hope. He was pleased to see that they had their nearby beautiful Bobbin Cottage available for him to spend the night in and they promised to take him out for a meal at the Curry Cabin.

Chapter Twelve

By the time that Sandy had got home to Ely on the Saturday afternoon, Hannah was already there. His dad was entertaining her while his mum had gone off to do a volunteering session at the cathedral – apparently someone was sick so she had gone in to help out.

No sooner had Sandy got himself changed when he heard the front door open, followed by the loud voice of his Grandad Tom. On getting back downstairs, he saw that Hannah had taken his grandad off into the conservatory.

'Where is Grandma?' Sandy asked him.

'At home, but Hannah wanted a quiet word with me this weekend so I have come along now.' Although Sandy knew how close Hannah was to his other grandfather and he also knew how fond of her Grandad Tom was, he was still a bit surprised by this comment. Hannah had his whole family in the palm of her hands, in particular his grandfathers!

'You can sit in and listen if you want, Sandy,' Hannah said. 'But you are so protective of other detectives it would have been pointless asking you what I wanted to know.'

'Why? Try me,' Sandy said, feeling and sounding quite hurt.

'I have a case conference on Monday for a brief I have just picked up. It is the case of a man who has allegedly set fire to four different premises. Two premises are pubs he was staying in, but the other two are residential addresses.'

'What has he been charged with?' Sandy asked, now trying to be overly helpful.

Tom said, 'Sandy, just wait until Hannah asks a question, don't butt in.'

Sandy now sat quietly; his grandad had spoken! Hannah, enjoying this, said, 'Yes, Sandy, keep quiet.' She smiled at him. 'Arson with intent to endanger life, times four, if you must know. The problem I have is that I have the initial set of papers and as far as I can see, the senior detective's key decision log is all over the place. I have no idea of the direction of his enquiry. I want to advise on what we need to do to get trial ready.'

As Sandy had quickly left the room, Grandad Tom said, 'I presume you have the evidence that links all four fires?'

'Yes,' Hannah said, as Sandy returned clutching two books. 'The fire service investigators and the forensics have linked them through a number of similarities. Of course, our defendant is present at each of the fires as well.'

'Look at one of my key decision logs,' Sandy said, as he showed Hannah the one's he had been writing his decisions in for the death of William Peveril. 'At the top is the decision, normally a strategy,' he said, showing her a page titled 'witness strategy'. 'Then I write a reason or rationale for that decision below it, and then what we are going to do about the decision.' Even his Grandad Tom was impressed when he also looked at the decision log. Sandy didn't know who he wanted to impress the most with his key decision log, but it was most probably his grandfather rather than Hannah. Unfortunately, Sandy thought, in the case of William Peveril, keeping a good decision log hadn't helped him to even determine if a crime had occurred.

'The one I have is nothing like this,' Hannah said. 'I am

not sure how I, as a young twenty-seven-year-old barrister, tell a seasoned senior detective his decision-making is not good enough!'

'Why do they think the defendant has committed these crimes? What is the senior detective's hypothesis for what he believes the motive is?' Tom asked.

'That is what is missing, you are wonderful!' Hannah beamed at Tom. 'Thinking about it now, the defendant was always present and the one to find the fires and the one to save people and get them out of the buildings. No one, luckily, was too badly hurt, other than through smoke inhalation.'

'Sounds to me almost like Munchausen's syndrome by proxy,' Tom said, then looking at the bewildered faces of his grandson and Hannah, he said, 'Munchausen was a Bavarian baron who made up wildly untrue stories of his exploits. He was looking for attention to be focussed on him. This is what I think you should suggest, Hannah. Start the meeting telling them that you want to prosecute this case based on your hypothesis that the defendant deliberately started the fires, to be the hero, for which he was personally getting emotional and psychological benefit from. You need the police and CPS to find someone to overview and link all of the fire evidence together and then for them to get all health records, where there may be some mental health illness recorded, and then a clinical psychologist to assist and provide a professional opinion.'

Both Sandy and Hannah looked at Tom in awe. The old detective then started to tell them about a similar case that he had had and how he and his team had managed to convict the defendant in that case.

By the time he had finished telling them about another

unrelated case, Katherine and Sandy's Grandma Margaret had arrived and Tom was told to stop his reminiscing as they needed to head home for their evening meal.

∞

After having a lie-in and a leisurely breakfast, Sandy and Hannah went out for a walk together. They walked the Ely Eel Trail. Sandy had wanted to take Hannah around this in the past, but other events had got in the way. They had, though, already run quite a lot of the trail when they had completed the triathlon.

The trail had been created to show off the heritage of Ely and was waymarked by seventy markers. The trail started at the Oliver Cromwell House, which had some parts of the building from the thirteenth century and had been home to the Roundhead Oliver Cromwell during the sixteenth century. Sandy thought of the one occasion when Hannah's father had visited Ely; he had been fascinated by Oliver Cromwell's house.

Because the trail went past his house's front door, they started there and walked in a circle from the house. Sandy was glad for the distraction as he was struggling to completely put out of his mind the emotions of an exhumation, of digging up a body, the extensive and totally intrusive post-mortem, and the emotions of talking to the family and the visibly upset Arabella Montague.

For what? he thought. Only for it to be an unascertained cause of death. Why hadn't he been stronger with Arabella when they had met at St James's Park Café? Why had he let Juliet talk him into visiting France and let himself be seduced by the excitement of being involved in the exhumation? He knew why. It was because he loved investigating and the opportunity to investigate a possibly suspicious death was too great for him to resist.

They took a diversion so Sandy could show Hannah where the Boat Race between Oxford and Cambridge had taken place just a few weeks earlier on Easter Sunday. The traditional race had been moved to Ely from the Thames for one year only and was held on the River Great Ouse. Although he hadn't been able to see the race, even though he actually lived facing the river, Sandy was proud to tell Hannah that Cambridge had won again, and he reemphasised the word 'again'.

The family were having Sunday lunch at the Old Fire Engine House restaurant. The Old Fire Engine House was very close to the cathedral in an old Georgian building that over a hundred years ago had housed Ely's fire engine, which had originally been a horse-drawn fire engine. Although the restaurant was a favourite of Sandy and his family, Hannah had never been and she was equally excited to see that John McFarlane was also joining them for Sunday lunch. He was going to give Hannah a lift back to Cambridge when they had finished so that she could prepare for her case conference the next day. Sandy was sure his Grandpa John would critique what his other grandfather had advised Hannah.

Not long after they had finished lunch and Hannah had headed off to Cambridge, while Sandy was walking home with his mother and father after they had gone past the cathedral and started walking through Cherry Hill Park, he received a phone call from Rich.

'Hello, Sandy, sorry to disturb you on a Sunday but I have just had a call asking for comment by a reporter who is freelance and sells his stories to anyone that will buy them. I am not a fan of him, but you have to take your hat off to him.' Sandy, sensing the call was going to take a long time, had stopped and waved his parents on. He stood and gazed over at the cathedral. The side view from the park was magnificent.

'What has happened then, Rich?'

'As we thought, due to the heavy police presence at St Peter's Church and in and around Edensor, social media was pretty electric in the area. He must have picked up on this.'

'Who is this person?'

'Patrick Hallam, he has been around a long time. Well, he went into the church to investigate this morning, pretending no doubt to be a parishioner. The vicar didn't tell him anything, but wandering around the churchyard afterwards he saw that the only grave that had been disturbed was the grave of the late Viscount William Harrison Peveril. He has pushed me quite hard for a quote and wants to know why we have disturbed the grave.'

'Sounds like he doesn't know we have had an exhumation and a post-mortem, does it?'

'Not sure he would know what an exhumation is. I agree with you, he was probably just fishing. I gave nothing away, but maybe tip off James and Arabella. James I am sure will know him – as the local MP for the Hope Valley their paths must have crossed.'

'OK. I will take the risk of not ringing them today but call them sometime tomorrow.'

∞

When Sandy heard his dad leave the house very early in the morning, having decided himself against the Monday morning train commute to London, he felt quite blissful as he turned over and fell back fast asleep.

Jane Watson had agreed he could work from home on the Monday but was needed back in the office on the Tuesday. Sandy took full advantage of the opportunity and went for a run first thing, getting home just as his mum left for her work as a primary school teacher.

He spent nearly all morning signing off files and reading and sending emails. It wasn't until the early afternoon that he remembered that he needed to speak to James and Arabella about the newspaper journalist. He rang James.

'Hello, Sandy, glad you called me as I was just about to call you.'

So the journalist had beaten him to it. Rich would not be impressed with him. 'I am sorry I didn't ring you yesterday. What did you say to Patrick Hallam?'

'Patrick Hallam, I know him, but have not heard from him for a little while. What is he after now? He always puts a negative slant on things and is sensational in his articles.'

'He has found out that there has been a disturbance at your father's grave and was fishing for information,' Sandy said, quite relieved that he had been in time after all.

'I won't say anything and neither will Arabella. I have only just left her. We have been to the solicitors for the reading of my father's will. That was what I was ringing to tell you. We forgot to say on Friday about it. As we were all here, we thought we would have the reading of the will this morning.'

'Was Monica there?'

'Yes, although very much her usual self, she was

actually quite chatty to both Arabella and myself. She must think nothing came of us wanting to dig our father up.'

Well nothing did come of it, did it, thought Sandy.

'My father's second wife was there and she was not very talkative.'

'Were there any unknown dramas with the will?' asked Sandy.

'No, pretty straightforward. I didn't know the details of the prenuptial agreements but everything that belonged to the Peveril family came to Arabella and me. He made a bequeath to each of my three children and a few charities in Derbyshire. Then his remaining personal money is to be shared between the two wives who came after our mother had died. He left them each something in excess of three hundred thousand pounds.' When Sandy whistled, James said, 'It is not really a lot. Monica has six months from our father's death to vacate Peveril House and that sum of money buys you nothing in London, if that is where she wants to stay.'

'Still, almost a hundred thousand pounds a year for the time they were married.'

James laughed. 'I suppose if you put it like that, not too bad then.' After he had finished laughing, James said, 'In all seriousness though, Sandy, she was much better off with my father alive than dead.'

Sandy knew that if there was any remote possibility that William had been killed by Monica this could be the only motive and James was ruling it out. Sandy, though, cheekily asked, 'What was your father's share of Peveril's valued at?'

James, who didn't seem offended by such a personal question, said, 'You would have to ask Arabella or Monty.

He would know as the finance director. Probably a lot more than you think.' Actually, Sandy did think quite a lot. 'An example is when we were at a charity event for a hospital in London. One of the owners of a big wine cooperative came over to our table and very loudly told my father that he would give us two million euros per hectare for Chateau Peveril.'

Sandy was quickly doing the maths as he knew from his trip to the chateau how many hectares they had there. Quietly to himself he went, 'Wow,' then said, 'Were any of you tempted?'

'Neither I nor my father was. The chateau has been in our family for a long time. Arabella might be though. As a businesswoman she knows if we put that level of money into the linseed farm and flax estate, we would be making far more money back than we do from wine.'

There was the sound of an announcer in the background and a train pulling in. 'Got to go, Sandy, speak to you soon.' With that, James had gone and left Sandy to ponder if this was the end of the line for the investigation into the death of William.

Chapter Thirteen

The loud buzzing noise that kept going off in his bedroom was slowly but surely making a sleeping Sandy come awake. For a moment or two he had no idea what the noise was, then he realised it was his phone making the noise. Sandy looked at the bedside clock in his bedroom of the flat he shared with his father in London.

The clock said it was only 6.05 a.m. On picking up his phone, he found that he had four missed calls from Arabella. 'What has happened?' he asked Arabella upon calling her number. 'Why are you ringing me so early?' Sandy said, almost whispering into his phone so as not to wake his father, who was sleeping in his nearby bedroom.

'When Monica left home yesterday evening, I followed her and she came to a house in Kensington and she has been in the house all night.'

So what? Sandy wanted to say, but now was not the time to do any straight talking to Arabella as he could pick up the excitement in her voice. 'Not really sure what you want me to do about it, Arabella.' He also wanted to say she is a grown woman in her forties, surely she can do what she wants.

'Please, please, Sandy, come here now. I am sure there is something going on.'

Sandy was also sure something was going on with Monica but he was not sure it was a police matter. With a big sigh, he said, 'OK, but I suspect it will take me forty-five minutes to get there.' He quickly got washed and dressed and slipped out of the flat just as his dad was getting up to get ready for work.

Just before seven a.m. Sandy walked around the corner of the road and into Cornwall Gardens in South Kensington. He could see ahead of him on the left-hand side of the road Arabella's big black Range Rover. Luckily for her this sort of car wasn't unusual in this area of London. Kensington is a wealthy and expensive place to live. Cornwall Gardens are one of a number of picturesque squares in London. It has private gardens running through the middle of the square for the use of the residents. The gardens looked well maintained and were full of bushes, shrubs and trees. The centuries-old London plane trees particularly stood out.

He gave Arabella a quizzical look as he got into the front passenger seat of the Range Rover. Arabella immediately said, 'Sorry, sorry. Thank you, thank you.' She really did look very apologetic and a bit sheepish. 'I just couldn't stop myself.'

Arabella, who had clearly been there all night, still looked amazing. Sandy said, 'Please tell me, which house we are looking at and then go back to the beginning and tell me why we are here, at seven in the morning?'

Pointing at a pretty two-storey terraced house with a bright red door, which was about four or five houses further down on their left-hand side, Arabella said, 'I have been asking James, what does Monica do with herself all the time? He had no idea and I think, quite frankly, no interest.'

'Why do you?' Sandy said. 'She will be out of your lives in only four months or so when she has to vacate Peveril House in Eaton Square.'

Totally ignoring the interruption, Arabella continued by saying, 'Monty and I came straight to London from the reading of the will in Sheffield as we have some meetings. When I saw her go out at nine p.m. I just had to follow her.'

'I presume she was walking. How did you follow her in this car without her noticing you?' an incredulous Sandy asked.

Smiling for the first time with her infectious smile that Sandy couldn't help but respond to in the same way, Arabella said, 'Of course not, I followed her on foot. She went into the house there and hasn't been out since. Monty brought the car along and stayed with me all night. He has walked home to get ready for the meetings today.'

The ever faithful, loving and dependable Charles Montague, Sandy thought. 'How do you know she hasn't left and gone out of the back of the house?'

'Monty went round there to check, and the houses on this side of the gardens just back onto the gardens of the street running parallel to this.'

Just as Arabella said this, a man came out of the front door and down the steps, and walked straight towards them.

∞

In order to hide their faces from the man as he got closer and closer, Arabella and Sandy moved their heads together as if to kiss. Because they were trying not to look at the man, they didn't know if he had seen them at all as he passed by. As it transpired, he had walked straight past them and continued down the road.

Sandy jumped out of the car and told Arabella not to go anywhere near the house and not to follow Monica if she came out. He would try and get hold of Juliet to attend and take over from Arabella. He didn't like to say to her that if Monica did come out of the house any time soon, surely she would recognise the car and, of course, her stepdaughter sitting in it. The thought of Monica being Arabella and James's step mum while being younger than them was something Sandy struggled to get his head around.

The man was walking quite quickly and purposefully, which meant that Sandy was able to keep a good distance behind him. When Sandy had been a detective sergeant in the West End of London, he had completed a foot surveillance course. He was not sure he had been any good at it though. In the back of his mind as he was following the man, he wondered if he was carrying out surveillance, and if so, he was racking his brain to wonder what authorities he needed in order to do this. Whatever happened, he was stuck with it now so he put any requirement for authority out of his mind.

While walking, he quickly, and as best as he could due to trying to keep up with the man in front and trying to keep his hand steady, sent a message to Juliet telling her to attend the address in Kensington and to be briefed by Arabella when she got there.

The man went straight across a road that dissected Cornwall Gardens and Sandy presumed he was going to go past the nearby museums that he could see ahead. The nearest one was the Natural History Museum and the one after that the Science Museum, then, if he crossed Exhibition Road, they would come to the Victoria and Albert Museum. The man, though, turned right onto Grosvenor Road and down towards the very busy

Cromwell Road, which he crossed.

Sandy had to hold back as the man waited for the pedestrian lights to go on and then he sprinted to make sure he could also cross when the lights were still green. Grosvenor Road underground station was definitely the location they were heading to.

In the underground station, there were not too many people waiting for the lift to go down to catch a Piccadilly Line train. Sandy took a risk and hurtled down the tight and numerous steps to the platforms. He almost crashed into a couple of slower moving people as he headed down the stairs. On reaching the bottom, he had a few moments of panic until he saw the man appear and go to the platform for the train heading east.

On the platform, as it was busy with people, Sandy had a chance to have a good look at the man he had been following for the last ten minutes or so. He was slightly shorter than Sandy, but not by much, and he was a bit older, but probably less than forty years old. He had very dark shoulder-length hair and was dressed in a smart suit with a pink, open neck shirt. Sandy had to admit he was devastatingly handsome.

Every time the man looked around, Sandy looked the other way. Don't get too close, he warned himself. The train arrived and Sandy found himself three carriages away. He found it quite difficult to see if the man got off and he had to keep moving from side to side of the carriage to peer out of the door as platforms were not all on the same side. Around Knightsbridge and Hyde Park, the train and platform got very busy so Sandy took a risk and moved to the carriage closest to the man.

With a sigh of relief, he could just about make out that

he was sitting in the next carriage and was reading that morning's Metro. The next stop was Green Park and Sandy readied himself to get off. He didn't know why but he felt this was where they were heading. As it turned out, he was wrong and it was the following stop, Piccadilly Circus, that the man alighted.

Due to it being so busy with rush-hour crowds, with people everywhere pushing their way through, it was easy to keep hidden but on the other hand equally hard to keep up. They didn't leave the station as he presumed they were going to but carried on towards the Bakerloo Line heading north.

∞

They boarded the train and unfortunately, because the train was already at the platform when they got there, Sandy had to jump on the train quickly and not think about how to keep himself hidden. As it turned out, he was in the same carriage as the man who seemed to be looking straight at him, very intently with more than a passing gaze.

A Metro newspaper that was lying discarded on a seat was what Sandy decided was the best answer to being as exposed as he was. When they stopped at the next station, Oxford Circus, hiding behind the paper seemed to be working as the man appeared to have stopped looking at him, if that was what he had been doing in the first place, and he was now looking around elsewhere.

Only one stop later at Regent's Park, the man got off. Having to get up pretty sharp to ensure he got off before the doors shut, Sandy held back as they went along the platform and up out of the station. He waited a few moments at the barrier to go out in order to give himself as much distance as possible from the man. Sandy sped up a bit as he went out of the station and into the street, to make sure he didn't miss which direction the man went.

He hadn't need to bother because the man was actually waiting for him. There the man was, hiding around the corner of the entrance. 'What do you think you are doing following me?' the man said very aggressively. He then moved himself to stand directly in the path so that Sandy could not try to get around him.

Gulping quite loudly and totally surprised by this turn of events, Sandy said, 'I am not following you. I don't know who you are.'

'Don't give me that.' The man was sneering now. 'I saw you at Grosvenor Road station. I wondered why you ran down the stairs when the lift was just arriving. I then saw you at Oxford Circus and here you are again. Of course you are following me.'

Sandy couldn't help but notice that the man had piercing blue eyes and they were at this moment staring like light strobes through him. Sandy had regained his composure and said, 'I am going to have a walk around Regent's Park, that is why I have come here. Why would I follow you? I don't know who you are.' He decided to keep saying this just in case the man slipped up and told him his name.

'Look, you are not very good at this, are you? You are dressed in a suit and you are carrying a backpack that no doubt contains a laptop. Just be honest with me, you are a solicitor and have come to serve me with some papers. I am not accepting them. Post them to me. Don't be so underhand like this.'

'If I was a solicitor, which I am not, wouldn't I have had

ample opportunity to serve papers on you already? I don't know you and I do not take kindly to being accosted in the street by you.'

'I haven't got time for this. I am going this way.' He pointed down Marylebone Road. 'And you are going that way.' He pointed into Regent's Park. 'Do not, for one moment, follow me any longer.'

After he finished saying this, he walked off along Marylebone Road in the direction of Madam Tussauds museum and Sandy, having no other alternative, crossed the road and walked into the park. One thing he was certain of was that he would have failed any foot surveillance course a number of times over. This might have happened as early on as Grosvenor Road underground station from what the man had said to him. He didn't look along Marylebone Road as he was sure the man would be watching to see if he did go into the park to be certain that he had stopped following him.

Chapter Fourteen

Having no alternative but to walk across the road and into the park, Sandy was inwardly kicking himself for being found out by the man. As he walked along, he looked straight in front of him, not daring, as much as he wanted to, to even glance at where the man was going. He was sure that he was being watched and that the man's beady eyes were keeping track of his every move.

Regent's Park, described as the jewel of the Royal Parks, covers one hundred and ninety-seven hectares and even includes a zoo, called London Zoo. Sandy had never been here to the zoo and now was not the time to do so either. He had though been into the park on a number of occasions and had walked along the lovely Regent's Park canal in the past. The park had been designed many centuries earlier by an architect, John Nash, a friend of the then Prince Regent, hence the park being called Regent's Park.

Not knowing how long to leave it before returning to the road and the underground station, he wondered if ten or fifteen minutes was enough as he wandered around aimlessly.

When his phone buzzed to tell him he had a call, he was pleased to see it was Juliet. 'Have you made it to Cornwall Gardens as yet?'

'Yes, done that and just leaving Eaton Square having followed Monica back home,' a slightly out-of-breath

Juliet said.

'Tell me what happened before I tell you about my nightmare experience.'

'Forget what I have done. What have you gone and done, Sandy?' an interested Juliet asked.

Sandy described to her what had happened and how the man had almost clocked straight away that he was following him. Juliet was laughing so much that Sandy had to pause his story on a number of occasions.

'So, you are in Regent's Park, just wandering about? Wait till I tell…' Juliet had to stop talking as she was laughing again. 'Them in the office and the boss Jane why you are late coming into work this morning.'

'Don't tell them anything,' Sandy tried to plead with her, knowing that the more he did, the more Juliet would be telling everybody. 'Tell me what happened to you before I stop this escapade.'

'Well, I sent Arabella away and told her to go straight back home with strict instructions that she must not speak to Monica about this. Lucky for her, no sooner had Arabella driven off than Monica came out and I followed her back to Eaton Square. She was walking a bit too quick for my liking.'

'Hence, you are out of breath,' Sandy said, trying to gain a bit of ground himself. 'I have been telling you for months that you need to get fit.' Juliet, obviously in a good mood this morning, was laughing again and it was so infectious that Sandy had forgotten his previous embarrassment and his mood had lifted.

'I did an electoral register check on the house and it has one occupant listed, a Dr Henry Adams,' Juliet said as she ended the call.

A doctor: it could mean a medical doctor, but not necessarily – he could be an academic doctor. No clues then as to where the man, who was probably this Henry Adams, had gone to.

Sandy walked the way the man had headed, thinking he would get the underground train to Westminster from a station along that road. He passed Harley Street.

Now, wasn't Harley Street where a number of very exclusive medical consultants had offices? Yes, he said to himself. Sandy turned onto Harley Street and knowing he had only one chance to pick a side of the road to focus on, for no particular reason walked down the right-hand side of the street, glancing at the various brass name plates on the outside walls by the doors as he walked past.

Bingo, Sandy thought, as he walked by one of the houses, as one of the brass name plates on the wall had in bold black letters, 'Dr Henry Adams, Consultant Gynaecologist'. Now, feeling very pleased with himself, he headed off to the nearest underground station and to the office for his workday to begin, even though he felt like it had been a long day already.

∞

The laughter and banter in the office where the consulate investigation team worked from was firmly directed at Sandy. As promised, Juliet had told everyone that Sandy had been seen by a person he was following almost immediately. This was not quite accurate, but Sandy was happy to be the one that was lifting the office mood that morning.

Juliet had completed some research online and found

the website for Dr Henry Adams who was located in Harley Street. It outlined the various services he and other associated medical consultants could offer – no doubt eye-wateringly expensive. She had shown Sandy his picture. It was definitely the man that he had been following and he could confirm that the man was Henry Adams, an apparently internationally renowned gynaecologist.

He decided to call Arabella, whose phone, for her, rang an uncharacteristically long time. Sandy presumed she had gone to the meeting with Monty, but she answered the phone eventually. 'Arabella, firstly don't mention a word to Monica that you know where she has been staying overnight. That would cause us a lot of problems.' Sandy envisaged a complaint from an extremely angry Dr Adams to his boss Jane Watson coming swiftly afterwards if she did.

'What do you take me for?' Arabella replied, yawning while she said it. 'Sorry, I had fallen asleep after being awake all night.' That was why she had taken so long to answer.

'What do you know about a Dr Henry Adams?'

'Is that whose house she was staying at?'

'Yes, we think so. What do you know about him?'

'Never heard of him. What sort of doctor is he?' a still very sleepy Arabella replied.

'We think he is a gynaecologist.'

'OK. Monica had an operation about three years ago, performed by a consultant gynaecologist from Harley Street. My father paid for it. Probably paid out a fortune. Yes, I think his name was Henry and I have seen him at a couple of hospital charity functions. Very dishy looking.'

'I am not sure I am able to comment on that description,'

Sandy said, although he had to agree with Arabella and would describe the man he had followed as something similar, maybe not though when he was a few inches from him telling him to walk away.

When Sandy had finished talking to Arabella, by asking her to send Monica's mobile phone number to him, he commented to Juliet, 'Didn't take Monica long to move on, did it.'

This sent Juliet into another fit of the giggles. 'What have I done or said now?' Sandy asked.

'You are a great detective, Sandy, but when it comes to love you are so naive. Luckily for you, you have found Hannah who is perfect for you. If not, you would still be waiting for love, possibly forever. I think Monica moved on from William Peveril to Henry Adams quite somewhile ago, and long before William died.'

The penny dropped immediately for Sandy and he phoned Rich straight away. 'Hello, Rich, is it possible to get call data for Monica's phone, please? We think...' Sandy looked at Juliet and then added, 'We are pretty sure that Monica Peveril has been, or is, having an affair with a doctor she has known for a few years.'

'I have put Operation Cornflower on the back burner at the moment because we have no cause of death, so nothing to investigate. I think we should wait to see what comes back from the toxicology first. Don't you?'

'Yes, I do understand that, but I just feel it will help to give us a picture of Monica and who she is calling and when she is calling, in particular this lover.'

There was quite a pause before Rich responded, 'The authority to collect phone call data needs a crime or at least a legitimate reason to obtain that data. What do you want me to put down, adultery? Not sure that is one of the categories, is it?'

'We are investigating an unexplained death on behalf of the coroner. Surely that will do?'

'Let me get the form up on my computer screen now,' Rich said. Sandy now felt he was going to get his way. 'Yes, I can put that on here as a suspicious death enquiry. OK, you win. I will get Lofty to do it later. I am still not doing anything else with Operation Cornflower though until we get more information back from Dr Stroud.'

∞

It wasn't until the Sunday that Hannah and Sandy had a chance to meet up. After they had had Sunday lunch cooked by Sandy's father, they decided to go for a walk along the River Great Ouse. There had just been the four of them at lunch because although Gregor was a good cook, he was not a confident cook.

They walked a different way to the way they normally went, this time going along the river to a small village called Little Thetford. There was lots of activity on the river that afternoon, with a number of boats going backwards and forwards.

Hannah had had a successful week and her case with the man who had set fire to at least four premises was progressing well. The senior investigating officer had been visibly impressed when she had put forward the two proposals of someone to provide an overview of the fires and to approach a clinical psychologist. He had contacted the National Crime Agency and they had commissioned this already.

As they walked along, Sandy looked at her and was immensely proud. He hadn't yet told her about his experience of foot surveillance in London and was just about to do so when his phone buzzed in his pocket.

'Hi, Sandy, sorry to disturb you on a Sunday but just getting caught up on my emails after a few days off.'

Sandy mouthed to Hannah, 'It's Lofty Dobson.'

'I have the call data for Monica's phone. Only text messages so she mustn't use WhatsApp. On glancing through the numbers she calls and which call her, there are only three that are constantly called. One stopped the day that Viscount Peveril died, so must be his, and the other two carried on being called or received.'

'I have William's number on my phone somewhere so I can check if it is his. Can you just send me the call data through? Hannah wants to have a word.'

After he passed the phone over, he could hear the banter between them about the triathlon and her and Sandy cheating by swimming in a pool and cycling and running on flat ground. All three of them were happily laughing together and Hannah had told Lofty her taking part in a triathlon was a one and only event.

No sooner had they left Little Thetford and crossed over the bridge to walk back to Ely, but on the other side of the river this time, when Sandy's phone buzzed again. He looked to see who the caller was as he knew he shouldn't take any more work calls while spending time with Hannah. It was Nicholas Stroud. He had to answer this. Mouthing, 'Sorry' to Hannah, he said, 'Good afternoon, Dr Stroud. Working on a Sunday or is this a social call?'

'I have the results of the fast-tracked toxicology back and you will want to hear about this as soon as possible.

Are you free for lunch tomorrow in Cambridge? You will need to get DCI Singh to be there if possible so he hears it first hand from me.'

'Please tell me now,' Sandy pleaded, intrigued and desperate to know why Nicholas seemed so excited. 'I understand that you want to tell me and Rich together, but I will have to reorganise a meeting as I am due to be in London tomorrow, and I've no idea about Rich Singh's availability.'

'It would be best that I share the results with you in person.'

Sandy sighed. 'Very well. I will message you as soon as I've spoken to Rich. Hopefully we will be able to meet you for lunch tomorrow so you can tell us your news.'

Hannah looked at Sandy quizzically and he just shrugged and said, 'Sorry, work.' For a couple who had such little time together this was a bit annoying, but Sandy checked the team diary on his phone and found out that Phil Harris was at work all week so sent him a message about the meeting. Phil, obviously another one who worked on a Sunday, made an immediate reply of, 'leave it with me'.

The next person he rang was Rich, who didn't answer his phone. This allowed Hannah and Sandy time to walk together, getting closer to Ely all the time. They crossed the bridge and returned to the riverbank that Sandy lived along. The usual ice cream van was in place just past Sandy's parents' house and no sooner had he ordered when Rich called back. He said he would have to get his recently retired dad to do the school run for him but could come to Cambridge.

After letting Dr Stroud know that they could make lunch, Sandy and Hannah walked into the house. Katherine said, 'Did you both enjoy your alone time?'

Before Sandy could reply, Hannah said, 'Yes, lovely thank you,' then muttered under her breath so only Sandy could hear, 'The alone time also with Lofty, Nicholas Stroud, Phil Harris and Rich. Yes, very alone.' However, she was smiling while she said it.

Chapter Fifteen

The train from Derby to Cambridge actually went through Ely first, so Sandy picked Rich up at Ely railway station. Rich loved Sandy's Morgan car and said the trip was worth it just to have a drive around in the open-top sports car. Sandy hadn't been able to resist the temptation to put the roof down even though it was an overcast day. They had gone into Ely so that Sandy could show the city off to Rich. They drove past the cathedral and also past his house along the river and then headed to Cambridge.

On the way, Rich told him that Lofty had completed subscriber checks on the three main numbers: one was Monica's mother and one was, as presumed, William Peveril. Sandy had been able to confirm this as well from his own phone records as he had previously rung William. The final one was someone called Henry Adams. When Sandy told him the foot surveillance tale, Rich could hardly stop laughing. This joke, Sandy thought, is now wearing thin.

They arrived at Brown's, the restaurant on Trumpington Street in Cambridge that they were meeting at. There was going to be quite a while before Dr Stroud arrived as he was giving evidence at an inquest in Cambridge and the case had been delayed. Rich and Sandy sat at one of the tables outside and enjoyed each other's company and watched the people of Cambridge walking by the front of the restaurant.

By the time Nicholas arrived, they were already on their second drink of tea and coffee and had ordered bread for the table, which had all been eaten. Nicholas had insisted that they ordered the food first before he told them his news. He, like Rich and Sandy, was also very hungry.

Finishing a large mouthful of his pasta, Nicholas said, 'This case started because of the gut instinct of Mrs Montague and the investigative tenacity of DCI McFarlane.'

'Stubbornness,' Rich said, making them all laugh.

'William Peveril did have moderate coronary artery disease, which might have caused although I don't think it's the case to cause a severe shortage of blood to the heart and a fatal arrhythmia.' Looking at the confused faces of Rich and Sandy, he added, before taking another large mouthful of his pasta, 'Dying from a heart attack.'

'Just so I have got this right, are you saying he may have died from a heart attack?' a very disappointed Sandy asked.

'I don't think so, but I am not able to totally rule it out. A witness to his last few moments, such as Lady Peveril, would assist greatly with explaining this.'

Seeing their disappointed faces, Nicholas quickly said, 'I did need to be honest with you, but, as I said, I don't believe that is why he died. I strongly believe that William died of morphine toxicity.' Again, seeing the confused faces before him, he added, 'A fatal overdose of morphine.'

'So, he was poisoned using morphine then?' a now more hopeful Rich asked.

'Well, that is for both of you to find out. It could be argued it was accidental. I don't think that it was a build-up of any morphine-based tablets he had been using, but further examination of the hair samples I took would help to determine this.'

Sandy, now making no attempt to eat any more of the fish pie he had ordered – his usual meal at Brown's – was getting very interested and said, 'I presume you can only get morphine-based drugs on prescription?'

'Very much so, yes. In tablet form, orally in a bottle or, what I think happened here, by the use of an injection. The injection would only be, or should only be used by a qualified medic, either a doctor or a nurse.'

Dr Stroud looked and smiled at both Rich and Sandy. He was enjoying playing centre stage to the two smartly dressed, very intelligent and extremely enthusiastic detectives sitting at the table with him.

He paused while the waiter cleared the plates away and then said, 'Based on the exceptionally high level of morphine we have found in the tissue samples, what possibly happened within a minute at the most of the injection, the molecules would make their way to the brain. Then, within about two minutes, William's breathing would have slowed, and within five minutes the breathing slowed so much that the brain was not getting any oxygen and he would have died.'

Rich and Sandy looked at each other and Sandy said, 'So, we are saying he was murdered then?'

'No, I am not saying that. My interim report will say that I believe he died of morphine toxicity.'

'We should though start a homicide investigation then?'

'I thought that was what you were doing already. If not, why and how did you get me to carry out a forensic postmortem.'

He had to leave but promised to send Rich and Sandy his interim report by the next morning. He couldn't promise a final report for a number of weeks as he needed all of the tests to have been concluded.

∞

They had clearly outstayed their welcome at Brown's as although no one said anything, the bill being placed on their table was a good sign it was time to move on. Rich and Sandy had a lot they needed to discuss so were looking to go somewhere else to talk.

While he paid the bill, Sandy had a thought and said, 'I know it is unconventional, but do you want to have a couple of people to use as a sounding board? They will keep everything absolutely confidential.'

'Yes, that would be good.'

Sandy made a couple of calls. He then gave Rich a whistle-stop tour of Cambridge, walking along King's Parade and past King's College Chapel as a couple of highlights. After about three quarters of an hour, they made their way into the rear of the Eagle pub.

The Eagle had been a pub for centuries, but its biggest historical significance was that in 1953, one of its regular drinkers, Francis Crick, came and told others in the pub that he and James Watson had discovered the double helix structure of DNA. One of, if not the greatest scientific discoveries of the twentieth century. Watson and Crick a decade later won the Nobel Prize for their scientific advancements.

Sat at a table at the rear of the pub were Sandy's two grandfathers. Rich looked quizzically at Sandy as if to say, who are these two old men?

'Rich, let me introduce you to my two grandfathers.'

They rose and shook Rich's hand. 'This is Tom Fisher and this is John McFarlane.' Rich still looked a bit quizzical, albeit he was delighted to see Sandy's grandfathers.

'Tom is a retired senior detective and John is a retired judge, but is still working as a barrister.'

Rich nodded as he now understood. The two men who were sat opposite him and Sandy had an incredible wealth of knowledge with which they could assist them. No wonder Sandy was such a good detective, he thought, with such great genes.

'I do apologise, Rich, that they might seem a bit like Laurel and Hardy and bicker with each other.' He gave his grandfathers a warning look. 'Shall we look at our case using the 5WH methodology?'

John said to them, 'I know a poem that 5WH is used in. It is by Rudyard Kipling and it is called "I Keep Six Honest Serving Men".' Even though Sandy and Tom pleaded with him not to recite it, Rich said, 'I don't know it and would love to hear it, Judge McFarlane.'

John said, looking at Rich directly but also glancing around at the other two at the table, 'I keep six honest serving-men. They taught me all I knew; Their names are What and Why and When And How and Where and Who. I send them over land and sea, I send them east and west; But after they have worked for me, I give them all a rest.'

All four of them burst out laughing. The old men in particular were loving their time with the two young detectives. John said, 'Sorry to spoil your enthusiasm, boys, but this isn't an English homicide; it must be a case that the French police lead on.'

Tom added, 'Also, Sandy, didn't your boss tell you not to go to France again without her permission? I would have thought that is the place that you would need to go if you are to progress this investigation.'

Rich and Sandy looked at each other dejectedly as they knew they were both right. Sandy left the table to get some more drinks and to make a call to Lieutenant Marius Legard in Saint-Émilion. Sandy explained to him that William Peveril had most probably not died from a heart attack but from morphine poisoning and they needed an authorisation from the French police to carry out further enquiries. The lieutenant didn't speak for a long period and Sandy wondered if he had not understood due to the language difference. Finally, he said he would send an email giving authorisation.

They all now felt a little happier and started thinking about the 5WH. After they made sure no one in the pub could overhear them, Rich briefed them on what they knew so far. Sandy was the one delegated to take notes.

'We know who the victim is, it is William Peveril,' Sandy said.

Tom questioned his grandson and said, 'But what do you really know about him? Has he had heart problems before? What were the tablets he was taking for his bad back? Where did he get them from? Did he have any enemies?'

'Can't answer any of your questions, Grandad.' Sandy then asked and answered his own question. 'What has happened? William has died. The forensic pathologist says he died of morphine toxicity.'

John said, 'Your investigation will need to be sure you have an expert cardiologist. If there is ever a court case and I was defending, I would ensure that I would be persuading the jury to not rule out a cardiac arrest.'

Tom said, 'That is the trouble with you barristers – prosecute one moment, defend the next.'

'A regular comment from detectives, I am afraid, and that comment is getting boring, Tom.'

Sandy asked and answered another of his questions: 'Where did this happen? In William's bedroom suite in Chateau Peveril.'

'This bedroom,' Tom said, finishing his drink and looking straight at Sandy and Rich, 'needs a CSI to give the whole room an in-depth examination. What clues were there in the room?'

John said, 'There may also be a second scene to think about. What about the place where the morphine was obtained from? And that might be in England.'

Sandy continued with his questions. 'When did this happen? There was a half an hour window in which William Peveril died. This was between Monsieur and Madame Chevalier seeing him alive and well and Monsieur Chevalier seeing him deceased.'

'Sandy, my dear grandson, what about Monica Peveril? You are totally blinkered on her being the offender. When did you speak to her? Surely, she could also be a significant witness. She was the last person to see him alive, not the Chevaliers.' John had put on his best barrister voice and was overemphasising his Scottish accent. Everyone laughed when he pulled on the lapels of his jacket.

Sandy asked and answered his penultimate question: 'How did this happen? If it was definitely morphine toxicity, which is what it appears to be – either tablets, oral medication or most probably an injection – a key action we must do is to search anywhere that the remains of the method for administering the medication could be.' There was no comment made about this from Rich or the two grandfathers.

'Why did this happen?' Sandy asked.

Tom replied first. 'You and Rich are going to have to rule out accident, self-administration.'

John said, 'What about suicide, that most definitely needs to be ruled out?'

Rich, in response to the alternative hypothesis the grandfathers were raising, said, 'Murder must be the main hypothesis though, mustn't it?' Sandy nodded enthusiastically at him, but when both John and Tom shook their heads, they all laughed.

John challenged them and said, 'There is only one obvious suspect: Monica Peveril. Thinking about the "why" question, why did she kill him then, if that is what she did?'

Tom said, 'What do you know about Monica then, Sandy? Anything?' Both Sandy and Rich had to admit that they did not know anything about her.

Rich looked at Sandy to answer John's question of why she would kill him. Sandy said, 'Not sure, but it could be for money. Could be for love in a negative way. She didn't love him anymore and wanted out of the marriage.'

'That would be a bit drastic, surely she could have just divorced him,' Tom said.

'I know, and another love motive could be that she had fallen in love with Henry Adams. Not sure we have the answer or will ever know, but we shall try our best to find out.'

Rich said, 'Apparently Sandy is a very tenacious investigator.' He pointed at the two men opposite him. 'I can now see where he gets that from. You two.'

They all laughed together again, then John said, 'He can be very stubborn.'

Tom added, 'He has always been like that, since he was a little boy.' What a pleasant afternoon they were all having together, but the amount of points that John and Tom had raised would involve a lot of extra work.

The time had arrived for Rich to catch his train. John was going to drop him off at the station. Just as he was about to leave, Sandy had a message from Jane . She had received a message from a lieutenant in the Gendarmerie in France stating that he was happy for his gendarmes to assist DCI McFarlane in his investigation, although she said this was the wrong way round – we should be assisting them. She was agreeing to only him and Clare to visit France for a very short period. This was to assist them – a point he must make clear to them on arrival in France.

Chapter Sixteen

The Eurostar pulled out slowly from St Pancras station even though it was running late that morning. It sped up though as it travelled through the English countryside. The Operation Cornflower team, for some reason, were struggling to get settled in their seats. This was mostly caused by Lofty Dobson, who needed to change seats so that he could sit comfortably with his long legs stretched out.

The team for the visit to Saint-Émilion was Rich, Lofty and a CSI from Derbyshire, along with Sandy and Clare Symonds. Jane Watson had stuck to her decision and even though Juliet had pleaded with her, she had not been allowed to make the trip.

The turnaround time in Paris for them to change stations and trains was much longer this time as their late-running Eurostar train had meant they had missed their connection. The Derbyshire team and Clare were surprised to see a slightly exasperated Saffron Dupont waiting for them. She had been there over two hours.

Saffy was wearing the same skirt suit that she had worn last time, the red and green check one, but this time she had on red tights, so slightly less glaring than the green ones she had worn the first time Sandy had met her.

As only Clare spoke any French, the reason Saffy had joined them became immediately clear and Rich congratulated Sandy for thinking about it. He took the praise but it was actually Juliet who had arranged for her to be with them during their visit and not him. Saffy entertained them with her incessant talking, mostly about wondering how long Lofty's legs were.

The train really sped up very fast through the French countryside and by the time Sandy had looked through the guidebooks for Bordeaux, which he had bought in Heffers in Cambridge, the train was moving through the outskirts of Bordeaux. Sandy and Rich discussed plans for what they wanted everyone to do during the two to three days they were spending there.

As promised, Marius Legard had sent one of his gendarmes in a car to pick them up and take them to Saint-Émilion. On seeing the six of them, he pronounced a number of exclamations, which Saffy translated as, 'He has been waiting for us for two hours and he can only take three of us. That means he has to come back for the other three and then he will be late off work to go home and he lives back towards Bordeaux. Well, that is basically what he said, taking out the swear words!' The way Saffy had said it made all of them laugh and made the French gendarme utter even more loud exclamations.

After the other three had left, Sandy had a thought. He asked Lofty and Rich if they wanted to climb the bell tower to the Cathédrale Saint-André. If they went now, and at speed, they would just about make it there and back in time, otherwise the gendarme would have to wait again, which set off all three of them laughing.

Rich didn't want to come as to reach the top of the Tour Pey-Berland belfry took two hundred and thirty-one steps. Lofty set off very quickly and left Sandy behind, puffing due to the pace being set. Lofty was well over ten years older than Sandy and a lot fitter than him. He realised that he had to work on his fitness to even come close to Lofty.

The bells that they saw as they approached the top of the tower were massive. The views on reaching the top were stunning, not only all across the city of Bordeaux but also looking down at the cathedral and its magnificent architecture.

Luckily for Lofty and Sandy, they got back just in time to be driven the relatively short distance to Saint- Émilion. Both Rich and Lofty marvelled at how pretty the rolling vineyards looked as they passed them.

On arrival at the hotel, they could see an excited Saffy talking in the bar area to a waiter. She beckoned for Sandy to come over. He saw that she had already changed into less striking clothing of jeans and a red blouse. Saffy obviously liked wearing the colour red. She told them that the waiter had some extremely important news and if Sandy could get sorted in his room quickly, she would translate what the waiter said for him.

∞

By the time Sandy had come down into the bar, the waiter had gone off. Saffy told him what the waiter had said to her. 'He says that one of the English ladies from Chateau Peveril was visiting an Englishman that they had staying here. They often spent time in his room alone. You know what that means don't you, Sandy?'

Sandy didn't want to tell her what he thought she meant. Could it possibly be that Henry Adams had stayed in this very hotel at the time that William Peveril had died? This was a good development.

Although the receptionist spoke good English, Sandy took Saffy with him to speak to him. The receptionist was very reluctant to show them the hotel registration book, but when Saffy mentioned that they were there helping Lieutenant Legard, the man reluctantly handed the book over. A quick scan through the book showed no trace of Henry Adams or, in fact, any English person staying during the crucial period they were looking at, even if an alias was being used.

His high hopes had been dashed. Sandy looked at Saffy as if to say, you must have got this wrong. Saffy, who read his thoughts, said, 'He did, he did, Sandy. He definitely told me this.'

By now the others had arrived and the six of them set off for their dinner. Apparently, there was a very good Vietnamese restaurant nearby, but Sandy didn't think it was right for them not to visit a French restaurant. Not far from the hotel was a rustic French restaurant that fitted the bill perfectly. He even thought about buying for the table a couple of bottles of the Chateau Peveril, that was until he saw the extremely large price each bottle cost.

When Sandy walked into breakfast the next morning, he found that Saffy had almost taken the waiter, who she had spoken to the previous evening, as a hostage.

Saffy told the waiter to repeat what he had told her. This he did, and it was as Saffy had reported. Sandy said, with Saffy translating, 'We have checked the hotel registration book and there is no record of the person you mentioned to Miss Dupont as staying here.'

'The book you looked at was for this year. The man stayed here sometime last summer,' the waiter said with Saffy translating. He was looking quizzically at them.

Sandy kicked himself for so wanting to believe it had been Monica and Henry having romantic trysts in the hotel bedroom. This could have been anyone, including possibly a wine buyer for one of the UK's large supermarkets or an independent wine retailer.

He got himself breakfast from the table, which was laid out in the dining room with meats, cheeses and breads, and ordered coffee from the waitress as tea always seemed to be weak and barely warm in France. Just as he started to chew a large mouthful of lovely, warm, fresh croissant filled with lemon marmalade, the waiter appeared with two large guest sign-in books.

To avoid getting crumbs and marmalade all over the books, Sandy got Saffy to look through the first book, which ended in June, whilst he looked through the second. There, in July, was an entry for a Dr Henry Adams, who had stayed for one week. By now Lofty had arrived at the table with his plate piled high with pastries.

On looking through his outgoing calls, Sandy found that entry he was looking for. It was as he remembered – he had phoned Viscount William Peveril in France at just this time last year. So, there was a high probability that it could only have been Monica visiting the hotel and Henry in his bedroom.

While Sandy took a couple of photographs of the entry, Lofty left his food and went with Saffy to the hotel reception. They both came back disappointed as the CCTV they were hoping would help with identification of the English woman visitor only stored recordings for one month prior.

After the team had all had breakfast, they held a quick briefing. The plan was for Clare and the other CSI to go to the chateau to commence their forensic examination, along with the French police forensic investigator who had just arrived. Lofty and Saffy would go around with a gendarme to all of the other hotels in Saint-Émilion to see if a Henry Adams, or a sole Englishman, had stayed during the period that William and Monica had been here, leading up to when he died. Rich, Sandy and another gendarme would also visit the chateau and speak to Antoine Chevalier and his wife. This gendarme apparently spoke English and would help to translate if there was a problem. Lieutenant Legard was looking after them well.

∞

When they arrived at the main house of the chateau, Rich kept saying, 'Wow!' as he was clearly impressed with what he was seeing. The driveway up to the chateau was an impressive way to arrive. The chateau itself wasn't as big as some of the others that they had passed but was still very impressive, hence Rich's reaction.

Before they went to meet with Antoine and his wife Claudette, Rich and Sandy went up to the bedroom suite that was William and Monica's. Clare and her team of two were fully dressed in all white CSI boiler suits, with masks on and their hoods up.

Sandy had briefed Clare and the Derbyshire CSI on the amount of people who had been in the room already. Obviously, William and Monica had been in the room as well as Antoine and Claudette. The others that Sandy knew of were the doctor, who had certified death, and the two funeral directors, but he was unsure of anyone else who had a reason to visit. He then suddenly remembered that both himself and Juliet had also been in the room.

Clare had reminded Sandy earlier of Edmond Locard's principle that 'every contact leaves a trace'. If someone had been in the room, even if the room had been cleaned, as it appeared Claudette had done, she and her team would find it. Edmond was, after all, a Frenchman, so his advice should definitely happen in this case. Clare had completed a crime scene assessment before they had started their work and the three CSIs knew what role they were going to perform. Sandy and Rich had left it to her specialist knowledge and allowed her to take total charge of this scene.

Although Sandy had been in the room before, he felt it was important for Rich and him to see the place where William had died and for them to both have a feel for the scene. This was something he always did when investigating a murder or suspicious death. It helped Sandy to focus his thoughts by thinking that a person had died there and he needed to do everything he could to find out how they had died. If someone had killed them, then he would do everything he could to find them and prosecute them.

Rich and Sandy did not enter the room but stood in the doorway and watched for a short while. This bedroom suite was what Sandy had designated in his notebook as scene one. He was glad that Clare and the team were being so thorough. They were looking for DNA and fingerprints and they were using tapings, which were in reality wide pieces of Sellotape, to look for fibres and other materials. The Operation Cornflower CSI was taping the chair that William had been sitting in and all of the carpet around it.

Clare had told them when they first arrived that the

French forensics officer had taken a three-hundred-and-sixty-degree video of the room and she had taken lots of photographs for them to view, when needed. Both of these would be extremely useful if a court case ever resulted from the investigation.

Clare also told them as they did each section of the room that they were also carrying out a proper search after their forensic recovery activity. Clare said they would also go back when totally finished and search again. She was aware that any medication, packaging and discarded syringes would be crucial if found. Clare had completed a search advisor course before she had joined the FCDO to supplement her CSI/CSM training.

One thing that was slowing them down was having to stop to log in any exhibits they were taking, so Clare asked if Lofty could come out and join them. Sandy told her that unfortunately he couldn't release Lofty from going around the hotels looking for traces of Henry Adams.

Rich and Sandy were just about to head downstairs when they saw Antoine Chevalier standing nearby waiting for them. Antoine was dressed just as Sandy had seen him before, smartly in a three-piece suit, albeit with an ill-fitting waistcoat, but that was only due to his button-bulging stomach. Antoine said, 'DCI McFarlane, I wonder if I could have a private word with you both. I have something delicate to tell you that I don't want Claudette to know.'

Chapter Seventeen

They followed Antoine outside and round to the rear of the house. The yard and the winery were busy with people and trucks moving about. Although the winery had some very old buildings, much older than the house itself, it also had a very large modern building that housed the main part of the winery and all of the large vats that contained the wine. Antoine said, 'The reason I want to talk to you privately is that I don't want Claudette to think badly about a member of the Peveril family.' Antoine dramatically looked around to make sure no one was listening. There was no one nearby so nobody was likely to hear anything. This didn't stop Antoine from then whispering, 'I have heard a rumour in Saint-Émilion that Lady Monica is having an extramarital relationship.'

Rich and Sandy looked at each other a little bit disappointed as this was not new information to them, but Antoine looked and acted like he had given them the key to the death of William. His proud face beamed at them.

'Who told you this?' Sandy asked Antoine, as he saw Clare putting a ladder against the outside of the house that went up to the first-floor balcony of William and Monica's bedroom suite.

'Apparently both of those two men,' Clare shouted across at them, pointing into the room, 'are scared of heights so I am the one to have to climb the ladder and examine the outside!'

When they stopped watching Clare climbing carefully up the ladder, checking vegetation as she did so, Antoine replied to Sandy's question, 'Suzanne Valadon.'

Sandy looked at Rich and said, 'I spoke to her when I visited Saint-Émilion last time. She registered William's death. She never mentioned anything to me.' He looked back at Antoine and asked, 'Did she say who this relationship was with?'

'Only that it was with an Englishman that Lady Peveril had brought with her from England to be her play-thing in the afternoons.'

Rich and Sandy couldn't help but laugh at the way in his broken English and with his French accent Antoine had said 'play-thing'. Antoine also laughed. 'I can see no harm in it, but Claudette will. My wife can be very straight-laced.' Sandy could only picture in his head that they were taking part in a scene from the BBC series 'Allo 'Allo! And that made him laugh even more.

Rich said, 'Is there a possibility that this Englishman could have entered the house without you knowing, on the night that Viscount Peveril died?'

'Obviously he could have come in the front door and not climbed up there.' Antoine indicated to the first-floor balcony. 'You are romantics. Climbing up to a balcony to meet your lover? I don't think so!'

'What do you mean, come in through the front door?'

'It wouldn't have been the back door.' He indicated to the door into the kitchen. 'We were in and out of the kitchen preparing and serving dinner.'

Sandy said, 'Do you mean that while the Peverils were having dinner, the Englishman could have slipped in through the front door and into the bedroom?'

'You are making it all sound very romantic again. You are young, DCI McFarlane, and believe in the magic of romance, don't you?'

'So, could this have happened?'

'Yes, of course.'

'But,' Sandy said, not rising to the teasing of Antoine, 'how did he get out?'

'Before Lady Monica came into the kitchen to get me to go up and see Viscount Peveril, she just let him out of the front door,' Antoine said as if it was obvious, which of course it was.

They went back inside and with the help of the gendarme officer, they went through the exact movements with Antoine of the events that had happened on the day and evening that William had died. They went back further into Antoine's involvement with the house and the Peveril family. There was no new information in what he had to tell them. The officer was writing the statement in French and would give them a copy, which Saffy had agreed to translate for them.

∞

They left Antoine in the kitchen and went into the dining room where Claudette was waiting to speak to them. She immediately asked them if they would like any coffee and off, she went to fetch them some. They could hear her; they presumed telling Antoine off in French for not offering them any drinks or cake. She was getting louder and louder with no response from Antoine, who was probably ducking for cover.

Having sorted out the coffee and some freshly baked

cake for Rich, Sandy and the gendarme officer, Claudette sat down and said, 'Please don't say anything to Antoine, but Lady Monica was having an affair with an Englishman.'

Rich and Sandy looked at each other in surprise. Sandy asked, 'Why don't you want Antoine to know?'

'He is, how do you say in English, such a prune. No, I mean prude. Please don't say anything to him. He would be horrified to hear anything bad about the Peverils. He, and of course I as well, am totally devoted to them.'

Well, he already knows, thought Sandy, and he asked, 'Who told you?'

'Suzanne Valadon told me.'

Again, Sandy and Rich looked at each other in surprise. What a gossip Suzanne is, they thought. Sandy said, 'How did Suzanne know? And did she know his name or tell you a name?'

'Saint-Émilion is in reality a small village; we now only have two thousand permanent villagers. No, she didn't know his name, I don't think so anyway. When talking to me she always referred to him as the dishy Englishman. Suzanne, Antoine and I went to school together. Suzanne always got the dishy boys and I got Antoine!' She pointed dramatically to the kitchen and all of them, including the gendarme officer, laughed out loud, so much so that Antoine must have heard them in the kitchen.

They went through the information that Claudette had told Sandy the last time he had been there and there were no changes to what she had previously told him. Sandy asked, 'How much cleaning in Viscount Peveril's room did you do after Monica left?'

'She was there for two more nights then went off. I then

had a chance to do a quick clean through, no more than that. I also changed the bedsheets, not that anyone will use that room anymore, not at least for a long time.' Claudette suddenly, after all the joviality, looked very sad and added, 'That is all I have done and I can't bear to go in there anymore. I hope that Arabella or James come to visit soon and make us all feel like a family again.'

'Could anyone have entered the house on the evening that Viscount Peveril died?' Rich asked.

'Yes, of course, we were in the kitchen. The front door is always open.'

There was nothing further that they could think of to ask. The manager of the winery, who had arrived to see Antoine, offered to show them around the vineyard and winery, which Rich and Sandy were delighted to accept. He firstly walked with them to the fields of vines that went on endlessly. There were twenty-seven hectares owned by Chateau Peveril. They were told that the vineyards produced some of the best Saint-Émilion wines because the chateau was located on the Côtes. The Côtes is a limestone-rich plateau and hillside on the right bank of the Garonne river. They never watered the vines to keep to their tradition.

Looking out in the sunshine over the gently undulating plateau and down the hillside was a breathtakingly beautiful sight. The vines were all in leaf and looked very healthy. The view was so picturesque that Sandy took a few photographs to show Hannah and his family. Apparently the Peverils were ahead of most of the other chateaux in the region as they practiced one hundred percent self-sustainable vineyard farming methods. They became a totally organic vineyard within two years of Arabella

Montague becoming the CEO. She had forbidden the use of herbicides and all pesticides as well.

They looked in on the large new winery and realised what a huge investment this must have been. Sandy had a taste of the wine, which he enjoyed very much, as did Rich who didn't normally drink alcohol very often. The gendarme officer had more than one wine tasting and if he hadn't been with the English police, would have probably had a lot more. The old buildings were full of shelves with stacks of wine bottles and they also had cellars full of wine as well.

As they headed back to Saint-Émilion in the car, Sandy told Rich that William Peveril had been offered fifty-four million euros for the chateau only a month or so before he died. The Peverils, he was sure, wouldn't ever sell.

∞

After they returned to Saint-Émilion, they walked off away from the hotel towards the town hall, to see the town manager, the infamous Suzanne Valadon. There she was stood at the window where Sandy had first seen her. She waved to him and beckoned them in.

Suzanne had on a yellow and blue expensive-looking dress and a string of what Juliet had thought were real pearls. Suzanne said as they entered, 'If it isn't my favourite English detective.' She was definitely flirting with Sandy this time and Rich looked from Suzanne to Sandy wondering what was going on. 'What can I do for you?'

Sandy asked, 'Why, when I was last here, didn't you mention Monica Peveril visiting an Englishman in a hotel here?'

'I am not one to gossip, young man.' This made Rich and Sandy both splutter as that was exactly what she had done to the Chevaliers and who knows who else. 'Who told you?'

'The Chevaliers told us,' Rich said.

'What gossips they both are. They love the tittle tattle as you say in England. Last summer the man stayed in the same hotel that you and your team are staying in, DCI McFarlane.'

There was no doubt that if anything went on in Saint-Émilion, it was known by Suzanne. Rich asked, 'A key question for us though is if this man was here when William Peveril died?'

Suzanne smiled provocatively at both of the men as if she knew she held a key piece of information and wanted to milk it for all its worth. She even touched her blonde streaked hair on a couple of occasions and then said, 'Yes, he was here. He stayed in the Grand Saint- Émilion Boutique Hotel. Very nice hotel. Lovely rooms and a lovely restaurant. Just around the corner from here.' She pointed in its general direction and then said, 'On the way and closer to the Chateau Peveril.'

Just before Rich or Sandy could say anything, Suzanne added, 'He was here waiting for her when she came to register the death.'

Sandy said quickly and quite abruptly, 'Why didn't you tell me that when I saw you last time?'

Suzanne looked at him and smiled sweetly. She had deliberately kept the information back. 'You asked and I clarified it if you remember. I said do you mean in here?' Suzanne very expansively moved her hands and arms around her room. 'No, he did not. He was waiting outside in the Viscount's Rolls Royce for her. After she had seen me and registered the death, I saw them drive off. You can see everything from that window.' She pointed to the window where Sandy and Rich had seen her when they had first walked up to the town hall.

When they got back to their hotel, they saw Saffy and Lofty sat outside in the late spring sunshine enjoying a cup of coffee. They were both grinning widely. After ordering coffee themselves and sitting down next to them, Rich couldn't contain himself, and while grinning widely himself said, 'Did you visit the Grand Saint-Émilion Boutique hotel at all?'

The way Saffy and Lofty's head jerked to look at each other was a picture and made both Rich and Sandy laugh. Lofty said, 'How do you know that Henry Adams stayed there up until two nights after William Peveril died?'

Sandy said, 'We only knew from the lady in charge of the town hall that it was an Englishman, but the same one that stayed here. Which was why we thought it was Henry Adams.'

Lofty, not wanting to be outdone, pulled out a CD from his backpack triumphantly and said, 'But we have lots of CCTV of Henry and also Monica in the hotel reception, and twice of them leaving the hotel together.'

'What about on the evening William died, did Henry leave the hotel?'

'Not that we can see. No. But there is an entrance through the restaurant and no CCTV there. So he might have left that way but I would have presumed that he would have come back through the hotel reception.'

They all agreed that it had been a good day for the

Operation Cornflower team and they planned that as soon as Clare and the other CSI returned, they would go to the same restaurant for dinner as the previous night. They knew that they should probably try somewhere else but Sandy fancied trying the cassoulet, which was one of the restaurant's specials.

Rich and Sandy had a meeting with Lieutenant Marius Legard at the courthouse in Bordeaux at ten o'clock in the morning to discuss the way forward for the investigation. Things were looking bright for them.

Chapter Eighteen

The next morning, Marius picked up Rich, Sandy and Saffy, who was coming with them in case any translation was required. Marius was very jovial that morning and talked about what an incredible place Saint-Émilion was and what an honour it was to be the person in charge of the police detachment there. The village, he said, was totally reliant on mainly the chateaux and their wineries, but also very much on tourism. The tourism brought the police only occasional moments of trouble. Sandy asked if he had signed up Suzanne Valadon as an informant, which brought laughter from all of them in the car. Marius clearly knew what Sandy meant.

They parked then walked the remaining short distance to the Bordeaux Law Courts. Sandy had not seen the building when he had been in Bordeaux before. He was completely amazed when looking at the architecture of the Law Courts. The building was stunning, a very modern design with great glass curtain walls under an undulating copper roof. They entered the courthouse using the main external flight of stairs, which led into the building.

There were in total seven courtroom pods. The pods from the outside of the building looked to Sandy like the oust houses you found in the county of Kent. The building also included the original old building and a section of the city's medieval wall.

They were shown into one of the courtrooms, which was

magnificently clad in cedar. There were two people already in the room and they introduced themselves. The two men were both dressed in sombre dark suits. The first man told them he was a public prosecutor and the second told them his name was Pierre Veil. He was the investigating judge who oversaw investigations in the area for the most serious and complex offences, such as the case of William Peveril. This was a different system to the one in England where the police led on this stage of any criminal investigation. In France, they primarily had an inquisitorial criminal justice system, while in England this was an adversarial criminal justice system.

After the introductions had finished and they had all shaken hands and sat down, the judge, who was clearly in charge of the meeting, said, 'I have read the interim autopsy report. Thank you for having it translated, it has enabled me to understand some of the medical terms. What I understand is that William Peveril could have died of a heart attack then? Which is what we have as an official record of his death.'

Rich and Sandy looked at each other in a concerned manner – where was this conversation going? 'Dr Stroud is quite clear in his report,' Sandy said, 'that he does not believe that it was a heart attack.' Sandy gulped as he had been caught off guard. 'Dr Stroud states that in his very experienced and professional opinion, the cause of death was a fatal dose of morphine,' Sandy said, trying to sound convincing and emphatic.

'But he is not able to rule a heart attack out, is he? And the dose of morphine could have been administered accidently or be a deliberate self-overdose,' the judge said. It was clear that he had no intention of commencing an investigation into the death or to go through the rigmarole of changing an official record of the registration of death.

Sandy looked at Marius to see if he could help. Marius just shrugged his shoulders as if to say, this type of stance was not something new to him and not something he would get involved in. Sandy said, 'We have no evidence to support either of those other possibilities that you suggest though.'

'You, on the other hand, have not one scrap of evidence to support a case of murder though, have you?' the judge said.

Rich, trying to help their case, said, 'We know that Monica Peveril has been having, and was at the time having, an affair with a Dr Henry Adams.'

The judge very robustly replied, 'I am not sure, officer, if having an extramarital affair is a criminal offence in England, but I don't think it is, and it is definitely not, thankfully, a criminal offence here in France.' This brought laughter from all of those in the room but not from Sandy, Rich or Saffy. They had a sinking feeling that all of their hard work had been pointless and a waste of time. The judge concluded the conversation by saying very firmly, 'We will not investigate this any further but you can take it to the Ministry of Justice in Paris to seek their views if you wish.'

That was it and they were all shown out of the court. The case was over. Marius told them that in his view there was no point in them going to Paris but he would try and arrange it if they wished, possibly for the following morning. Sandy, as tenacious as ever, said a firm yes, that was what they wished. He did this without even consulting Rich, who really should have been the one making the decision. Rich did however feel the same as Sandy – they couldn't just leave France without trying all they could to find justice for William Peveril.

∞

Three very despondent people walked back into the hotel. No other member of the team was there. They were all at the police station ensuring that the exhibits were all correctly recorded, labelled and placed in the correct storage area.

Rich and Saffy went to their rooms while Sandy went and walked to the police station to tell the others the news. He slinked by the town hall, glancing furtively up at the window that Suzanne normally stood at, but there was no sign of her.

On a whim, and in order to lift his mood, he went and climbed the one hundred and ninety-six steps of the monolithic church's bell tower. The church and tower were a marvel and it looked like, and probably was, carved out of the rock it stood on. The view from the top was spectacular, not just of Saint-Émilion with its winding and undulating narrow streets and its cobbled squares, but the view of the whole region and across the endless rows and rows of vines in the surrounding vineyards.

Just before he was going to start the climb down, Sandy saw he had a message from Marius. There was a meeting booked in Paris at the Ministry of Justice for ten the next morning.

He realised that there were two people he hadn't updated all week. He had been holding back, firstly to get the autopsy interim report in writing, and then he was swept along with the visit to France. Sandy decided to stay at the top in the viewing area and he made his first call to Arabella, who didn't answer her phone, but the ringing tone sounded like she was abroad somewhere.

James answered straight away. 'Sandy, how are you getting on in Saint-Émilion?'

How did he know, I hadn't mentioned it, Sandy thought, as he took his phone from his ear and looked at it with a puzzled expression. Then he realised, of course, it must have been one of the Chevaliers that had told him. 'I thought well, but not great now I am afraid. Where is Arabella?'

'She is in Barbados. It was all very last minute. Monty felt she had to have a break. Our neighbours in London, you would have heard of them, the movie actors, Vivienne Jones and Adam Scott, have a small villa in Sandy Lane, Barbados, and they have let Arabella and Monty stay there for a week.'

Wow! Nice, Sandy thought without saying it. James asked, 'Why not so good there?'

'I am sorry I haven't updated you but I really wanted to do it in person when I returned. The post-mortem pathology results do say your father had some heart disease but they don't think he died from that.' Sandy knew that it wasn't right to be telling James this on the phone, but he now had no choice. 'There is a strong probability that he may have died from a morphine overdose.'

The silence was deafening and although Sandy knew he shouldn't fill the silence, he said, 'The French though don't want to investigate further how this could have happened. I have an appeal process that DCI Singh and I are going to attend in Paris tomorrow morning. Do you want me to continue to pursue this?'

Still silence from James, then he eventually said, 'Sandy, as you know, Arabella and I trust your judgement completely. We will support whatever you think best. Please come and see us next week, not at the London House as Monica will be there. I am not going to tell Arabella the probable cause of death until she comes home. I feel so sad all of a sudden. Sorry, I am feeling a bit overwhelmed. You see I loved my father so much and I am missing him. It comes in waves and I feel that I am drowning a bit at the moment. Luckily, I need to be in the House of Commons in ten minutes, so normality will take over.'

James's palpable sadness had washed completely over and into Sandy and he was determined to try and do whatever he could to find justice for this family.

He reluctantly climbed down from the top and went off walking dejectedly to let the others at the police station know what was happening with the case.

∞

The train into Paris was right on time. The punctuality of the French rail network was mostly excellent. Rich, Sandy and, amazingly for her, Saffy were very quiet almost all the way from Bordeaux to Paris. The very early morning taxi ride from Saint-Émilion to the station in Bordeaux may have had something to do with it. Clare, Lofty and the others had remained in Saint-Émilion and planned to leave later in the morning.

Their taxi pulled up outside the Hôtel de Bourvallais on Place Vendôme, which housed the French Ministry of Justice. It was an incredibly beautiful building. It had originally been built in 1708 and then enlarged after a fire at the end of that century. The French flag was flying high from the flagpole above the corniche.

All three of them looked around in amazement as they entered the building and were shown into a meeting room. Looking at the marble, the flooring, the paintings and the chandeliers almost made them for a moment forget the reason why they were there.

There was no one else present in the room until the investigating judge, Pierre Veil, walked in. Sandy and Rich glanced at each other knowingly. This was not a good sign having the dismissive Pierre being at the meeting. Pierre was accompanied by two other men, one of whom was a very senior public prosecutor and the other a senior investigating judge. The minister was running late but turned up at ten forty-five a.m. Apparently some crisis had delayed her.

The minister was a junior minister for the French Republic's Ministry of Justice. Danielle de Gaulle was extremely elegantly dressed and reminded Sandy of the poise and sophistication of Suzanne Valadon, albeit there were no pearls on show by the minister. As it turned out, the minister wasn't the last to arrive; it was two senior police officers, one from the National Gendarmerie and the other from the Police Nationale.

Wow, quite a cast list, thought Sandy, and amazing that they had been able to be organised at such short notice. The minister asked Pierre to tell them all why they were there today.

'There has been the death of a British citizen at a chateau in Saint-Émilion. The British citizen's family own a very prestigious winery there, which they have owned for almost one hundred years. This British citizen died of a heart attack.'

Sandy interjected. 'Is it possible please to use his name, which is William Peveril. Also, we don't believe he died from a heart attack.'

Pierre glared at him. Danielle de Gaulle, however, agreed that William should be called Monsieur Peveril. Sandy wanted to interject again and say, he is actually called Viscount Peveril, but thought it wise to keep quiet at this stage. Pierre continued, 'Monsieur Peveril's death has been registered as a cardiac arrest.' He emphasised the word 'registered'. 'His body was repatriated and a week later buried in England.' He paused to look at his notes. 'In a graveyard in Derbyshire, England. Then, without any conversation or informing us, the body of Monsieur Peveril was dug up and an autopsy performed on him, again without our knowledge.'

Rich spoke before Sandy could. 'We had all of the necessary permissions to do this. The exhumation and autopsy were totally legal.'

Danielle waved her hand at Rich, telling him she understood, but wanted Pierre to continue. 'The autopsy, which only has interim findings, states that a heart attack is possible.' Pierre glanced across at Sandy as he started to squirm in his seat, no doubt wanting to intervene again, but Pierre continued. 'The British pathologist however believes Monsieur Peveril had a fatal dose of morphine, but no conclusion as to how or why that could have happened. I accept that we could investigate further, but if there has been any criminal activity, all suspects and all family members are in England. So, I have decided we have no investigation here in France.'

Danielle asked Sandy what his view was. 'I am not able to disagree with Monsieur Veil on any point,' Sandy said. 'But if Viscount Peveril was murdered, surely, we owe it to him and his family to find out what happened. The European Convention on Human Rights has as a protected right in Article Two, the right to life. That includes where that person has died. They had a right to life. We will do everything that we can…' He looked at Rich, who nodded vigorously. 'To help and support a French investigation into how Viscount Peveril died.'

Danielle de Galle said, 'Thank you, both. In my mind there are only two options. One, we remain with our registered death decision of death by cardiac arrest. Or two, we have the body exhumed and brought back to France.'

Sandy was horrified by this idea and thought about Arabella and James and all of the authorities that needed to be obtained again, and probably refused. He said, 'We have already done this, you have the autopsy report.'

The senior investigating judge said, 'The British pathologist is not registered in France though. We will need our own legal medical institute to carry it out.'

Danielle continued what she had been saying. 'Option two, as I said, is to bring the body back here, we can do the autopsy at one of the medical institutes here in Paris, then we can see what investigation needs to be carried out.' She looked around the room and then said, 'I prefer option one, don't you?' There were lots of nods and agreements by all of them present. The decision really belonged to the judiciary and not the politician, and of course Pierre and the senior judge were in agreement. Saffy wanted to stand up and shout for them to investigate but Sandy held her tightly so she didn't. Saffy was a diplomat here in Paris and it could be career suicide if she did shout out.

Reluctantly, knowing that James and Arabella would trust his judgement, after looking at Rich they both nodded in agreement.

The investigation was over. Sandy though kept thinking all the way back to London on the Eurostar that there must be a third option, but he just couldn't think what that was.

Chapter Nineteen

The early May long bank holiday weekend was an opportunity that Sandy had taken to relax, rest and not think about work. The disappointment of the result in the Peveril case had not gone away but he had managed to place it towards the back of his mind. The only downside that weekend was that Hannah was not about as she had gone to spend the weekend with her father in Harrogate.

Monday was a warm day and after an early morning run, Sandy sat on a bench for a couple of hours reading a book. He was also watching the world go by. It was a very busy day along the Great River Ouse tow path, both in front of their house and across the river at the marina. The ice cream van just down the road from where he was sitting was having a roaring day of trade with a consistently long queue of people waiting.

When he went back indoors, Sandy went out to the back of the house to help his father cook the food for the family barbecue.

Not long after Sandy had started flipping burgers and chicken legs and wings, his Grandad Tom arrived to supervise him, or that was what Tom thought he was doing. He instructed Sandy, 'Don't burn them this time.' Tom was laughing when he said, 'How did you and that nice young man, DCI Singh, get on in France?'

'Not good at all, Grandad,' a very disappointed-sounding Sandy replied. 'They didn't want to commence an investigation in France and even if they did so, they gave us an option of having another exhumation, which would have been unpalatable to the family.'

'You will still need to do a limited investigation for the coroner though, won't you? He could declare at inquest it was an unlawful killing.'

'I didn't think about that,' Sandy said pondering what his grandad had just said. 'That might just be enough for the family.'

'But not enough for you.'

'No, not really. A criminal investigation and hopefully a trial would be enough for me,' Sandy said, smiling at his grandad and quickly turning all the food over on the barbecue before it got burnt.

'I had a case...' Tom said, about to launch into telling Sandy one of his old case experiences. He paused and looked at Sandy and was pleased that, as usual, his grandson was one of the only people in his family interested in the cases that he had been involved in or knew of. 'Where a local man had gone to Thailand and committed an offence against a boy there. We had video evidence and tried to prosecute him here as the Thai police didn't feel able to prosecute as they couldn't find the boy. Unfortunately, there was no law that allowed it to happen here at that time, so a colleague and I worked hard to get the law changed.'

'Is that for all offences?' a hopeful Sandy asked.

'No, it is only for sexual offences as far as I remember. It is in the Sexual Offences Act.'

A thought suddenly came into his head, and passing over the barbecue tools to his grandad, Sandy whizzed into the house and up to his bedroom. He pulled out a box from beside his wardrobe and started frantically picking books and papers out and throwing them onto his bed. He was starting to have a sinking feeling that he had left what he was looking for in the flat in London, when he triumphantly found it.

He had found his very first day book from when he had started working at the FCDO in London. He was sure he had made an entry about something Juliet had told him. He flipped through the pages and there it was. In his incredibly neat writing, the note said: 'There is a law from over one hundred and fifty years ago that states if a British citizen murders someone abroad, they can be tried for that offence in this country.'

Sandy started smiling and took the book downstairs and into the garden and saw that his dad had taken over the cooking on the barbecue. He went up to his grandad and gave him a hug and kiss and wondered that if this law was still in use, that just maybe he had found the third option.

∞

As he strode across Manchester Square in London and through the entrance of the Wallace Collection, Sandy knew he was running late to see Arabella and James. He had been distracted in the office by emails and reports that he had needed to look at.

Already there and sitting at a table were Arabella and James. James stood when Sandy walked up to their table and went off to buy Sandy a cup of tea and a pastry. How well this family knew him! Arabella looked well and tanned from her week in the Caribbean – obviously a good move by Monty to take her away.

After returning, James said, 'I was going to wait until you told Arabella the findings from the post-mortem, but thought it best to let her know last night when she returned from holiday. I knew that she would be upset so thought it best to happen then, rather than now in a public place.' Sandy looked at Arabella, who just nodded in acknowledgement of what James had just said. Arabella was wearing a bright yellow sundress and seemed totally in control of her emotions.

James said, 'We want you and DCI Singh to do everything that you can to find out exactly what happened to our father.'

'The French gave us two options for them to lead an investigation. One, to keep the record that your father died of a cardiac arrest.'

Arabella, almost shouting, said, 'No, that is not right.'

'Second option is that they seek to exhume again, take your father's body back to France and perform another autopsy.'

Sandy could see two horrified faces looking at him and he had hardly got the words out before Arabella, almost whispering but now definitely crying, said, 'That would be horrific.' She wiped her eyes and cheek. 'I promised myself I wasn't going to cry. Gosh, my emotions are all over the place.'

James held her hand and said, 'They have got us between a rock and hard place. No, definitely no to any further disturbance of our father's body.' He squeezed his sister's hand firmly.

'We have another option,' Sandy said and seeing that they both looked at him hopefully, continued by saying, 'We could continue with our investigation and submit the findings to the coroner for him to hold an inquest.'

'Or,' James said, 'I can see by the way you just said that, that there is something else.'

'I know that it is from a long time ago, but the Offences Against the Person Act 1861 has a section within it that states, in cases of murder and manslaughter, whether they occur here or abroad and providing the person that is a suspect for the murder is a British citizen, that person may be dealt with, inquired of, tried, determined and punished here in this country.'

Seeing the stunned silence from the brother and sister opposite him, Sandy asked, 'I know nothing about Monica, is she a British citizen?'

Arabella said, 'Yes, from Brighton. In fact, she is there at the moment with her mother and is due back in a couple of days, when I will be safely away from her and back home in Norfolk. I would say that the coroner option sounds the easiest option.'

'I would favour the investigation option,' James said, looking at Arabella.

'I didn't say that was what I favoured, James. If I had wanted an easy option, I wouldn't have met Sandy in the first place.'

'It is not really my decision but DCI Singh's, and we would need to talk to CPS and the coroner. Is that what you want me to do?'

The nods gave Sandy all of the support he needed. He left Arabella and James in the café and paid for the entrance into the gallery. He knew he had lots of work waiting for him back at the office but he couldn't resist a quick visit.

The Wallace Collection was, in Sandy's opinion, one of London's best art galleries and a view into eighteenth-century aristocratic life. The Wallace family art collection had many highlights, including paintings by Rembrandt, Titian, Rubens, Joshua Reynolds and Thomas Gainsborough. Sandy particularly admired the Laughing Cavalier by Frans Hals. The chandeliers and staircase reminded him of the French architecture he had recently seen at the Ministry of Justice building in Paris.

∞

A video conference had been organised by Rich after Sandy had rung and told him about the relevant section in the Offences Against the Person Act 1861. Rich had been very excited by this new information.

They had then discussed on the video call the principle of the building blocks to an investigation that they both knew well as: preservation of life, preserve scenes, secure evidence, identify victim/witnesses and finally, the key building block they were now discussing, to identify suspects.

Rich told Sandy that he had now raised the level of Operation Cornflower to be a murder investigation. He had designated Monica Peveril and Henry Adams as suspects.

Sandy said, 'I presume, Rich, you have recorded a decision to that effect?'

'Yes, exactly that, giving reasons for why I believe there are reasonable grounds to suspect them of the offence of the murder we are investigating.'

'Have you recorded an arrest decision as yet for them both?'

'No, what do you think?'

'You can record a decision delaying arrest to make sure

we do a coordinated arrest and search. I think we could do that early next week.'

The next time they both spoke to each other was when they saw each other at the video conference that Rich had arranged. Online with them were two CPS lawyers and they could all see that the coroner, Arthur Ramsbottom, was online but they couldn't see or hear him.

Sandy said, 'Mr Ramsbottom, sir, could you please turn your camera on?'

There was a deathly silence and nothing happening when suddenly they could see Arthur and someone, who must have been an assistant, walking away from him and his laptop. They could see Arthur talking animatedly at them but no sound. Sandy said, 'Mr Ramsbottom, you are on mute.'

They then could see Arthur looking all over his screen looking for inspiration, but to no avail. He then, clearly for all to see, was shouting for help as the assistant then came running back in and turned the mute button off.

Rich and Sandy were glad they were on mute themselves as they couldn't help but giggle at the situation, as did the two CPS lawyers, who it turned out were senior lawyers from the Complex Casework Unit.

Arthur said, 'I hate these things. We should always meet in person.'

Rich said, 'As you all now know, we are investigating the suspected murder of William Peveril. I sent round the details of the Act and section we want to use to investigate, then hopefully charge and prosecute the offenders.'

One of the CPS lawyers raised the digital hand that the meeting system had, then said, 'What have you been using to investigate so far? You have had a forensic post-mortem, haven't you?'

Arthur jumped in before Rich or Sandy could respond. 'My authority, young lady. My authority.'

The lawyer unperturbed said, 'So, you haven't been using the Police and Criminal Evidence Act to investigate so far then?'

'No, well yes,' Rich said and scratched his head. 'No. I am not sure.'

Sandy jumped in and said, 'We have been, at the request of the French police, investigating the death of William Peveril. When they felt they no longer wanted to investigate, we took over and PACE is exactly being adhered to.'

The lawyer was still displaying her digital hand, which she eventually put down telling them it was a legacy hand that was still raised.

Arthur, not giving up, said, 'Young lady, as the senior coroner for the Peak District, when one of my residents has died in suspicious circumstances, whether here or abroad, as William did, I instruct my officers' –Sandy and Rich weren't exactly sure that they were his officers – 'to investigate and find out exactly what happened, and that, I assure you, is what is going to happen in this case.'

Arthur, although he came across as very pompous, was very compelling. Rich said, 'Thank you, Mr Ramsbottom. What I want though is an assurance from CPS that if we get to a place where charging the offender, or offenders, is possible, you won't raise an issue that the actual murder occurred in France?'

The same CPS lawyer said, 'Is the suspect, or suspects, British citizens?'

'Yes, we have made enquiries and both are British

citizens.'

'OK, but I warn you that for this sort of case we will need a full, or close to full, file before we will ever sanction any charges. We will need in writing a document that tells us the French will not be prosecuting this case, and as well as that, any French evidence must be translated by the police before we will consider it.'

The objective that Rich had set for the meeting had been achieved, albeit with it, the setting of an even higher bar by the senior CPS lawyer. Another problem they had to overcome was that there had been no record made of their meeting at the Ministry of Justice in France, although Sandy had on the train home made some excellent notes that they could use as a basis for the document.

Chapter Twenty

On the Sunday, Hannah and Sandy accompanied Katherine to the service in the cathedral. After this they went quickly in Sandy's Morgan Roadster from Ely to Cambridge. They walked through the centre of Cambridge, which was busy that afternoon with people walking about laden with shopping bags. It looked like the shops in the Grand Arcade and around the market place had done well so far that Sunday.

They went across a bridge over the River Cam and headed along the Backs looking across at the magnificent Cambridge colleges as they walked. After they had headed through Queen's Road, they set off to the nearby village of Grantchester. It was much quieter over this side of the Cam than in Cambridge city centre.

The early afternoon was pleasant and warm and as they walked into and through Grantchester Meadows, they kept close to the bank of the River Cam. They could see cows minding their own business on the meadows and it was amazing that within only a few hundred yards or so, the scene they were walking in could have been, and in fact was, in the middle of the English countryside. It could also have been a scene from centuries ago, unchanged over time but for the tarmac paths.

As they walked along, Hannah asked Sandy if she could rehearse her opening speech for court the next day. It was to be the first day of her trial of the arsonist, and although she was excited, she was very nervous.

Hannah, as if facing the jury, said aloud to him her opening speech.

Sandy clapped and gave Hannah a hug and a lingering kiss, which brought a cheer from a passing boat and a group who were punting, who had made it a lot further out of Cambridge than people punting usually managed. It was obvious to Sandy that Hannah was already, even in these very early stages of her career, an excellent barrister.

As they walked on, no one was swimming at the popular spot along Grantchester Meadows where children and families often swam on warmer days.

On reaching Grantchester, they went quickly, due to them running a little late, to the very old and wonderful Blue Ball Inn, where they had an excellent Sunday lunch.

A walk around the village followed their meal. Sandy told Hannah that he had read somewhere that more Nobel Prize winners lived in Grantchester than anywhere else in the world. Their walk included a look in and around the Church of St Andrew and St Mary, which features prominently in the ITV series Grantchester, based on the books by James Runcie. Both Sandy and Hannah were big fans of the TV series set in the 1950s. They particularly liked it as you saw scenes of Cambridge that they both recognised. Sandy told Hannah about his drink with Rich in the Eagle with his grandfathers, which brought a big smile to Hannah's face – the pub was another regular place shown in the series.

They passed the house that the poet Rupert Brooke used to live in and was now owned by a very famous author.

As they slowly made their way back to Cambridge hand in hand to Hannah's home, Sandy told her about his exciting week ahead to arrest two suspects for murder. Rich had organised this to take place on Tuesday morning, but they both had a few last-minute issues in relation to staffing to resolve before it could go ahead.

∞

The meeting room in Belgravia Police Station was full of people. The room was actually quite pleasant and had a round table that they were almost all able to sit around. It even had windows looking out onto the street and a large screen with a projector, which was now whirring to life. The biggest downside, as Sandy saw it, was that there was no tea or coffee available. He always thought a meeting went better if there were refreshments.

Rich and Sandy stood at the front ready to begin the briefing for the simultaneous arrests of Monica Peveril and Henry Adams. Present at the meeting from Sandy's team were Juliet and Clare. Also present was Lofty and at least five other members of the Derbyshire Operation Cornflower team. Sandy presumed that one of them was a CSI and there was probably a digital media investigator. The others could be interview officers. There were four uniformed Metropolitan police officers who were going to help with prisoner transport.

There was an incredible amount of noise in the room as everyone was chatting to each other. Rich, who was leading the briefing, asked for quiet and then said, 'We are this morning going to carry out actions to arrest these two individuals.' The projector was now displaying the pictures of Monica and Henry. Sandy could tell they were media photographs that Rich must have got off the internet. 'The person on your left is Monica Constance Peveril, forty-three years old, and on your right, Henry Fredrick Adams, thirty-eight years old.'

'I thought it was the other way around,' some bright spark in the room said. Rich even had a smile about this.

'We are going to arrest Monica at her home in Eaton Square. She resides on the first floor, but there is a communal area that all the family use on the ground floor that we will search as well. Juliet, you will lead the team that goes there. Any questions?'

'What offence am I arresting her for?'

'Good question, Juliet,' Rich said, having forgotten to mention this. 'We are arresting both of them for the murder of William Harrison Peveril.' The screen was filled with a picture of Viscount Peveril – a sobering picture but a good move by Rich to focus the team on the whole reason that they were there, which was to try and get justice for this man's life being taken from him. Rich said, 'The interim post-mortem report from Dr Stroud says that William died as a result of a fatal dose of morphine. These two suspects were, and in fact are, in a relationship with each other. Henry has ready access to morphine. Both were in Saint-Émilion, France, on the evening of the murder. Monica was in the room when William died.'

The atmosphere in the room was best described as electric, and you could have heard a pin drop as Rich outlined the circumstances of the death.

'What do we do if James Peveril is at home and gets in the way?' Juliet said.

Sandy looked at Juliet and said, 'We have someone outside the house in Eaton Square who will let us know when James leaves for the Houses of Parliament. We will enter then. We know Arabella, who also sometimes resides there, is in Norfolk.'

Rich continued with his briefing. 'We are going to arrest Henry at his surgery on Harley Street. This gives us the best place to search for how the drugs may have been obtained that got into William Peveril. I will lead this team.'

Sandy added, 'We also have someone outside in Harley Street that will let us know when he gets to his surgery, and we will need to make sure that he hasn't got a patient with him at the time of our entry.'

Rich continued by saying, 'The arrests must be carried out simultaneously, so DS Ashton, please wait until I give you the go-ahead to enter and make the arrest. Is that understood, Juliet?'

'Yes, perfectly, and we hand over the prisoners to our uniform officers and will we need to book them into detention here ourselves?'

'Yes, please. Leave Clare to carry out the forensics and the search. I want you then to let me know after Monica is in a cell before I bring Henry in, so they don't see each other at this time.'

'Right,' Sandy said. 'Time to go and get ourselves in position nearby to each of the premises.' As he said this, everyone seemed to leap into action. The noise quickly built up again by the very excited detectives and police officers about to go out to arrest suspects for murder – not an everyday occurrence in their police careers.

∞

Each of the convoys had three vehicles in it. The Metropolitan police uniformed officers were leading the way in their black van. The convoy that Juliet was in only had a relatively short distance to travel. Sandy, who was in a car with Rich and Lofty, had further to go to Harley Street.

They drove at speed and Lofty, who was a good driver, was struggling to keep close to the police officers leading the way. This was due to the volume of traffic and the continuous sets of traffic lights they kept coming across. Motorbikes kept darting along in and out of the traffic. The same was happening with taxis pulling in front of them and then heading off at speed down side roads. Lofty was continuously pressing his horn, which brought about a cacophony of noise as other drivers copied and pressed their car horns as well.

They hurtled up and around Hyde Park and along Oxford Street, where they now not only needed to be mindful of the traffic but also pedestrians, some of whom seemed to have a death wish by stepping off the pavements and into their path. They went left into Cavendish Square before the police van leading the way came to an abrupt halt just into Harley Street, causing Lofty to break hard, the movement of which threw Rich and Sandy forward in their seats.

The two big and burly uniform officers jumped out of the van and Sandy could see that they were wearing belts that carried a small extendable baton, a pouch for their pepper spray and a massive set of handcuffs known as Quick Cuffs. They split up and one went to see if there was a rear entrance and the other walked towards the front of the house. Lofty said as they walked away, 'I wouldn't need any of that kit!' Lofty did seem a little bit agitated that morning; it might have been the stressful drive or the excitement of the forthcoming arrests, or a combination of both.

Rich had received the message that Dr Adams was in his consulting rooms, which were located downstairs. A number of other consultants had their rooms on different floors of the house.

Rich, Sandy and Lofty moved forward quickly and deliberately. Sandy walked up to the front door and pressed a brass buzzer for one of the upper floors. He said, when it was answered, 'I have an appointment with...'

He read one of the names from the brass plates on the outside of the building to the person answering, who said, 'You have pressed the wrong button, people are always doing that. They are on the floor below. I will let you in.' The door buzzed to open and in the three of them went.

Rich called Juliet and said the words, 'Strike, strike, strike.' They were in a small entrance hall and the excitement and tension they felt was palpable. Sandy felt his heart beating very hard and he had butterflies in his stomach. At that very moment, a lady and her husband came out of Dr Adams's consulting rooms and it was quite a squeeze for them to pass by and go out into the street.

Now was the time to enter the consulting rooms. Rich rang one of the uniform officers just before they entered to tell him that they were in the premises and about to carry out the arrest.

On entering the room, they found it to be a large reception area with a very expensive-looking red leather armchair and a sofa. There was a rectangular low table with magazines neatly placed. Along one side was a big oak desk with a lady standing behind it. She was smartly dressed, in her mid to late fifties with very short brown hair and wore glasses.

Seeing the three men enter, she looked them up and down and said, 'Excuse me, you must have come to the wrong consulting room. Dr Adams is a consultant gynaecologist.'

Sandy said, while showing her his police warrant card, 'That is exactly who we have come to see – Dr Henry Adams.'

'The police!' she exclaimed, putting both her hands to her face. 'What has happened?'

As soon as she mentioned the police, they went straight to the door at the side of the room. Sandy went to open it quickly and go into the room to make the arrest, but as he went to open the door handle, the door was being locked from the inside. Upon pushing it, he found that they couldn't now get into the room.

Chapter Twenty-One

The door looked substantial and would need something like a door opener to smash it open. It didn't seem possible that a shoulder charge would be able to shift the door. Sandy hoped that if there was a window out onto the rear of the house, one of the uniform police officers was in position to cover it.

Lofty pushed Sandy out of the way and to one side of the door. Lofty then took two or three steps backwards and somehow, when running at the door, he jumped so that he put both of his feet in the air and they simultaneously crashed into the door, making a loud crashing noise and breaking the door lock. This was clearly by the smoothness of the movement – something that he must have done before.

Regaining his footing, Lofty opened the door and went in. Sandy quickly followed him. There, stood behind a desk in the room, was Henry Adams. He was dressed in a blue suit, not wearing a tie. He was in the processes of throwing his mobile phone onto the desk. 'Who are you?' he shouted. 'You are not the police. You must have come to rob me.' Henry picked up some surgical scissors that were in a dish behind him. 'Don't you dare come any nearer. I will stab you.'

Sandy now took charge and placed a calming hand on Lofty's arm. He shouted behind him, 'Rich, take the receptionist out onto the street and do not let anyone else in here. We need back-up – get them to wait in the reception area until I give them a signal to come in.'

Rich did as asked and he could be heard calling the uniform officers for back-up.

'You,' Henry said, waving the scissors at Sandy, 'I knew you were following me.' He clearly now recognised Sandy from the other day.

Sandy said, 'Henry Adams, I am DCI McFarlane and I am arresting you on suspicion of murder. You do not have to say anything but it may harm your defence if you do not mention when questioned something you later rely on in court. Anything you do say may be used in evidence against you.'

He had hardly been able to say the whole caution before Henry said, 'Murder! Who have I murdered? Don't be ridiculous.'

While the two of them were talking so intently with each other, unnoticed by Henry, Lofty was inching closer to getting around the side of the desk. Sandy had noticed this and in order to further distract Henry, said, 'The murder of William Harrison Peveril.'

There was a flicker of understanding that could be seen in Henry's eyes. He shouted, 'I have never met this person.' As he said this, Lofty made a giant leap and the two of them went crashing down onto the floor, sending the tray with the surgical instruments flying. The large chair that was there also went backwards and smashed into the wall.

For a moment there was no sound from the two on the floor. As Sandy ran around the desk, he saw Lofty was lying more or less on top of Henry. 'Please don't be hurt, Lofty,' Sandy said, not even in a whisper. The pair on the floor were clearly stunned and as Sandy tried to pull a groggy Lofty up, he was pulled out of the way by the uniform officers who had come crashing into the room.

Lofty got up and moved quickly out of the way. The uniform officers flipped Henry onto his front and handcuffed him behind his back. They pulled him very vigorously and unceremoniously to his feet and marched him out of the room.

Unbelievably there were no injuries, and Rich, who had also now entered the room, picked up the scissors that had been knocked onto the floor and under the desk. 'That went well then,' he said, which made all three of them laugh.

The two other Derbyshire officers in the third car from the convoy were in the reception room with the very shaken receptionist. She was sat down but got up and said, 'I desperately need a cup of coffee. Do any of you want one too?' She went and put the kettle on, where nearby on a tray were some extremely posh-looking bone china cups. She then said, 'Will Dr Adams be back today? If not, I presume I need to cancel his appointments?'

∞

The plan they put in place was to leave Lofty, the CSI and the other detective on Harley Street to search the reception room and the consulting room. Rich and Sandy were going to attend the custody area of Belgravia Police Station to ensure that the prisoner, Henry Adams, was booked into detention successfully.

They had only just set off when Juliet rang Sandy. 'I have arrested Monica. Clare and the team have started searching her rooms on the first floor, but Monica has told me I am not a high enough rank to arrest her.'

'What?' Sandy said. 'Just get the uniform officers to come in and take her off to the police station. Who does she think she is?'

'Apparently she is Viscountess Peveril, that is what she keeps telling me! I need to know my place in society.'

'OK,' Sandy said, reluctantly, 'I will come now and get Rich to drop me off outside the house.'

When they arrived outside the palatial Peveril House in Eaton Square, they found standing outside looking up at the front door of the house a small crowd of people, which included Vivienne Jones and Adam Scott. 'Is that who I think it is, the movie stars?' Rich asked, almost pointing at them.

'Yes, they live next door,' Sandy said, as he got out of the car. Rich was going to quickly head off to the Belgravia Police Station but instead hovered around to have a good look at Vivienne and Adam, before driving off in the car.

As Sandy passed the small crowd, Vivienne and Adam nodded at him as he strode up the stairs at speed and through the open front door. Juliet was stood in the hallway just outside the main reception room. Stood with her were the two uniform police officers. They were unsure what they should do as they had told Juliet that they didn't feel right to have to roughly move the elegant Monica Peveril. Well they just might have to do that, thought Sandy. If Lofty was here, he would charge in, pick Monica up and put her over his shoulder and out into the van.

On walking into the room, he saw Monica was wearing a beautiful pink silk dress and wearing exceedingly high black stilettos. She was sat in a chair reading a magazine. 'Oh, it's you,' she said on looking up and seeing Sandy. 'Can you tell your sergeant out there' – she gestured dismissively to the hallway – 'that they most certainly haven't got the rank to arrest me. I would have thought it would have to be the Commissioner at least to arrest a Viscountess.'

'DS Ashton, have you arrested and cautioned Viscountess Peveril?' he asked Juliet, who had now come and stood by his side.

'Yes, at least fifteen minutes ago,' a very patient, calm and experienced Juliet replied, not looking at Sandy but directly at Monica.

'Your ladyship' – Sandy thought he would play to Monica's vanity – 'the law says that a constable can arrest anyone, whoever they are, if they have reasonable suspicion to do so. A detective sergeant therefore most certainly can.' He saw that Monica put her magazine down and was listening. 'Outside are some of your neighbours watching what is going on in here, as clearly this is not something that happens in Eaton Square. On my orders, very shortly these two' – he pointed to the two uniform officers peering around the door – 'are going to pick you up and carry you off handcuffed to their van and everyone will see you reduced to that humiliation.'

Monica was definitely listening now. Image, well her image, was one of her most important priorities – that was clear by looking at how she was dressed. She said, 'What is the other option that you are obviously going to be telling me next?'

'No handcuffs. You, me and DS Ashton go to the police station in an unmarked police car.'

Before Sandy had finished speaking, Monica had stood up and said, 'Come on then.' She was playing with them, taking total control of the situation and it had been working.

Sandy was a bit bemused when she went out into the hallway and she placed on her head a blue wide-brimmed hat and picked up a very expensive-looking handbag. He was not really sure her outfit fitted a day trip to the cells of Belgravia Police Station.

∞

The Met Police had given them use of the meeting room that they had held their briefing in earlier that morning. Rich and Sandy met in there with the Operation Cornflower interview advisor and the two detectives who were going to carry out the interviews, Bob and Pete. They had returned early from the searches. Even though Rich and Sandy outranked the interview advisor, she was quite clear – in fact, adamant – that even though they wanted to, Rich and Sandy were not going to be the ones carrying out the interviews. Bob and Pete regularly carried out suspect interviews; Rich and Sandy rarely did these days, if ever. It was a, 'No brainer,' she insisted.

They had already discussed what they needed to disclose to the two suspects and their solicitors, who had been called and were en route to the police station to advise their clients. They would disclose straight away the interim post-mortem report. Then, during the interviews at an appropriate stage, disclose the association between the two suspects from phone records and the hotels in Saint-Émilion.

The interviewers were experienced in the PEACE model of interviewing, which was to P, plan and prepare – that was what they had been doing and were doing now; E, engage and explain; A, account and challenge; C, closure;

then finally E, evaluate.

After she had booked Monica into custody, Juliet joined them. She made them all laugh when she described the open mouths of the custody sergeant and the others in the custody block when Monica walked in. She had still been wearing her hat. The custody sergeant couldn't bring himself to place the elegant, well dressed and incredibly beautiful Monica in a cell but instead had sat her in an interview room to wait for the arrival of her solicitor.

Now the prisoners were safely in custody, Sandy thought he had better let James and Arabella know that they had been arrested. He rang James. 'Hello, James—'

Before he could say anything else, James said, 'You have been busy this morning arresting Monica. I should think that was an experience.'

'How do you know?'

'The housekeeper rang me, almost immediately. What is going to happen to Monica?'

'We will interview her during today. Not sure what will happen after that though. We have also arrested a Dr Henry Adams as we suspect they were in it together.'

'I don't know him, but Arabella, when she was playing Miss Marple, tells me Monica often spends the night with him.'

Suddenly a thought popped into Sandy's head. It was something that Rich and he had overlooked. 'Where is your father's Rolls Royce? We know Monica had that in France with her and drove back in it.'

'Gosh, I have forgotten about the car. The Rolls is my father's personal property and I will need to dispose of it to give the money proceeds as part of his will to his ex-wife and Monica.'

'But where is it now, James?' Sandy asked, believing that the evidence from the medication would be in it.

'It is in a garage, just off Eaton Square. I will excuse myself now from the House of Commons and find the key for one of your officers and then take them to the garage myself.'

Having overheard this conversation, Juliet stood up with the intention that she would go and meet James at Eaton Square. Sandy didn't feel that he had anything to gain by ringing Arabella, so he sent a text message to James, firstly to let him know DS Ashton was on her way to meet him and also to ask if he could let Arabella know what was happening.

No sooner had Juliet left when Lofty walked into the room. 'How are you feeling?' the welfare-conscious Sandy asked. 'Not much fun being threatened with sharp surgical scissors.'

'I am fine. How are you, more to the point? You were threatened as well and you posh southern boys are not made of the same stuff as we are in the north.' This brought some welcome laughter from all in the room, albeit Bob and Pete, the interviewers, were unsure they should be laughing at the senior officer, which Sandy was, but when he laughed, they assumed it was OK.

The only thing of interest from the consulting rooms on Harley Street was that Dr Adams had prescribed in the past – some were well before William Peveril had died, but a couple recently – standard morphine tablets of fifty-milligram dosage to three separate patients, then to two different patients, two hundred milligrams of diamorphine in injections. Lofty said, 'Dr Adams's practice is in reality a one-man band. The receptionist is actually his only full-time employee and she also acts as the practice manager and secretary all rolled into one.'

'Did she say if this prescribing and dispensing was unusual?' Rich asked.

'In relation to the tablets, this was not unusual, but the injections, yes. He does prescribe them but this is normally after he has performed the surgery in a nearby hospital and while the patient is still in hospital. I have the names and addresses of the patients.'

Chapter Twenty-Two

The interview monitoring room in reality could only accommodate two people but somehow, the interview advisor, Rich and Sandy had crammed themselves into the room. They sat around a blank screen, which quickly burst into life, and they could see present in the interview room Monica – without her hat – and an older man, who they presumed was her solicitor. Also present were Bob and Pete, who were busying themselves getting ready for the interview.

When they were ready, Bob said to Monica, 'Please can you give us your full name?'

'You know my full name.' Monica pointed to a form that Pete had just filled in. 'You have just written it down there.'

'I am asking for the purpose of the recording.'

'Very well. My name is Viscountess Monica Constance Peveril. What are your full names? I should think your parents gave you funny middle names, didn't they? I quite like Constance. I don't use it enough though.'

Bob, undeterred, asked the solicitor to introduce himself then introduced himself as did Pete.

'DCs. I am not being interviewed by a lowly rank of a DC. I told that DCI McFarlane that I was not being arrested by a DS and I am certainly not being interviewed by a DC.' Monica's solicitor whispered something to her.

Bob, still undeterred, repeated the same caution that

Monica had been told when Juliet had arrested her.

'You have said that wrong,' Monica said, which made Bob look at Pete for reassurance. 'The DS that arrested me said it differently. You are not too good at your job, are you – you can't even caution me correctly. Are you sure you both are detectives? You don't look like detectives.'

'Tell us, in your own words, about how you met William Peveril.'

'I am sorry, whose words would I use if not my own words?' Rich and Sandy started sniggering when they heard her say this. This brought glares at them from the interview advisor. Monica looked intently with her smouldering blue eyes straight into Bob's eyes and said, 'Viscount Peveril to you. I met him at a charity event I was organising four years ago. He had just gone through a divorce and we initially courted, then got married quickly, and there I was, all of a sudden, a Viscountess.'

'Did you have a happy marriage?'

'Are you both married? Do you have a happy marriage? What do you mean by that? Do you mean did we have a sex life? Were we friends or companions? Sorry, stupid question.'

Bob said, 'Let me rephrase the question then. Did you and the Viscount have rows and arguments?'

'Another stupid question. Do you mean did we have an argument about where to go, what to eat, what to buy?'

Bob, who was starting to get uncomfortable and jiggling about on his seat, said, 'Was he, or were you, ever violent to one and other?'

'No. You two are not very well dressed, are you? Look at you both wearing what looks like polyester suits, cheap white shirts with ties halfway down and your shirt top buttons not done up. Shocking way to present yourselves at work, wouldn't you say?'

Unconsciously, both Bob and Pete did their top buttons up and straightened their ties, which made all three in the monitoring room smile and Rich and Sandy laugh softly.

Bob, desperate to try and take control of the interview, said, 'We are going to need you to take this interview more seriously. Just before he died, the Viscount had a bad back. What medication were you giving him?'

'I am not sure how you think I am not taking this interview seriously. I have been arrested for the murder of my husband. You know what I am going to say to what you have just said, don't you? Not a good question again. It is as if you are saying to me, sit up straight, answer the questions like a good little girl, exactly how we want you to. Confess to us, we are so good at interviewing you have no other option but to confess. Is that what happens or do you have other more extreme methods to make me confess to something I haven't done?' After sighing loudly and looking at her solicitor dramatically, Monica said, 'I have no idea what the medication was. I just got something for him and he was taking it.'

'Where did you get this medication?'

'In Saint-Émilion.'

'Are you sure? We have checked and we can't find anywhere in Saint-Émilion that the medication could have been obtained from.'

'Check again. Where do you get this furniture from? This table is not even made of real wood. These chairs…' Monica stood up and pointed to the furniture's metal frames. 'Cheap awful stuff, and don't get me started on this flooring.'

Bob and Pete had almost swooned when they saw Monica standing. No doubt just the effect that she had wanted. When Monica sat down again and crossed her legs, this created an unnerving effect for both Bob and Pete. The interview advisor muttered to herself, 'Men! You are all misogynistic!' Luckily, Rich and Sandy were not smiling or swooning at Monica.

Bob got out of his folder a copy of the interim post-mortem report. 'You have had a chance to read the report and talk to your solicitor about it. What do you think about it?'

'I thought it was well written. There is, though, lots of medical jargon within it and therefore it is not written in plain English. The paper is cheap, thin photocopy paper, not what I would suggest an important report should be printed out on.'

Bob and Pete looked at each other and Bob tried again: 'What do you think of the findings?'

'Very interesting question, at last.' Looking straight at Pete, Monica said, 'You haven't said too much, Pete, what do you think?' Looking down at Pete and Bob's shoes, she then said, 'Do you two ever clean your shoes? William would never go out without his shoes being highly polished. Obviously, you two don't care about your appearance.'

Bob tried the question again, but at the same time trying to rub his shoes on the back of his trousers. 'The findings say that William, I mean the Viscount, died of a fatal dose of morphine.'

'It says he had cardiac disease and a doctor in France told me he died of a heart attack. I have seen the registration of death and it says heart attack, so stop trying to say otherwise. Please read the report, it is in there.'

It looked, at last, like Monica was getting a bit rattled; however, on realising this, her solicitor asked for a break and for him to consult with his client.

Bob and Pete left the room and the interview advisor rushed off to see them and discuss the next phase of the interview.

∞

When the interview recommenced, Pete asked the first question. 'When we finished talking earlier, we were discussing the post-mortem report.'

'Are you asking the questions now? Is this a case of good cop and bad cop? He was a pretty awful good cop,' Monica said, pointing at Bob. 'Are you going to be an awful bad cop or are you better at questioning than him?'

Pete, not sure whether to ask his first question again or make a response to what Monica had just said, responded by saying, 'I am just the one asking this set of questions in the interview.'

'What is an interview?'

'It can best be described as a conversation with a purpose.'

'What is the purpose of this conversation then and why don't you get to that purpose?'

Already getting rattled and trying to get back to his first point, Pete, in a worried motion, ran his hands through his hair, and just as he was about to speak, Monica said, 'You really need to see a good hair stylist – they will give you much needed advice on shampoo and conditioner. You need them to also add in a bit of colour to hide your very greying hair. You will look much younger for it.'

Rich and Sandy couldn't help themselves but had to laugh at this comment. The interview advisor, on the other hand, was furiously talking into the earpiece that Bob had in his ear.

Bob, having no doubt been told by the interview advisor to intervene, said, 'Dr Stroud in his post-mortem report says that Viscount Peveril died of a fatal dose of morphine.'

'I don't care what Dr Stroud says, I know differently. William died from a heart attack.'

'Did you kill him?'

'No, I did not. Stop talking rubbish now.'

'You don't seem very upset or grieving that your husband has died?'

'Gosh!' Monica feigned surprise and looked around at everyone in the room, then said, pointing at Bob, 'I guess we didn't know we have in this room an expert on the grieving process. Please tell me how I need to act as a widow so that I can grieve properly.'

Bob now looked very sheepish and said, 'I am sorry, I feel quite stupid now.'

'Don't worry. I am sure that is how you feel on a regular basis.' Monica, who was in full flow, kept talking. 'William was thirty years older than me and was always going to die decades before me. Sad that it happened so early in our marriage, but that is life and I accept it.'

Pete said, 'Tell us about how you know Henry Adams?'

At the mention of Henry's name, Monica smiled. 'He is a gynaecologist and performed an operation on me.'

'You are in a relationship with your doctor?'

'Yes, I admit we are in a relationship. A bit of excitement in my life, but he hasn't been my doctor for over two years or even longer.'

Looking from Bob to Pete, she said, 'What do you both do to get some excitement in your lives?' Monica was flirting with them both.

'He came to be with you in Saint-Émilion,' a blushing Pete said, while he showed around the room a photograph that he had taken out of his folder of Monica and Henry from the hotel reception in Saint-Émilion. 'He was there when the Viscount died.'

'Yes, I admit that he was there then.'

Bob and Pete and those monitoring the interview got suddenly extremely excited. 'So, he helped you to kill the Viscount with his medical knowledge?'

Monica looked intently at Pete for several moments. Was she going to crack? Bob and Pete were going to let her fill the silence. Monica then picked up the photograph and said, 'You said he was there when William died.' Pointing at the photograph, she said, 'Yes, he was *there* in the hotel when William died.'

All the Operation Cornflower team, as quickly as they had got excited, were now feeling deflated. Monica was still talking. 'You two need to get out more. Get yourselves a hobby or find someone to have an exciting relationship with. Look, boys, spending all of your time in artificial lighting in rooms like this is doing your complexion no good. You are both too pasty-looking. I am worrying about you.'

Monica, it seemed, had taken charge again. Bob said, 'Tell us then, in your own words. Yes, of course you would only use your own words,' he hastily added, not wanting to be pulled up again by Monica. 'What happened in the moments before the Viscount died?'

'Although very uncomfortable with his back, William had been fine at dinner. Monsieur Chevalier had poured him a brandy, which he took up to our rooms.' Monica paused for a moment as if picturing what happened or making sure she got the next bit of her story straight. 'He got changed into his night clothes, sat in his chair and just died of a heart attack.'

There didn't appear to be anything more to discuss so Pete tried to bring the interview to a close, and Monica, as her last comment, said, 'If there was a TripAdvisor for interviews or if you have one of those feedback sheets, you know the ones, "tell us how we did", well, I am sorry boys, but two stars from me is the best I can go to.' This final comment brought a big smile not only from her solicitor who had enjoyed the whole experience, but also Bob and Pete. The interview advisor, as she got up to go down and see Bob and Pete, said, 'Not even one star from me!'

Chapter Twenty-Three

The interview advisor had told Sandy and Rich that although Bob and Pete's confidence had been clearly dented by the interview with Monica, they were determined to elicit all the information they could from their next interview.

Bob and Pete walked into the interview room where Henry Adams and his solicitor were waiting. Bob completed the introductions and Sandy smiled when he saw that Bob read the caution from a card that he produced from his pocket. Monica had clearly rattled him.

Bob said, 'Please tell us how you know Viscountess Monica Peveril?'

'One or both of you smoke, don't you?' Henry asked, curling his nose up as if he was experiencing a bad smell.

Here we go again, thought Sandy. The doctor was right though, as Sandy had seen them both smoking in the rear yard of the police station while talking to the interview advisor just a few minutes earlier. Henry continued by saying, 'I can smell it on your clothes. As a doctor let me tell you, very bad for your health.'

Bob tried his question again: 'Monica Peveril, how do you know her?'

'Monica was my patient three years ago. I performed surgery for her that I am unable to elaborate on due to doctor–patient confidentiality. I was then responsible for this particular physical aspect of her care for four or five months until she was fully well after the operation.'

'So, you have had a relationship with one of your patients?'

Henry looked angrily at Bob. Henry clearly had a temper. Sandy and Lofty had seen that in action at his consulting rooms. Doing his best to keep his cool, Henry said, 'No, that is not correct. When Monica and I met again, almost a year ago at a hospital charity event, we were drawn to each other and started our relationship then. So no, I did not, and have not, had a relationship with one of my patients.'

'That timeline fits perfectly,' Rich said to Sandy, 'with the call data for Monica and Henry's phones when they first started contacting each other.'

'How well did you know Viscount William Peveril?' Bob asked.

'Not at all and I never actually met him.'

'What do you mean by actually?'

'He attended two or three events that I was also present at. For example, he was there at the event after which Monica and I got together.'

'You have been to Saint-Émilion when they have been staying at William's chateau?'

'Yes. The first time was very soon after Monica and I got together. We couldn't bear not to be together for a whole month. After she had gone to France I went for a short while.'

'You were also there when William died, weren't you?'

Henry looked at his solicitor, who shrugged his shoulders at him and Henry then replied, 'I am not sure exactly what you mean by "there". Yes, I was there in Saint-Émilion, but in my hotel.'

He looked again at his solicitor, then said after quite a bit of hesitation, 'I was shocked when Monica called me to say William had died.' Sandy thought he had to be lying now. He was no expert in body language but Henry had been touching his face then his hair as he had said it, and for the first time Henry had not looked directly into the eyes of Bob as he replied, but towards the table.

'Let us now go to the post-mortem report,' Bob said as he got it out of his folder.

'Interim post-mortem report,' Henry said firmly.

'Yes, interim. Dr Stroud says that the Viscount died from a fatal dose of morphine. You have easy access to morphine, don't you?'

'No comment.' This surprised all of them monitoring the interview and clearly Bob and Pete, who quickly looked at each other. The interview had been flowing so smoothly up until this point.

'Are you making no comment because you don't want to incriminate yourself?' Bob asked.

Henry, almost shouting, said, 'Seriously, I am a consultant gynaecological surgeon and you are asking me if I have easy access to a drug that some of my patients need for pain relief. Yes, of course I do. As does any other medical doctor.'

Good, he was talking again, Sandy thought. Bob said, 'Did you provide morphine to Viscountess Peveril or administer the morphine yourself to William Peveril so that he died?'

'No comment.'

'You are not denying it then?'

The solicitor then said, 'Officer, you know better than this. My client does not have to say anything, and it is my advice that he makes no comment.'

Henry then, for the rest of the interview, made 'no comment' answers to everything that Bob, and then Pete in summary, asked him. In fact, he never looked at them directly again, but in a sort of bored-looking manner just focussed on a spot on the wall behind Bob and Pete.

∞

The team went back to their meeting room to evaluate what had happened in the interviews. Already waiting in the room were Juliet, Clare and Lofty. Even though he was desperate to ask Juliet what she had found in the Rolls Royce, Sandy knew it would be best for her to share that information in a structured meeting.

Leading the meeting, Sandy asked Lofty to let everyone know the highlights of the search at the Harley Street consulting rooms. 'Nothing of note at all,' Lofty said. 'The only possibility is that we have the details of five of Dr Adams patients whom he prescribed morphine to in the last few months or so before Viscount Peveril died.'

'Where do the patients live?'

'In London and Cambridge.'

Looking at Rich, Sandy said, 'Juliet and I can visit those patients if you want over the next week or so?' Rich just nodded in agreement.

'Clare, what did we find at Peveril House?'

'Well,' Clare said, rolling her eyes and shaking her head, 'if you want to take a tour of designer label clothing and footwear, Monica Peveril's dressing room is a good place to start. Thousands and thousands of pounds worth. Other than that, nothing to help our investigation I am afraid.'

'Clare,' Sandy said, 'have we had anything back from the forensic search at Chateau Peveril yet?'

'Yes, sorry. I should have told you a few days ago. We have DNA from William Peveril and one other person that we haven't got a record of.'

'Could that be from either of the Chevaliers?' Rich asked.

'Not theirs. I took their DNA and fingerprints when we were there and also the French doctor and the two funeral directors – the brother and sister Gerard. It's none of theirs. However, Antoine's fingerprints were all over the phone in the room.'

'Could be Monica's, or hopefully, Henry Adams's DNA.'

'We have only just taken theirs, so I will process their DNA as a priority.'

Rich had to leave the room as he had to make a call to CPS and also had some other authorities to complete.

'Juliet, please tell us that you found some great evidence in the Rolls Royce,' Sandy said, trying not to sound too excited.

'Sorry to disappoint, but the car was clean.' There was an audible sigh of disappointment around the room.

'OK, all I can say about the interview with Monica is that it was pure theatre. It would be a TV hit if we could ever show it,' Sandy said, which brought laughter from the room, but on looking round and seeing the subdued faces of Bob and Pete, he added, 'What we have got though is a firm confirmation from Monica that she was in a relationship with Henry and he was in Saint-Émilion when William died. Bob, tell us what else we found out from

Monica.'

Bob puffed his chest out. He was a very experienced and long-standing major crime detective and although Monica had given them the run around, he had got information to share. 'She is sticking to the position that her husband died of a heart attack. We will need expert evidence to support us to refute what she is saying.'

He looked around the room and everyone seemed pleased – that was a good result that they could work from. Sandy would have much preferred a confession, but he was an optimist. He asked Bob to tell them about the interview with Dr Adams.

'He also fully confirmed he was in a relationship with Monica and he had been to France on two occasions to spend time with her, including being in Saint-Émilion at the time of the death. He made no comment in relation to how the death happened or when we asked him about the findings from the post-mortem report.'

The DMI told everyone in the meeting that he had downloaded information from the suspects' phones. There were no messages or activity between them on WhatsApp. Monica didn't even have WhatsApp on her phone. There were hundreds of text messages. 'So last century,' someone in the room said, bringing further laughter.

Another said, 'It is all snapchat now you know.' From a quick scan of the messages, none of them were incriminating or were even loving or romantic, just about arrangements for meeting up. Sandy was not surprised because Monica, in his opinion, was a cold fish.

Just as the meeting was finishing, Rich came back in the room and told them all that the interviews and searches hadn't changed anything. CPS had insisted on a full file before they could make a decision and the two suspects had to be bailed. Sandy had fully known that this was what would happen but he was surprised how accepting everyone in the room was. They were so excited at the beginning of the day, arresting people for murder, and although they had completed a key task, their one step forward had taken them no nearer to a result.

∞

They were able to add conditions to the bail; Rich had organised this with the custody sergeant. The main condition for both of them was not to contact James and Arabella or any of their family. Sandy had rung James to let him know what had happened in relation to Monica being granted bail. Sandy also told him that Monica was going to live with her mother in Brighton but she needed some of her belongings from Peveril House in Eaton Square – no doubt lots of her designer clothes and shoes. She would send someone to collect the rest of her belongings in due course. The other condition that Monica and Henry had was to surrender their passports. One of the officers bringing her back to the house to collect some of her belongings would take it from her when they went with her into the house.

Rich had allocated Juliet and Lofty to take Monica to Eaton Square. Sandy asked James to either keep himself firmly to his floor or better still, if he could be away from the house for a couple of hours it would be helpful. James was happy to do this but was concerned that Monica may take some his father's personal items, for example, he had a very expensive watch that was over fifty years old, one he had been presented with on his twenty-first birthday. This had been left to his grandson George. Sandy told James to have a very quick scan through the rooms, not touching anything of Monica's, and to take what he knew, as the executor of the will, was left to others. But he had to be quick as she would be home shortly.

After she had been bailed, Rich placed Monica in a room near to the entrance of the police station for her to wait for Juliet and Lofty while they brought the car around to collect her. After only a couple of minutes of waiting in the room, Henry walked in, also to wait for his lift, which was from a couple of the Operation Cornflower DCs. They were equally surprised to see each other.

One of the authorities that Rich had organised and had been given written permission to carry out, was for them to be covertly monitored, both visually and verbally in this room. The only other person that was aware that this was happening was Sandy. They hadn't even told Juliet or Lofty.

The two lovers, Monica and Henry, embraced each other and kissed. They then sat holding hands.

Monica said, 'I am sorry to have roped you into this. What did you tell them?'

'I told them nothing,' a smiling Henry said to her. 'What did you tell them?'

'I told them everything.'

'What!' Henry said, swiftly pulling his hands away from Monica. 'What exactly is everything?'

Monica grabbed his hands back and held on to them. 'That we had been in a relationship for almost a year and you had come to France twice to be with me.'

Showing clear relief all over his face, Henry said, 'That

is OK then because I told them that as well. What did you tell them about how William died?'

'As agreed, of a heart attack.'

'Good. The post-mortem result doesn't completely rule it out. I made no comment, as my solicitor advised me to. Especially as I am a doctor, they would ask me to give a professional and informed response, which could have got tricky.'

They then sat there in silence for several moments before Henry said, 'We now need to end our relationship. I think that would be for the best.'

Sandy and Rich were monitoring the conversation along with a person from the Met Police covert team who was logging the conversation. Showing the most emotion that Sandy had ever seen Monica display, they saw Monica pull her hands away in fury from Henry, and she jumped up to her feet and struck Henry straight across his face with her hand. She had hit him with such force that the reddening mark of her hand and fingers was quickly starting to show. Monica said, after she had struck him, 'You—' She was unable to say her next words because Juliet and Lofty had just at that moment entered the room.

'Too soon,' Rich shouted at the monitor. Sandy and Rich were kicking themselves that they hadn't delayed Juliet and Lofty longer. They may have just missed a crucial piece of the jigsaw puzzle of how William had died. They both looked at each other in pure frustration.

No sooner had Monica left than the two DCs arrived and took Henry – who was gently rubbing his face with his hand – away with them. The DCs looked at him and then each other and not knowing what else they should do about Henry's face, decided to just give him a lift and not ask him anything about it. Henry was returning to his home in Kensington.

Sandy had rung the General Medical Council earlier in the day as they oversee the discipline for doctors. The lady he spoke to told him they needed him to send a written report for them to put in place the hearing of an interim orders tribunal. This tribunal, they told him, might take no action against Dr Adams, nor impose conditions on him to limit his doctor's practice or even to suspend Dr Adams while they investigated. Due to the circumstances that Sandy had provisionally told them, they would, at the moment, continue to allow him to practice.

Chapter Twenty-Four

It was not until the end of the day that Sandy had a chance to contact Hannah. She had been very upset for two days now because after all of her preparation, planning and practice, her trial had been put off on the Monday morning. The defence had put in a request to consult their own expert clinical psychologist. The defence had been served with the prosecution expert papers the previous week, which they said was too little time to consider the impact of them. The judge had put the case off for two weeks.

This highlighted for Sandy a huge issue for the case against Monica and Henry. They would need an incredible number of different experts if they were going to prove their case. Once an expert was found by the prosecution, the two defendants – not just one as in Hannah's case – would want their own competing expert. No other way to describe it other than a nightmare scenario.

An experts planning meeting was organised. This was to be chaired by Rich, with Clare and another CSI present. Dr Stroud, who had supplied his now completed report, was also going to be in attendance. His findings were yes to cardiac disease, but his conclusion for the cause of death was morphine toxicity. Rich had also invited two members from the National Crime Agency who had a database of experts that included medical experts. Although Dr Stroud had some ideas of who to use to assist with providing expertise, the NCA would be of invaluable assistance.

The plan that Rich had was that he would get on with finding appropriate experts, while Sandy and Juliet saw the five patients who had been prescribed the morphine.

The first patient's address Juliet and Sandy visited was in a nice area of London, Notting Hill. To be fair though, at the prices that Dr Adams charged, all the areas they were going to visit would be probably very expensive. The name that Juliet had was possibly a Russian name. They knocked on the door of the large, terraced house. A man answered and it turned out that they had presumed right – he told them he was Russian and as a result he didn't speak very good English. He was in the middle of a business telephone call and told them to go into the front room, where his wife would join them shortly.

The lady who joined them was as elegantly dressed as Monica always was. Juliet, after explaining who they were, said, 'We are looking into some medications that Dr Adams of Harley Street has prescribed to his patients. You were one of his patients, weren't you?'

The lady spoke much better English than her husband and said, 'An absolutely fantastic doctor. Yes, he treated me for a few weeks at the beginning of this year.'

'Were you prescribed any tablets for pain relief by him?'

'Yes.' After having said this, the lady got swiftly to her feet and went off out of the room. They could hear her tapping up the stairs in her high heels. Sandy was not sure whether she had put the shoes on to see them or actually wore them all day in the house. If she did, surely that would be incredibly uncomfortable. The tapping, after a very short while, came back down the stairs and the lady entered carrying a box of tablets.

'I used about half of them.' She pulled out of the box the tablet blister packet, which showed some empty slots. 'Then I didn't need them anymore. I should dispose of them, but I kept them in case. Can you give them back to Dr Adams for me?' She passed them to Juliet, who had no intention of taking them from her to pass back to Dr Adams.

In the end Sandy took them, as he thought, just because this doesn't help our case, it does to a certain extent help the defence, so we had better take them as possible exhibits. Juliet took a quick statement then they left feeling a lot less hopeful than when they had first arrived.

∞

The next house they visited was in Mayfair. They pressed the button of an equally impressive large town house but this was split into three flats. The one they wanted was on the ground floor. They got no reply. Just as they were about to give up and leave, a woman walked out of the front door. Sandy said, 'We are looking for Mrs Tudor, do you know where she is?'

The woman looked at Sandy and said, 'You are too late I am afraid, she died two months ago. I have the phone number for her daughter.' The woman promptly went back inside and a few minutes later she returned and handed Sandy a piece of paper with the name 'Harriet Tudor' on it and a phone number. He couldn't make out which area it came from. 'Where does Harriet live?' he asked.

'She is an investment banker and lives in New York,' the woman said, before rushing off, clearly now running late after their conversation.

Sandy checked his watch and although it would be early morning in New York, it wasn't too early for a call. He made the call. 'Hello, who is this?' Harriet said.

'I am DCI McFarlane calling from England. We are at your mother's apartment. We came to see her about a medication that a Dr Adams prescribed for her. I am sorry to ask you this, but how did your mother die?'

'She died of ovarian cancer.' There was then a sob on the other end of the phone and a pause for a few seconds until Harriet said, 'I was told to come back home as my mother didn't have too much time to live. I came as soon as I could.' More sobs and tears. 'I really did. Living the other side of the Atlantic doesn't work too well to get back to England quickly.' Sandy just knew what Harriet was going to say next. 'I must have been mid-Atlantic when she died. I never made it home in time and never saw her again.'

Sandy said, 'I am so sorry for your loss. I really am.'

'What was this medication that you are talking about? We had a private nurse who lived in the apartment and would know all about any medication. I will send you her details to this number that you have called me from. I need to go and reapply my makeup as I can't go into work looking like this,' a very sad-sounding Harriet said.

They headed off to the last address in London and had just got to the house in Hampstead Heath when the message with the contact details for the private nurse arrived from Harriet. Juliet, putting her phone on speaker, rang the number, then, when answered, the person said, 'Hello, who is this?'

'I am DS Ashton; I am making enquiries into some medication that was prescribed to a Mrs Tudor.'

'Which of the medications are you interested in? Mrs Tudor took so much medication every day. I might not be able to remember doses but I should be able to remember types of medication.'

'The one we are interested in was a morphine injection, prescribed by Dr Henry Adams.'

'What a lovely man. He is an excellent doctor.' Surely not another member of the Henry Adams fan club, Sandy thought, as the nurse continued by saying, 'He was so kind and gentle with her. I gave Mrs Tudor only five milligrams of the injection twice a day. It just took the edge off her pain. There was some left but I disposed of it down the sink and put the needles in the sharps bin.'

Another dead end. Juliet arranged to meet the nurse to take her statement early the following week. They knocked on the door where they had been waiting outside and were let in by a woman. When they explained why they had come to see her, she swiftly went and got a whole packet of the drugs containing morphine. It turned out that one thing she didn't like was taking any medication, in particular for pain relief; she preferred to deal with pain holistically using meditation and yoga. Dr Adams, she said, was just being over cautious. But no doubt charging you a fortune for the drugs as part of his bill, Sandy thought. Sandy took the lady's statement and possession of the unused drugs but not before the lady told them what a wonderful and incredible doctor Henry Adams was.

The two remaining people to see weren't in London. One was in the centre of Cambridge and the other actually lived in Grantchester. Sandy wished he had known that when Hannah and he had recently visited Grantchester as he could have visited then. Sandy called Rich to say that they had drawn a blank from a prosecution point of view with the morphine prescription enquiries. Rich suggested that they didn't need to visit the other two people. Sandy felt differently and told him that they needed to as what they currently had found out helped the defence, so they should see it through.

Rich informed him that his meeting to find experts had gone well and there was going to be a seriously large number required if they were going to get anywhere near a prosecution. Between Clare, the NCA and himself they had spent the rest of the day contacting some of the experts and were making progress.

One thing they didn't have as yet was any idea where the morphine had come from that William happened to have in his body. There had certainly been no steps forward but lots of steps backwards today in relation to this aspect of the investigation.

∞

On the way into the FCDO offices the next morning, Sandy received a message from Detective Superintendent Jane Watson asking him to see her as soon as he got into the building.

On entering her office, he was surprised to see that Jane wasn't on her phone as she usually was. 'Sandy, sit down.' she said. As he sat down Sandy had a feeling that he was in trouble again. Once he was sitting, Jane said, 'I am very concerned about the amount of time you are spending on the William Peveril case.'

Sandy, trying to defend himself, responded, 'We are at a crucial time in the investigation. We have completed arrests and had interviews and I am checking out a number of patients that were prescribed a similar drug to the one we believe may have killed William.'

'No, not any more you're not. Let DCI Singh from Derbyshire complete those enquiries. It is no longer a case for us as it is not a case from abroad.'

Totally shocked by Jane's response, Sandy tried to recover some involvement in the case and said, 'It is a crime that happened in France.' Seeing that Jane now had an expression of interest, he continued quickly by saying, 'The offence still happened in France and we are just using the Offences Against the Person legislation to investigate and, hopefully, prosecute here in England. The only connection DCI Singh has in the investigation is that William Peveril is lying dead in a grave in Derbyshire. There are no enquiries in Derbyshire, they are here in London or in France.' Seizing his moment, he said, 'I have two more possible witnesses to see and I was going to see them on Friday with Juliet.'

'No, Sandy. We have to demonstrate that we are being equal to all families. I need Juliet for a couple of family meetings on that day and I also need you to go to a couple of meetings for me on Friday, so you will not have time to see the witnesses.'

A very subdued Sandy got up to go but made one last attempt to still be involved in the investigation. 'As the witnesses are in Cambridge, can I visit them on my day off this Saturday?'

Jane could see the disappointment in his face and replied in a much softer tone. 'I am not saying you can't still be involved in the future. I get your point, and I am sure DCI Singh could be having the same conversation with his boss in Derbyshire about whether they should be involved or not. It is just that we are getting pressure, quite rightly, from families to do more for them in relation to their loved ones that have died abroad.'

Just as he was about to walk out of the office, Sandy, almost in a whisper, said, 'And Saturday?'

'Yes, of course. If Clare is in the office send her in to see me as I need to rein in her spending of the forensic budget on the case.'

After Sandy had briefed an equally disappointed Clare and Juliet, he debated for a few seconds who he should contact next. Hannah won the day. He told her he couldn't meet her on Saturday until later in the afternoon. He suggested that rather than her travel to Ely, he would see her outside the Round Church in Cambridge, and to make up for it he would take her for a meal somewhere special that evening. Hannah sent him a thumbs up emoji. Sandy hadn't got the hang of emojis.

He then contacted his mum to say there was a change of plan, he wouldn't be home that evening and not until Friday, when he might head straight to the Cutter Inn as he would be in desperate need of a beer by then. No emoji reply from his mum, just 'OK'.

He decided not to share Jane's conversation with Rich but just told him that he would see the last two medication witnesses on Saturday and not tomorrow as planned. No response from Rich – he was not too quick at replying to messages and phone calls were normally the best way to contact him.

Late on Saturday morning, Sandy pulled up a very imposing drive in Grantchester. This was a very imposing house, not far from the church he had visited with Hannah a few days ago.

The occupant, Muriel Longbottom, ushered him into a garden room that showed off an extremely well looked after walled garden. On the other side of the walled garden, Sandy knew, was the River Cam. After taking a seat, Sandy said, 'We are looking into medication that was prescribed to you by Dr Henry Adams.'

'What medication do you mean? I haven't seen Dr Adams for over a year.'

'Were you prescribed almost three months ago a morphine injection?'

'No, not at all. In fact, never.'

Chapter Twenty-Five

After returning from his car, where he had gone to collect some blank statement forms, Sandy found that a man in his early sixties had joined them. He was probably slightly older than Muriel. He introduced himself as Michael Longbottom and said, 'What a beautiful car your Morgan sports car is. I have always admired them.'

Muriel said, 'I called Michael in from the garden as I am a bit confused about what you are telling me: that I was prescribed a morphine injection but didn't receive the medication. Is that right?'

Michael added, trying to be helpful, 'Dr Adams was an excellent doctor for Muriel. Very thorough and he looked after her well and she has had no problems since.'

Sandy looked straight at Muriel as he needed her to be the one that answered, as it would be her statement and not hers and Michael's. 'Towards the end of February, you were prescribed the medication then.'

Muriel looked round at Michael and said, 'I hadn't been treated by Dr Adams for over a year by then. Are you sure you have the right date?'

Sandy was sure that Lofty had got the right date, but asked, 'Have you ever then been prescribed a morphine injection by Dr Adams?'

A now clearly frightened Muriel said, 'Should I have been? Have I missed something that would have helped my pain over a year ago?'

Before Sandy could say anything else, Michael said, 'Why are you asking, DCI McFarlane? What has happened?'

Trying not to give away too much at this stage as the time for that might come if they made it to a trial, Sandy said, 'A person has died in suspicious circumstances and morphine may have been the cause of the death. We are making enquiries to ensure all prescribed morphine has been accounted for.'

Michael put his hand on the arm of his wife and said, 'I think I understand, and I can see you want to take my wife's statement to say that she hadn't received the medication. Let me make us all a cup of tea while you do that. I can also provide you with the medical bill from Dr Adams. The cost of it will make your eyes water, but I can assure you, having gone through it all with a fine-tooth comb, there was no prescription that I had to pay for that included morphine.' He nodded to Muriel in a reassuring manner as he stood up and went out into the kitchen.

∞

Sandy was feeling extremely optimistic as he headed to the next, and last, medication witness. The witness lived in a large house on Jesus Green in the centre of Cambridge. Sandy parked alongside the River Cam and crossing a bridge, walked up to the house. A lady in her early to mid-forties answered the door. Although she was comparatively young, the way she had her almost white hair rolled into a bun on her head made her look a lot older than her actual age was likely to be. After introductions, it turned out the woman, Edwina Booth, was an economist and a visiting professor at the University of Cambridge. Sandy said, 'Can you tell me, when you were treated by Dr Adams, if he prescribed any morphine-based medication for you?'

'Yes, he did.'

Sandy's feeling of optimism fell again. 'Do you remember when this was?' he asked.

Edwina went out of the room and clearly went upstairs in the house and returned with a half-used packet of morphine-based tablets. On looking at the packet, Sandy saw that it had been prescribed the previous September. 'Have you had any more prescribed since you were given these?'

'No, I finished as his patient last October and then transferred to Addenbrooke's Hospital locally for them to finish my treatment.'

This was hopeful, Sandy thought, as he took Edwina's statement. The key was going to be making sure there wasn't just a mistake in the recording of dates in her patient record. Edwina, like all of the other patients, told Sandy what a wonderful doctor Henry Adams was. This was not something that he was going to put into the witness statement. The vision of Lofty and himself being threatened with the surgical scissors was not the actions of the person the patients were describing.

∞

Looking at his watch, Sandy thought he had plenty of time to meet Hannah. He rushed to his Morgan car as one thing that had been worrying him was leaving the car parked beside the River Cam, possibly overnight, if he had an alcoholic drink with his dinner. He got to Hannah's house, still in a suitable time, but on getting no reply realised she must have left already. He ran to the Round Church where they planned to meet.

Of course he was late by the time he got there and although she said she wasn't upset, it felt like it. Sandy kept apologising for being late and for cancelling most of their day together. Hannah told him if he mentioned it again, then there really would be a problem with him being late.

The Round Church was first built between 1115 and 1131 and was based on the Holy Sepulchre in Jerusalem. As Sandy's Cambridge college was very close by, he had passed it probably hundreds, if not thousands, of times. He had though only been inside rarely and Hannah had never been inside.

They enjoyed the time looking inside and on leaving the church they headed to Jesus Green in a good mood together. Sandy desperately wanted to call Rich and let him know about the exciting developments for their investigation that he had discovered. However, he was sure that would not go down well with Hannah and as he had planned for them to have a fantastic dinner together, he didn't want to spoil things.

Jesus Green, where Sandy had been only an hour or so earlier, is a large park and Hannah and Sandy walked along the avenue of London plane trees. Although originally part of Midsummer Common, which is where they were heading next, it was called Jesus Green because of it being adjacent to Jesus College. On their way to the border with the River Cam, Sandy said, pointing to the large house he had been in earlier, 'That house belongs to a Professor Edwina Booth, I was there seeing her earlier this afternoon.'

'What for and why did you not leave your car nearby?' Hannah asked, but before Sandy could reply, she said, laughing, 'You couldn't let your car be left here, could you? I do believe you love that car more than anything else in the world.'

'Maybe not anything else in the world.' They looked at each other knowingly, but Sandy knew there was more than a grain of truth in what Hannah had just said. Sandy pointed out to Hannah the Lido swimming pool and suggested that they must come to the Cambridge Beer Festival, which is held every year on Jesus Green. Hannah didn't seem too keen on this idea though.

While they sat on a bench alongside the River Cam by the Jesus Lock, Sandy said, 'Professor Booth was very helpful for our investigation into the death of Viscount Peveril.'

'I am glad that this investigation is progressing well. I wish my arson court case was going as well. I have managed to get the judge to insist that the case will start a week on Tuesday, after the defence asked for another adjournment, as the offender refuses to see the defence clinical psychologist.'

After spending a very pleasant hour watching the boats go through the lock or turn around and head back up the River Cam, they walked into Midsummer Common and Sandy told Hannah about Strawberry Fair that he used to attend every year and how popular it was, as were the other fairs that were held on the Common.

The restaurant that Sandy had managed to get them into was one of the best in Cambridge. He had been lucky that they had had a late cancellation. Midsummer House is a Victorian villa converted into a restaurant and backed on to the River Cam. It is in its own private gardens and looks out on the cows of Midsummer Common from the front. As they went into the dining room, which was in the conservatory, Hannah said, 'Sandy, you shouldn't have brought us here. This will cost us a fortune.'

'This will make it up to you for us missing our day together, and as we didn't celebrate the first year since we met, I thought this would be the perfect place for us to be in. I will be paying.'

'Not that you weren't forgiven, but you definitely are now,' a smiling Hannah said while reaching across and holding Sandy's hand.

There would be no doubt in anybody's mind in Midsummer House that early Saturday evening that these two young professional people were definitely in love.

∞

There was no love lost between Arabella Montague and Monica Peveril. Sandy knew this already but could be in no doubt of this on the Monday morning when he received a phone call from Arabella just as he arrived at King's Cross railway station.

'Sandy, she is outside the house looking at me. I thought you told James that she is not allowed to have contact with us.'

'Arabella, slow down, I am confused. Why is Monica' – he presumed that was who she meant – 'in Norfolk?'

'Not in Norfolk, I am in Peveril House in Eaton Square. She is just standing outside looking at me.'

Sandy thought it best if he went straight to Eaton Square rather than the office. He decided to call a London black cab, telling the driver to get him to Eaton Square as quickly as possible – a mistake most probably, but he needed to get there quickly.

He had two things troubling him. One, there was no way that Monica could actually see Arabella whose apartment in the house was on the third floor. So, by standing outside, was she breaching her no contact bail condition? He didn't know. The next thing he was worrying about was that police officers were not normally meant to meet people on bail unless they got, for example, a senior officer's permission. There was no way he was going to contact Jane Watson, after her telling him only a few days ago not to do any more work on the case.

Other than the odd dart down a side street at speed, the cab journey hadn't been too traumatic, mostly due to the large volume of traffic slowing them down. As soon as he got out of the cab, Monica walked straight up to him. 'DCI McFarlane. I knew she would go running to you. She hates me, doesn't she? Well, that's OK. I have always hated her. William and James have placed Arabella so high up on a pedestal, just like they did her mother.'

Sandy looked at the visibly upset Monica, who was dressed in a black trouser suit and looking immaculate as usual. He had seen her use her right hand to devastating effect, so warily stepped out of arm's length. 'I am not really meant to talk to you on bail but what are you doing here? Your bail conditions were no contact with Arabella or James.'

'My solicitor contacted James and I have a delivery van arriving any moment to collect all of my belongings. I am moving out of Peveril House today, forever.'

Sandy looked at Monica and for a fraction of a second

felt sorry for her. Before he could say anything, Monica said, 'Where did it all go wrong? What have I done?' Was he going to get a confession, Sandy wondered. He thought if he cautioned her, as he should do, that would break the moment, so he kept quiet.

It was not to be though, as Monica then said, 'I can sense Arabella in the house. They are not meant to be in there, only the housekeeper.' Sandy squinted up to the third floor; you could possibly see someone if they stood right at the window. A woman's intuition is a wonderful thing, he thought.

Sandy rang James rather than Arabella. 'James, did you receive a letter from Monica's solicitor asking permission for her to move her belongings out of Peveril House and for you not to be there when this happened?'

'Yes, and I have stayed in Derbyshire to allow it to happen. I have already removed, as you know, all of my father's family possessions.'

'Well Arabella is in the house. Why is she here then?'

'Sorry, sorry. I didn't tell her as I thought she was in Norfolk. I didn't know she was going to be there. She must have a meeting in London today. I will ring her now and get her to leave immediately.'

Sandy relayed the news to Monica just as her large removal van arrived. No doubt it was large so as to fit in all of her clothes and shoes. He moved Monica round to one side as he watched Arabella and Monty leave the house and walk off out of Eaton Square.

As Sandy headed off to work, he thought he had a lot to update Rich on and that would be his priority right after he got a Danish pastry and a large coffee for himself.

However, before he had got to his office at FCDO, his phone rang. It was Antoine Chevalier.

Chapter Twenty-Six

I wonder what Antoine wants, Sandy thought as he answered the phone. Antoine said, 'DCI McFarlane, there has been a reporter from England asking about the death of Viscount Peveril.'

'Who told you about the reporter, Antoine? No, don't tell me, let me guess: was it Madame Suzanne Valadon?' While Sandy was saying this, he was smiling to himself.

'Yes. Amazing, how did you know?'

'What was the reporter's name?' While he was asking this, Sandy suddenly thought it must be the reporter that Rich mentioned to him a few weeks ago, who had worked out there had been activity at William's grave, so he asked, 'Was his name Patrick Hallam?'

'Yes. Suzanne said his name was Patrick, anyway. She showed him the death registration.'

'Has he been to the chateau as well?'

'He hasn't been to the main house but went on a tour of the winery and asked lots of questions. The winery manager says he took lots of pictures, including lots of the main house.'

'If you can,' Sandy said, knowing that this would be hard for Antoine and his little gang, 'please don't tell him anything about the English police's involvement and tell Suzanne, if she possibly could, to try for once in her life not to tell him everything that is going on and whatever happens, not to mention Monica's English boyfriend.'

'Suzanne has never listened to me before, so why would she listen to me now?' Antoine said, laughing at his own joke. After a few moments, Sandy realised that Antoine expected him to laugh as well. He tried to laugh, well sort of, and it was enough to please Antoine who laughed even more loudly.

'Well, just try, Antoine,' Sandy said emphatically.

A phone call to Rich was now urgently required, but this time, definitely not before a very large coffee and two Danish pastries at least.

'Rich, I have a few updates for you,' Sandy said, just as he finished a large mouthful of pastry and a sip of his already half-finished coffee.

'Good. I have a couple of things to update you on as well.'

'I will go first then. The last two people I saw on Saturday never received the morphine.'

'Wow!' a very excited Rich said. 'Looks like we have where the morphine came from. Yes!' he exclaimed.

'I have their statements as well as the three from the patients that did get the medication. I will scan them and send them to you after our call.'

'Great news, Sandy. Really well done. Shall I tell you my news now?'

'Two more bits from me first though. I met Monica this morning and was sure she was going to confess but just couldn't bring herself to do it.'

'Where did you meet her?'

'She was clearing her belongings out of Peveril House in Eaton Square. She's gone back to Brighton now.' There was a pause while Sandy had another sip of coffee and finished his second pastry. 'Sorry about that, Rich, it's been a long morning, from leaving home in Ely till now. Antoine Chevalier rang to say that Patrick Hallam was in Saint-Émilion asking questions.'

'He could really mess things up if he finds out about the Monica and Henry connection, couldn't he?'

'You could contact Patrick and tell him you will give him an exclusive story when we are able to?'

'There are a number of other journalists that I would happily do that with, but not Patrick Hallam. I do not trust him, Sandy. Well, my news was that I have sent Lofty and another DC to France. Let's hope Patrick and Lofty meet there. I know who would come out on top.'

'What are they doing in France?'

'Firstly, they are seeing if there is any CCTV of Monica and Henry at Calais on their way home to England and when that was. Then they are going to collect all of the French statements and let each of them know that we have an investigation in England and they may be required to give evidence, if we ever get to trial.'

'We have quite a few French witnesses, don't we?'

'Yes, eight at least. The trial will be a logistical nightmare. You will not believe either how many experts we have currently sending in statements.'

'Are you regretting taking this on? If so, I am sorry I have roped you in.'

'Are you joking, Sandy? This is so exciting. Exactly the type of complex crime I want to be investigating.'

'Good, because I think so too. I am loving it and we might just get justice along the way for William Peveril.'

Rich and Sandy were very like-minded spirits. They were just about to ring off when Rich said, 'I forgot the most important piece of news. A week today I have a meeting with CPS to see if they are going to prosecute, hence sending Lofty urgently to France, and I need those patients' statements as soon as you can please.'

∞

The team meeting had just finished by the time Sandy arrived in the consulate investigation team's office area. He quickly looked around and was pleased that there was no sign of Jane Watson. He wasn't keen to tell her why he was so late this morning.

No sooner had Sandy sat down when Clare came and sat next to him. 'How did you get on with Jane last week and her talk about the budget for Operation Cornflower?' Sandy asked.

'She was fine.' Well, she wasn't with me, thought Sandy. Clare continued, 'We have covered half the exhumation costs and agreed we will cover all forensic costs from France, but Derbyshire will pay all other forensic costs, including expert fees. Rich has agreed to it.'

'That sounds very pragmatic of you and Jane.'

'I have the results of the outstanding DNA comparison from the room in Chateau Peveril and they are Monica's. No sign of Henry Adams's DNA there. That is not to say he wasn't in there, but from a DNA point of view, no help with proving that.'

This information was a bit of a blow but there was nothing that could be done about it. Juliet had gone off to scan the statements they had taken from the patients the previous week to send to the Operation Cornflower incident room. Sandy then received a message from Rich that read: 'Can you chair a video meeting for me please as

I am snowed under? It is with the DMIs at any time that suits you this afternoon.'

When Juliet returned, they agreed that they could meet with them at three o'clock. As Sandy was about to reply to Rich, he gave Juliet the two statements that he had taken on Saturday. He asked her to read them and then scan and send them to the incident room. He told her she would be pleased with what he had found out. As he replied to Rich, he thought that since Jane had told him that he should do no more work on the William Peveril death, that was all he had done.

Three o'clock soon arrived and Juliet and Sandy had positioned themselves in a small meeting pod and looked at the screen of Sandy's laptop. There were on the screen three male detectives who were DMIs for the investigation.

After introductions, Sandy said, 'I know all about the caller data, but can you confirm who owned the three predominate numbers that calls were made to and received from?'

One of the DMIs, the one who looked the eldest of the three, said, 'Monica Peveril's mother with an area code in Brighton. William Peveril, but that stopped presumably the afternoon before he died. She was with him after that evening so no need to call. The final one was Henry Adams and they started conversing in the July of last year and that was still ongoing when we obtained the phone records.'

'Anything of note between Monica and Henry in terms of messages or lengths of calls?' Juliet asked.

'Nothing on the messages, but where we originally thought there was a call an hour after the death, we had failed to take account of the time difference, so it might have been that that call was possibly made before the call to the doctor.' Juliet and Sandy looked at each other confused. If it were as they thought, one of their hypotheses being that Henry administered the morphine, would they be calling each other? Most probably not.

'Tell us about the cell site data please for the two phones?' Sandy said, while writing furiously in his notebook.

'Not quite sure what you mean, or that we have done this?'

'Sorry,' Sandy said, stopping writing, 'Have we any cell site data that links the two phones together in a similar location?'

A knowing smile came from one of the other DMIs, who said, 'This could be a huge job if you want us to go back until when there was first phone contact between the two phones. What DCI Singh asked us to focus on was the day of the death and the few days afterwards. Will that be OK?'

Realising that he had asked a mammoth task, Sandy said, 'Yes, of course, have you got that focussed data for us now?'

'Yes, we received it at the end of last week from the French phone providers. Both phones were apart in the morning in the Saint-Émilion area. Then they were together for two hours in the afternoon, then apart again until the next morning.'

Sandy and Juliet looked at each other again. 'So are you telling me that Henry was not with Monica at the time of death?'

The DMI looked a bit surprised and said, 'No, not telling you that. What I am saying is that the two phones were not together. He could have left his phone in his hotel room.'

Very unlikely, Sandy thought, as he tapped his phone in his pocket. He was never without it unless he was playing rugby and then it was nearby. He even took it for a run with him.

The DMI said, 'Then the phones were together for an hour or so.' Registering the death, Sandy thought, as he pieced together the movements.

'Not together again for the rest of that day and all of the next day. Then together for the next three days as they travelled through France, stopping in Paris and not moving from one location for two days. Then home to England, which is when we stopped the tracing.'

'Where in Paris did they stop?' Juliet asked, just before Sandy said it.

The DMI put his glasses on and scrutinised his records, then said, 'Place Vendôme.'

Sandy was very surprised by this answer and said, 'I only went there recently, that is where the French Ministry of Justice is!'

Sandy sought to bring the meeting to a close but had forgotten the third DMI, who had not spoken and did so now. 'I have examined the computer for Dr Adams's patient records.'

Both Sandy and Juliet were very interested in this information, having been the ones conducting this line of enquiry.

'The receptionist or office manager keeps immaculate up-to-date records. Dr Adams, when he adds entries, this is normally completed much later that day or the next day. That is his pattern.'

'What about the records for Edwina Booth or Muriel

Longbottom? Who made their recent medication records out?'

'That was Dr Adams. There was a big gap in their records up until this point, which was the day before he must have gone to France. He made the record up immediately and dispensed the drugs himself from his supplies, which he then registered all appropriately.' Not quite, Sandy thought, as he never did actually give the drugs to those two patients.

∞

The next two days were very busy with work for the FCDO and Sandy didn't have a chance to think about the Operation Cornflower investigation. On the other hand, Juliet Ashton was still thinking about it and came to Sandy one afternoon, clutching a couple of newspaper articles she had printed off. 'Look at these,' Juliet said, thrusting the papers on the desk in front of Sandy. 'Our Henry Adams really is a heartbreaker. Here are photographs of him with two beautiful women and in one of the articles he has been named as the other man in a very acrimonious divorce hearing in the high court. The woman wanted, but didn't get, the twenty million-pound settlement for which she was hoping.'

Looking at the smiling Juliet and flicking through the articles, Sandy thought there might be something in this. It might explain why getting rid of William could have been better than another messy divorce with him splashed all over the tabloids. 'What is the timeline for these relationships in relation to Monica?'

'The divorce hearing one directly before her, looks like

that relationship came to a finish about two months before Monica came on the scene. Then the other one a fair while ago. I am sure there must be one in-between.'

Passing the papers back to Juliet and smiling, Sandy said, 'Can you let Rich know so that he can allocate someone to visit the women?'

'I can do it, Sandy.'

'Jane told us not to do anything more on the investigation without her permission.'

'No. She told you not to do any more on the investigation, not me, so leave it with me. I will try and see them in the next couple of days,' said a smiling Juliet and off she walked to her own desk, winking at Clare as she walked past her.

Seeing and hearing the information that Juliet had provided him with had spurred Sandy to want to think about the investigation again. He rang Rich. 'Hello Rich, how is your preparation going for the meeting with CPS next Monday?'

'All good. Thanks for chairing the DMI meeting. Their reports are coming in slowly to add to the file, as is the experts' evidence.'

'After hearing the cell site information,' Sandy said, 'I have been wondering about the missing two days in Paris. I wonder if Lofty could make some enquiries there to find out what they were up to?'

'Too late, Lofty has had a whirlwind trip, seen everyone, got the statements and has just rung me from Calais, where he has got CCTV of them boarding a ferry there and he is on his way home.'

'We could go to Paris then.'

'What? Sandy, I couldn't possibly spare the time to do

this at the moment.'

Suddenly realising what he had just said and laughing, Sandy said, 'Sorry, thinking aloud. When I said we, I meant that Hannah and I could go to Paris.'

Laughing himself now, Rich said, 'That's more like it, my boy. Forget looking at what Monica Peveril was doing and just have an enjoyable time together.'

This sounded like a really clever idea, but Sandy had two women problems that he had to overcome to make it happen. He decided on talking to Jane first. As he stood outside her office waiting for her to finish on the phone, he debated with himself what could be the best tactic to use. When he entered, he said, 'I know, Jane, you told me no more work on the William Peveril case at the moment. But we need to make some enquiries in Paris. Please can I do this? I would do them this weekend so as not to disrupt my work here but would need Monday as an annual leave day to travel back.'

Taking her glasses off and motioning for Sandy to take a seat, Jane sighed. Oh dear, Sandy thought, this was not going to go well. 'Sandy,' Jane said, 'as this is an overseas enquiry that needs to happen, of course you can do it and I do not want you to take an annual leave day on the Monday, it is a working day.'

Wow! This was a positive change of heart from Jane, Sandy thought, but she kept talking. 'Look, Sandy, I am not stopping you doing any work on the investigation. We just need to be transparent as you know extremely well. We have obligations for many other families that we are unable to assist with and if we spend too much time on one, where other police forces could do those enquiries, we have less time to spend on other families.' Jane was right and this was something Sandy knew only too well when looking at his in-tray of cases.

Hannah was the next person to contact about visiting Paris. He knew she was in court so sent her a message asking if she fancied a trip to Paris. His phone rang; it was Hannah.

'Yes, of course I would love to go to Paris with you this weekend, but it is too tight with my court case starting on Tuesday next week.'

'We could get an early Eurostar train if you stay over at the flat with me on Friday and an early Eurostar back on the Monday, so home for you to Cambridge by early afternoon at the latest?'

'OK, why not, that will be absolutely wonderful.'

A delighted Sandy started to look at booking their train but realised the one thing he had failed to mention to Hannah was that he actually needed to spend some time working in Paris that weekend.

Chapter Twenty-Seven

The Eurostar train was on time as it pulled into the Gare du Nord in Paris on Saturday morning. Other than a really early start to their day, both Hannah and Sandy had thoroughly enjoyed their journey. The tea and breakfast as they left London had especially been appreciated as well as spending the time together.

The topic of having to do some work in Paris hadn't been raised by Sandy until they had gone through the Channel Tunnel and were in France heading to Paris. Hannah had taken it all in her stride, admitting that she had suspected Sandy was up to something by him coming up with the idea of the trip at such short notice. Hannah told Sandy that she would prefer that there would be no work today on the Saturday, but they could go around together to make enquiries in the Place Vendôme on Sunday morning before they visited the Louvre gallery, as that wasn't too far from that area. Sandy couldn't help but smile to himself. What a lucky man he was and he knew he mustn't abuse Hannah's trust in him.

The walk to their hotel was a fantastic introduction to Paris. The mixture of wide boulevards and then small, cobbled side streets that they walked down were a fascinating and intoxicating sight. They often had to step out onto the road to avoid the sprawling café tables on the pavements where the sound of French voices rang out, and the smells of fresh bread and patisseries drifted in the air as they walked past a boulangerie.

When they reached the River Seine, they took a slight detour to see the Notre-Dame cathedral, located on a small island on the Seine. The cathedral had been built over a two-hundred-year period and was finally completed in 1345. Notre-Dame had been badly destroyed by fire only a few years earlier. The result of the fire was there to be seen by Hannah and Sandy. The roof had gone completely and the cathedral's spire had collapsed catastrophically into the building itself. Perhaps one of the most incredible sights they saw while walking around and looking from the outside, was how the scaffolding, that had been erected to carry out the restoration work at the time, had been melted together due to the fierce heat of the fire.

They strolled around slowly, looking in wonderment at the hive of activity going on as literally hundreds of construction workers were busy restoring the cathedral in record time and speed to return it to its former glory, certainly not taking two hundred years as it had originally taken to build.

As soon as they had deposited their bags in their hotel room, Hannah had them out again. They only paused at a boulangerie to buy them both a filled French stick and a coffee as they made their way around to see the Eiffel Tower. Sandy was keen that they go in and join the long queue to go up the tower, but Hannah was happy to just look at it and take a few selfies of them both with the iconic tower in the background. In her view, they couldn't afford the time on their whirlwind trip to be standing in a long and time-consuming queue.

The wrought iron tower had been completed in 1889 for an exposition that was held in Paris. There could be no doubt if anyone saw a picture of the Eiffel Tower that they would also think of Paris. The two were inextricably linked to each other, hence why Hannah hadn't wanted them to miss seeing it.

The next place that Hannah had planned for them to visit was the Arc de Triomphe and then on to the Champs-Élysées, a very broad and very chic Paris boulevard. The Arc de Triomphe was commissioned by Napoleon but was not finished until a number of years later. Hannah and Sandy dodged through the traffic to see the Arc and wander around it. As they ran through the traffic, they both laughed, thoroughly enjoying their time together in Paris.

They had a quick march along the Champs-Élysées, where Hannah didn't look in any of the designer fashion shops, much to Sandy's delight, before they then went back over the River Seine to their hotel. They had a quick change and headed out to dinner. Sandy, who hadn't been to France for years, was enjoying his third trip in only a few weeks. The côte de boeuf, grilled over a wood chip fire in the rustic French restaurant opposite their hotel, was a particular highlight for Sandy, as was buying Hannah and himself a bottle of red wine, unfortunately not Chateau Peveril, but still from a chateau in Saint-Émilion.

∞

The next morning, as the hotel they were staying at didn't provide breakfast, they sat on the banks of the Seine soaking up the morning sunshine, drinking coffee and eating warm croissants. The previous night Sandy had told Hannah that as he only spoke a little bit of French, he had asked Saffron Dupont to join him that morning. He explained that Saffron, or Saffy as she was known, was a British diplomat who worked in the British embassy in Paris and had also been a student at St John's College, a few years after him though.

As they both got a refill of coffee, Sandy said, 'Two things about Saffy I need to warn you about. The first thing is that her dress sense is quite bright and colourful. She likes wearing red.' He took a large sip of his coffee before he made his second point and while he did, looked carefully at Hannah. 'I also think she may be a bit fond of me.'

'So, Sandy, you bring me to one of, if not the most romantic place on the planet and what do you do, you invite a member of your fan club to join us?' Hannah said in such a tone that Sandy couldn't work out if she was cross or teasing him.

'I am not sure I have a fan club, but it is just a feeling that I have, sorry.'

When they arrived in Place Vendôme outside the Hôtel de Bourvallais, which housed the French Ministry of Justice, which had been the last place he had seen Saffy, she was there waiting for them. Saffy was wearing grey trousers and had on a blue blouse; even her glasses today were brown rimmed. Hannah looked at Sandy as they walked up to Saffy and said, 'What did you say about how she dresses?'

Sandy was momentarily speechless but then said, 'Saffy, good to see you again. Please can I introduce my 'girlfriend'.'

Hannah put her arms around Saffy and said, 'I am so pleased to meet you. Sandy has told me so much about you, even the fact that you went to St John's in Cambridge. I had a visit there only a few weeks ago, an unbelievably beautiful and amazing place.'

Saffy seemed to be delighted to be with both of them and was so happy that there was a chance that the investigation into the death of William Peveril was progressing.

There weren't many hotels that could fit the area that the cell site analysis of the mobile phones had revealed. The first two hotels they called at, Clarins and the Mandarin Oriental, were slightly further away from the area. They weren't surprised when the receptionist said they had had no one staying there on the days they were interested in that could fit the couple's description.

As they walked to the Hôtel Vendôme, Hannah, who was sensing that this might be a waste of time, said, 'You know that you could actually have phoned or emailed these hotels from London rather than visiting Paris yourself, don't you, Sandy?'

This brought lots of laughter from Saffy, who added, 'The receptionists' English is perfect, so you also didn't need to drag me along on a Sunday, either.' Hannah and Saffy linked their arms together and walked into the hotel reception ahead of Sandy.

As they stood there waiting for the receptionist to acknowledge them, Sandy tried to stick up for himself by saying, 'Of course I thought that, but there may be an Airbnb or CCTV that could help.' He couldn't say anything else as the receptionist was now free and after checking her records, she couldn't find anyone that fitted the couple's description during those days either.

The last hotel before having a quick search for possible other places that they could have stayed in was the Ritz Paris. Sandy had been for afternoon tea with his Grandpa

John on one occasion to the Ritz in London and this Ritz hotel looked equally as opulent and impressive.

The receptionist wasn't able to help them so called a manager to see them. The manager looked up the dates and said, 'Yes, we had a Viscount William Peveril and Viscountess Monica Peveril staying here for those two nights.'

Hannah and Saffy almost cheered but Sandy glared at them and motioned with his hand for them to step back out of the way so he could deal with the manager. He, though, couldn't help himself and grinned widely. Sandy took photographs of the entries and could only say, 'Wow' when he saw the bill for the two nights: including room service on both nights, it came to five and a half thousand euros. The bill was paid by Viscountess Peveril on a joint credit card. Sandy had some blank folded-up statement forms in his backpack so while Hannah and Saffy went outside, he took the manager's statement. The only disappointment was the CCTV in the lobby had been out of order at that time, but was apparently working well now.

∞

A very happy couple left Saffy, having organised with her to meet them for dinner later that evening along with her boyfriend. He was staying in Paris with her for a few days. When Saffy had mentioned that she had a steady boyfriend, Hannah had looked quizzically at Sandy, who realised that he had miss stepped by mentioning anything about Saffron Dupont to her.

The Louvre was only a short walk away and due to time constraints, they made the decision to just view the highlights of the world famous gallery. Having whizzed around a few key paintings, among which the Wedding at Cana and the Lacemaker particularly interested Sandy, they then arrived in an extremely busy room where they joined a long queue that just shuffled by the Louvre's star attraction: the Mona Lisa. Hannah, although she enjoyed art, was not an art lover to the degree that Sandy clearly was, and she could see the disappointment in his face as they moved forward slowly in the queue. Leonardo Da Vinci was Sandy's favourite artist and the few moments he had been allowed to savour his work that afternoon was not enough by any means.

They walked through the gardens and over the Seine and after a short distance arrived at the Rodin museum. Seeing the sculpture of The Thinker, in Sandy's view, made up for the disappointing experience of how they had seen the Mona Lisa.

The next morning, having had a very pleasant evening with Saffy and her boyfriend, they took a taxi to the Gare du Nord station. Sandy had never seen Hannah as tense and on edge as she was that morning. As they walked into the Eurostar section of the station, they were met with a large amount of crowds and the noise level was loud, very loud. On looking at the large electronic departure boards, Hannah said, 'I don't believe it. This can't happen to me.'

Sandy looked up and saw that their train had been cancelled. In a panic, he looked for an information desk or a ticket booth. He saw a long queue at a ticket booth, which he walked towards, ushering Hannah along with him. While they were waiting, Hannah seemed to be getting even more tense. The chance of missing her court case the next day was unacceptable and almost career ending.

However much he tried, Sandy did not seem able to calm her down.

On checking his phone, he saw that he had an email from Juliet, no doubt giving him an update on her interviews with Henry's previous girlfriends. He didn't look at it but instead looked at flights to England from Paris. There was a good number leaving all afternoon and into the evening. He now felt much calmer and told Hannah they had options.

As it turned out, they managed to get on the midday train to London. The stress levels returned to normal for a short while before rising again when the train was announced as being delayed by an hour. Another reason the stress level was high was the amount of people in a similar stressed state all crammed into a relatively small space.

When the train was announced so that they could board, Hannah and Sandy made their way at speed to get on the train. Sandy's phone went off and on looking at it, he saw it was from Rich. 'It is Rich calling. I need to take this call, Hannah,' but on seeing Hannah's face, he knew that he wasn't going to answer his phone.

Once they were safely in their seats and their breathing had returned to normal, Sandy rang Rich. 'How did it go, Rich, with CPS?'

'Tell me how it went with the beautiful Hannah in Paris first.' Rich was clearly going to tease him by dragging this out.

'I came here to work actually.' The two of them laughed together. 'It has gone extremely well here. Monica and Henry stayed in the Ritz Paris, the bill was huge and they never left their room.'

'Excellent. Well I know you want to hear this.'

'Just tell me, Rich, have we got a case?'

'More than a case. They have authorised me to charge them both with murder and Henry with supplying a controlled drug.'

Sandy shouted, 'Excellent news!' which caused everyone in the carriage to look around at him. Hannah, who knew what had just happened, gave Sandy a big kiss. 'When do you hope to do this?'

'This Wednesday, to get it done asap and for them to be in Crown Court. CPS have already appointed lead council to prosecute. We have come across her before, it is Ebony Forbes-Hamilton QC. She is in the process of selecting a junior to assist her.'

'Mrs Forbes-Hamilton is excellent,' Sandy said.

He hadn't noticed that Hannah's phone was ringing. 'It is from my clerk. If he is ringing to tell me that the case tomorrow is cancelled, I shall go ballistic!'

Sandy thought he might need to duck if that was the case. He did pick up odd bits of the conversation though, such as, 'I feel really honoured,' 'I must speak to Sandy first,' 'She knows about me and DCI McFarlane.'

When Hannah came off the phone, she looked at Sandy and said, 'I have been asked to be involved in the case of the Crown against Peveril and Adams.'

Oh no, not again, thought Sandy, recalling a bad experience of Hannah working for the defence in a previous case he had been involved in. 'Mrs Forbes-Hamilton QC has personally asked me to be her junior. I will only do it if you say yes.'

'This is your decision not mine, but from my point of view, of course, yes,' Sandy said, as they then passionately embraced and kissed. All of the people in the carriage had not taken their eyes off the two of them, watching the drama and theatre emanating from their seats.

Chapter Twenty-Eight

The next morning, waiting for Sandy as he arrived in the office at the FCDO was an excited Juliet. Before she could speak, Sandy, who had a very wide grin on his face, said, 'CPS have agreed for them both to be charged with the murder of William Peveril.' Juliet got out of her seat, gave a shout of joy and did a jig. Clare, who as usual was sat next to Juliet, also got up and hugged both Juliet and Sandy, giving them both a kiss. The other members of the consulate investigation team and civil servants who were sitting at their desks in the open-plan offices looked around at the three of them, wondering what was going on.

When they had settled down, Sandy told them both what he had found out at the Ritz in Paris. Clare said, 'I am disgusted with Monica.'

Juliet commented, 'I am not surprised by Henry, he is a total Casanova.'

'Right, Juliet,' Sandy said, getting his Operation Cornflower notebook out of his backpack and poised to write, 'tell me what you have found out please?'

'I have seen Pamela Hollins – she was the lady whose husband divorced her and cited Henry in the divorce papers. Apparently, she only got a two million-pound settlement instead of the ten million she felt she deserved – the minute Henry heard about being cited in the divorce he ran away from her as fast as he could. Her husband had a private detective following their every move.'

Sandy could see that Juliet didn't have any paperwork with her and said, 'I presume none of them made any statements, did they?'

'I saw three women in total. All of them loved him and had a fantastic time with Henry. He was the one who broke it off with all of them. They, in reality, didn't have a bad word to say about him and they all refused to make statements. Nothing to do with Henry, but more wanting to protect themselves and their reputations.'

'I presume all ex-patients of his?'

'No. None of them. All of them though were picked up by Henry at charity galas.'

'Same as Monica, then,' Sandy said, as he got up to see if Jane Watson was in her office.

He was pleased to see that Jane was in her office. She had her glasses on and was busy typing away, peering at her laptop screen. As she was, for once, not on her phone, Sandy said, 'Jane, I have some good news on the Peveril case.'

Jane immediately looked up at Sandy and took her glasses off. Sandy sat down opposite her and continued: 'CPS have agreed that we should charge both Monica Peveril and Henry Adams with murder.'

'Great news,' a genuinely pleased Jane said with a big smile to her face. 'Your judgement never ceases to amaze me, Sandy.'

Sandy also told an amazed Jane about what he had found out in Paris, not that he had been so disappointed by his Mona Lisa experience but about Monica and Henry's tryst in the Ritz. He then said, 'I know you don't want me to do too much on the investigation, but it should be me that takes Arabella Montague and Viscount James Peveril's statements.'

'Of course, Sandy. We are in a different situation now with the charges being brought – you can do much more on the case.' A pleased Sandy got up to leave when Jane said, 'Sit down, Sandy, I need you to talk at a conference organised by families of victims who die abroad next Monday. I should have gone but have some personal issues to sort out. It is here in London. I will email you the presentation I have put together. However, I would use your investigation from India to illustrate how it can work but also to highlight how much resource it takes to achieve that sort of investigation.'

Sandy couldn't say no and was quite happy to be able to help his excellent boss out in whatever way he could.

He had just got back to his desk when he had a call from Rich. Before an excited Rich could say anything more, Sandy told him about what he had found out in Paris. Rich then said, 'Right, Sandy, eleven a.m. next Monday at Belgravia Police Station we will be having an interview to clarify certain matters with Peveril and Adams, then charging them, then off to court.'

Sandy had a sinking and despondent feeling when he realised that he had only just agreed to talk at a conference that day for Jane. He couldn't be at Belgravia Police Station and Rich told him that it was all arranged with CPS and the court and couldn't be changed. The bright mood he had been feeling had soon lost its shine. He did, however, manage to organise seeing Arabella and James in Eaton Square on the Thursday morning.

Later in the day there was a message from Hannah, letting Sandy know that her opening speech in her trial had gone down well with the jury, who were very attentive. The preparation and practice, she had told Sandy, had all been worth it.

∞

On his arrival in Eaton Square, Sandy saw that Juliet was already waiting outside for him. 'Waiting around to catch sight of the movie stars, Vivienne Jones and Adam Scott, are you?' Sandy said to her, laughing. 'They will have the police onto you for stalking at this rate.'

'I do feel that I am visiting this address on a regular basis at the moment,' Juliet said, laughing with Sandy.

Arabella let them into the house and into the ground floor reception room. James was in there but there was no sign of Arabella's husband, Monty. There was a lot to do on the farm in Norfolk, so he couldn't be spared.

'I have some news that I wanted to share with you in person,' Sandy said after they had all sat down with a cup of tea. 'Obviously, I know that you will keep this information confidential. Monica and Henry Adams are going to be charged next Monday with the murder of your father.'

Although Sandy had been unsure how they would react to the news he was now telling them, their stunned silence surprised him. The brother and sister just sat there alongside each other on a large settee; they were now holding each other's hands and looking at each other. Juliet and Sandy could see that they both had a tear in their eye and a look of total deflation, rather than one of jubilation.

After what felt like a huge amount of time, James said, 'I am sorry, Sandy and Juliet, that our response to your news is not what you would have expected or even hoped for. It is not that we are not truly grateful for all that you have done on our family's behalf, but the sense of loss of our father feels pretty overwhelming at this very moment.' As James said this, the tears started rolling down his face as they had been already for Arabella.

'Not at all,' Sandy replied, struggling hard himself not to let the lump that had formed in his throat stop him speaking and the slight wetness of a tear that had formed in his eye roll down his face. How could anyone not feel for the two people sat opposite him in a complete state of grief and mourning.

Juliet decided to take over from Sandy and very softly said, 'We had hoped to take a statement from you both outlining your last contact with your father, and to ask you to put some thought into letting us have a photograph of your father that we can share with the jury. We also wanted to ask you to start to give some thought, if we get a conviction, to a victim impact statement. We can of course come back another day in a week or two so you have some time to process what we have told you.'

James, visibly pulling himself together, after looking at Arabella for confirmation, said, 'Please, let's do the statements now.' He then pointed to a number of photographs on the large walnut side table and said, 'Will one of those photographs do?'

After standing up and looking at the photographs, Sandy said, 'Sorry, not really as they all have other family members in them.'

Arabella said, 'I thought the one with my father and his three grandchildren, George and his two sisters, was the one I would pick, but I get your point. I have one of him upstairs, when he was the High Sheriff of Derbyshire. I think that is what I would like. He looks so proud as he is serving the county of his birth.'

'That would be perfect, and if I come with you to collect this, I can write your statement and Juliet can write yours, James. I have already written notes from what you told me originally so we shouldn't intrude any longer than we have to.'

∞

After a very quiet weekend where Sandy had only seen Hannah for a few hours on the Saturday afternoon, he arrived early for the conference that was taking place at a hotel in Westminster.

There were only a few people present as he helped himself to a coffee and a breakfast pastry. He had been running late for his train from Ely to London so this was his first opportunity that morning to grab something to eat and drink. One of the organisers – a lady who seemed lovely and was in her early seventies, so not much younger than his grandparents – told Sandy her story, while he drank, ate and listened, of her son dying abroad in Spain after he had been stabbed in a bar there. No one was ever held responsible, and she had spent almost forty years fighting for justice, firstly for her son, then for all other families where their loved ones had died abroad following a homicide. The lady's story resonated with Sandy and he vowed to keep fighting and investigating for as many of these families as he could.

He was the last speaker before the lunch break and followed an FCDO civil servant, whose presentation was in relation to facts and figures relating to British citizens who die abroad. Sandy told the story of his investigation into the suspicious death of Robert Smythe, an accountant from Northamptonshire, who had died suddenly in Vadodara in the Gujarat in India. All of the questions and conversations over lunch were from families telling him about their loved one who had died abroad and what could he suggest in terms of investigating their deaths further. If Jane Watson's intention, by getting him to attend the conference, was for Sandy to feel the pain, anguish and helplessness of these families, she had most certainly succeeded.

Over lunch, Sandy kept checking his phone but he had received no call from Rich. As he walked the fairly short distance from the conference to the FCDO office, he was starting to feel a little bit nervous that something may have gone wrong with the charging process for Monica and Henry.

He shouldn't have worried as later that afternoon, while sat at his desk, the call he was expecting came. Rich said, 'Hi, Sandy, both of them have attended court and have been charged. The next hearing is in the Crown Court for plea and directions, which is four weeks from today. The judge is going to be someone we already know well, Mr Justice Francis Kane QC, and the trial will be at the Central Criminal Court, the Old Bailey here in London, in about eight to ten weeks' time.'

'How did they react to being charged?' a relieved Sandy asked.

'They were pretty nonplussed, I must say, and in fact quite subdued. I asked the custody sergeant to make sure she completed a full suicide risk assessment for them both. No comment by either of them to our questions before charge. Even Bob and Pete couldn't get a reaction from Monica.'

'Any media interest?'

'Not yet, but I am sure the likes of the reporter Patrick Hallam will be all over the story soon. Don't forget, we are only going to make as a media comment that two people have been charged with the murder of Viscount William Harrison Peveril and there is a Crown Court hearing pending. One bit of concerning news for our investigation is that a professor of cardiology from the University of Oxford has submitted a statement for the defence team on behalf of Henry Adams, which states that William could have easily died of heart disease.'

This bit of news did concern Sandy, who said, 'Well we must just get a more qualified expert than him.'

'Apparently this professor is regarded as a worldwide expert!'

Sandy sent a quick message to Hannah asking how her case was going and telling her of the charges and the date for the next hearing, which he presumed she might be at. He then sent a message to James and Arabella letting them know.

Finally, he made calls to his two grandfathers to let them know of the developments. He was going to tell them the previous weekend but hadn't seen either of them. Both of his grandfathers were thrilled with his news that the suspects had been charged. His Grandad Tom was so impressed that he had even failed to mention his usual statement following a charge: now the hard work begins – you have to keep investigating until conviction and not stop when someone has been charged.

Sandy felt buoyant as it is not every day you have a case

where someone is charged with murder, a case you have been working on and have invested so much in. He felt so buoyant that he got Juliet and Clare to come with him so he could buy them a drink before they headed to their homes.

Chapter Twenty-Nine

The four weeks until the plea and directions hearing passed by really quickly. Hannah's trial had taken the whole of the four weeks to come to a conclusion. Only the previous Friday she had won the case. Her defendant had been convicted of all four of the arson with intent to endanger life offences. Sandy and Hannah had celebrated on the Saturday night at their favourite restaurant, the Oak Bistro in Cambridge.

One thing that had been happening on the Peveril case was the continuous plethora of expert witnesses making statements on their findings, not only for the prosecution but also for each of the defendants.

When Sandy made his way into the Old Bailey on the Monday, he was already running late. He walked into the area where the old courts are and gazed up at the marvellous dome and all the artwork in this area. There was no sign of anyone and all the courts there were busy. He sent messages firstly to Hannah, who had gone to court before him, but received no reply. His message to Rich was answered and it turned out their hearing was in one of the newer courts in another part of the building. Never assume, he told himself as he rushed to find the courtroom.

When he entered the courtroom, he saw a lot of very concerned faces on the prosecution team. Ebony Forbes-Hamilton had on her black gown and white horsehair wig. She smiled at Sandy as he came up to them. Ebony was

Scottish, well, born in Scotland. She was married to a Scotsman and had two children, also born in Scotland, but she was black and was very proud of her Antiguan heritage. They had met before during a previous court case.

Hannah, who had not put her wig on as yet, whispered to Sandy, 'The judge is in a foul mood this morning.' Sandy glanced up at the dais where Mr Justice Francis Kane QC should be sat but there was no sign of him at that moment. He also glanced at the defence barristers and was not pleased to see that Charles Holloway QC was the barrister for Monica. On seeing Sandy looking at him, Charles nodded very smugly. Their paths had also crossed in the past. Charles was an extremely formidable opponent who they would need to watch closely. On glancing further along, Sandy couldn't see who was defending Henry but looking to the back of the court saw Vaughan Slade QC, another barrister he had met before, talking to Henry. Sitting as far away from Henry as possible was Monica. She was dressed as elegantly as always. She was not smiling but did nod at Sandy in acknowledgement of seeing him in the court.

Before he could ask anything further to try and find out what was going on, the court usher said, 'All rise,' and the judge entered. Sandy and Rich quickly found their seats.

The clerk asked the defendants to stand and then read out the two charges to Henry of murder and supplying a controlled drug. When asked how he pleaded to each charge, he replied, 'Not guilty.'

Monica, when asked to respond to her charge of murder, looked straight at Henry and said, 'Not guilty.'

Justice Kane said in an irritated and bored tone, 'Very well, sit down.' While saying this, he indicated with his right hand for Monica and Henry to sit. 'These medically based trials,' he continued, adjusting his glasses to see over them to look at the barristers sat in front of him, 'are too difficult for juries to follow. It is often one expert's word against another. What, and who, are they to believe? The expert with the most qualifications? The expert who is the most eloquent in the witness box?'

It was now obvious what had been happening in court that morning prior to Sandy's arrival. The judge had no interest, or in fact intention, of the case going to trial. The smug smile on the face of Charles Holloway said it all.

Justice Kane continued talking. 'I have just counted at least thirty experts and some for an expertise I haven't even heard of. These are mostly from the defence.' He looked down at Charles and Vaughan when he said this. 'The trial is listed for four weeks. We will need four months at least at this rate. Four months of my life I am not prepared to give up by having to listen to these so-called medical experts. What have you to say for yourself, Mrs Forbes-Hamilton?'

Ebony lifted herself slowly and deliberately to her feet and said, 'I do agree with the point your lordship is making. However, establishing the cause of death is at the heart of the prosecution case. We, and I mean our medical experts, are clear: Viscount William Peveril died from morphine toxicity. So, we need the experts to tell that to the jury.'

The judge nodded at Charles, who then stood and said, 'I wholeheartedly agree with you, my lordship. Impossible for a jury to follow all of these experts, who to believe and who not to believe. They will all use medical terms that even us learned lawyers wouldn't understand.' He laughed as he said this but no one else did. His attempt at humour had fallen flat.

Sandy started to get very agitated in his seat and the judge looked at him intently. He was about to ask Vaughan his opinion when he said, looking at Sandy, 'DCI McFarlane seems to want to say something. What is it officer?'

Sandy rose to his feet. He had heard his Grandad Tom mention on a number of occasions a case where they had held an experts meeting before the court case itself. Rich looked at him worryingly, having no idea what was coming next. Sandy walked forwards so that he was clearly seen by the barristers as well as the judge. He saw that Hannah was looking at him, as concerned as Rich. 'Your lordship,' he said, 'I am so sorry to interrupt, but couldn't we have in this case an experts meeting, the type of meeting that is clearly outlined in the criminal procedure rules?' For a moment he was worried that he might have remembered what his grandfather had told him wrongly, but seeing Ebony smiling and nodding, he continued by saying, 'We can then focus on what the key medical evidence is that the jury needs to hear.'

Charles was on his feet in a flash. 'Preposterous. My experts will never agree to this meeting.'

'Sit down, Mr Holloway,' the judge said loudly. Then he said, 'Mrs Forbes-Hamilton, your thoughts please?'

'I absolutely agree with the officer. If we hold this meeting in four weeks and then meet straight afterward, you, my lordship, can then decide if we have the correct level of experts for the jury to listen to. In my experience, we underestimate the ability of a jury to see what is right and wrong.'

Vaughan was given a chance to speak this time and true

to form went with what he saw as the path of easiest resistance.

So, an experts meeting was decided by the judge and the barristers went off to their robing room to agree on the questions to be asked in the meeting. The smile that Sandy got from Hannah was worth his intervention, let alone he might have saved the case.

Rich needed to call the Operation Cornflower incident room straight away to get someone to start contacting experts to ensure they were ready for the experts meeting. Justice Kane had been clever and had said that the experts must be given a formal witness order to ensure attendance at the court for the meeting.

∞

The reason the judge had been clever soon became apparent to the Operation Cornflower team, as almost all the experts when contacted told the officers that they couldn't make the meeting. They had clinics or something else they had to do, or, more likely, anything else that they would rather do. However, the fact that there was a witness order in place did focus their minds. The only people excused attendance in person were the American experts for the defence.

The day of the meeting arrived. Rich and Sandy took the brunt of the bad feeling that a lot of the experts were venting off as they arrived and waited for the meeting. A courtroom had been designated as the room for the experts to meet in. This courtroom had excellent IT capability for the four or five American experts to be able to attend via video link.

The only one who was enjoying himself was Dr

Nicholas Stroud. He was going to chair the meeting and had in his hand the three sets of questions to be resolved by the medical experts. There were present forensic pathologists, a toxicologist, chemists, pharmacists, anaesthetists, trichologists and, most importantly, three clinical cardiologists, including the eminent professor of clinical cardiology from the University of Oxford Medical School.

The amount of eminent medical people all in one room was unbelievable. Sandy wondered how many academic degrees the almost thirty people had between them. Must be well over one hundred. There was nothing much for the Operation Cornflower team to do other than keep a watchful eye over the proceedings. The barristers and the judge were not present, but the judge had decided that they would all assemble in another court with the two defendants to take stock at two p.m.

They made their way to the café to have a drink and Nicholas said he would ring them if there were any developments. Sandy wondered if he should go back to the FCDO offices for a couple of hours as he had a few things he could work on there. He didn't need to wonder for long as he had a message from Nicholas asking if Rich and him could come to the courtroom.

When they arrived, Nicholas had a large grin on his face and said, 'There are a few defence experts that have just said in the meeting that they feel their evidence is not required and another three say they agree with the prosecution case.'

This sounded like really good news but as he was unsure, Sandy said, 'What do you mean?'

'The two defence forensic pathologists, who didn't

carry out a second post-mortem as William's body had already been buried again, had in essence just completed a review of my notes and both of them said there was no dispute. If they had done an examination themselves it might have been different, but they hadn't.'

'Anybody else?'

'Oh yes. The chemists, pharmacists and anaesthetists all agree with the prosecution case. They are saying that they agree that the morphine levels found in William's body would cause death, as we have described.'

A wide-grinning Sandy said, 'Looks like we have won the case. This is incredible news.'

'Sorry to burst your happiness bubble but it most certainly doesn't tell us who administered the dose or their motive, or even if it was self-administered,' Nicholas said, looking at Sandy and trying to calm his youthful exuberance.

A more subdued Sandy asked, 'What is happening now then?'

'We decided it was a good time to have a break, then we'll deal with the American experts next. Although early morning there in America, it is at least almost working hours. The last thing we will discuss is the cardiology expert evidence.'

As they walked back to the café to let the other members of the team know of the developments, Rich said, 'Well, I am sure that whatever happens, we will now have a trial.'

It turned out that the American experts were a little harder to shift. Eventually two of them agreed with the prosecution but a defence trichologist – the one for Henry Adams, who was clearly after a trip to London – could not be shifted from saying that the hair samples he examined showed long and consistent use of morphine by William Peveril. 'Absolute nonsense,' the prosecution expert announced. He vowed to go away and find out everything about the American as he was sure he was a charlatan.

At almost two p.m. outside the court ready to go in and see Mr Justice Kane QC, Nicholas told Ebony, Rich and Sandy that there was no shifting the defence cardiologists and that was where the battleground would be fought. He had to admit himself that he couldn't argue with their reasoning.

Justice Kane was not in the slightest bit grumpy this afternoon and was extremely pleased with the result of the experts meeting. Charles Holloway was not. He said, 'My Lord, I believe this was a wholly improper meeting. What has just occurred is an annihilation of my carefully chosen medical experts without us being able to legally challenge their findings and decision-making here in court.'

'Are you, Mr Holloway, saying that you believe that what has just occurred has been a breach of the application of the appropriate section of the criminal procedure rules. If so, how?'

Charles for once seemed not to be as confident as he normally was. 'I am not saying that exactly, but I have all of a sudden, from what I had this morning, lost almost all of my defence experts.'

Ebony decided to offer an opinion. 'Your experts agree with the prosecution case according to the notes from the discussion. I have no objection to you calling them to give evidence.' This comment brought about laughter from everyone, including the judge and Monica, but not Charles or Henry. And surprise, surprise, Vaughan had nothing that he wanted to add to the discussion.

The date of the trial was set for the first week of September. The judge and the barristers were confident that it would last no longer than four weeks. The listing officer for the Old Bailey who was present agreed that as long as the trial ran to time, he would allocate court number one for them.

Chapter Thirty

The month of August was normally a quiet month in the FCDO with lots of members of staff on leave. Juliet had gone home, as she called it, to Barbados for three weeks with her family. Parliament was in recess so there was no minister asking for a piece of urgent work to be done. However, this August it had become extremely busy very quickly, because following the US leaving Afghanistan, Britain had followed suit. The blind panic scramble to get British citizens out of the country had brought a hectic atmosphere to life in the FCDO building on Great Charles Street. Although Sandy was not directly involved and felt for all of the people trying to get back from Afghanistan, he felt a certain personal buzz to the excitement.

Hannah and Sandy had managed to have a long weekend away together. They went to The Lodge hotel in Old Hunstanton on the North Norfolk coast. It was a place that they had stayed at previously and thoroughly enjoyed. Hunstanton was close to the Peveril Farm but Sandy had deliberately not mentioned his visit to Arabella.

∞

As the beginning of the trial approached, Sandy asked his father, Gregor, if Hannah could stay with him for the duration of the trial in their flat in London. Gregor, true to form, told Sandy to ask his mother. He knew his dad would defer to her so wondered why he had asked him in the first place. Katherine, when he asked her, had said yes. Hannah, on the other hand, had said no, other than she might occasionally stay over if they had to work very late. Sandy was not sure what to think about her response. As he processed his thoughts, he realised that Hannah was her own woman and wanted to be focussed on her role in the murder trial and not her role in their relationship, which he totally respected but he was still a bit confused about how they should relate to each other during the court case.

On the morning of the first day of the trial, as Sandy walked to the Old Bailey, just as he turned the corner to turn left towards the court, he glanced along the road and gazed at the magnificent St Paul's Cathedral up ahead. He could hear a loud noise of some sort of demonstration that must be going on outside the courthouse.

Waving at him from the window of the café that was situated on this corner of the road was Antoine Chevalier with his wife Claudette and Suzanne Valadon. Sandy went in and joined them.

'Monsieur McFarlane,' Suzanne, blatantly flirting with him, said. 'Please can you tell Antoine not to worry, he is so very nervous of having to be in an English court. We have told him if he is imprisoned, we will visit him.' Suzanne and Claudette giggled together like little girls. Poor Antoine must have his leg pulled by the pair of them unmercifully. Sandy couldn't help but laugh himself.

The three of them, on the insistence of Arabella, were staying in Eaton Square. While in London, as well as them all having to give evidence, they had planned to see a couple of shows in the West End and the women also wanted to do some shopping.

It appeared that Antoine, even though he denied it, was really nervous. Sandy knew how he was feeling as the excitement, anticipation and trepidation of the murder trial made himself, that morning, feel a high level of nervousness.

While Sandy was talking to them, he was conscious that he had been getting messages on his phone and had also had a couple of missed calls. After he left Suzanne and the Chevaliers, he looked at his phone as he walked to the court and saw that the missed calls were from Hannah and Rich. He had also had a message from them both, which said: 'Come to court quickly, we have a big problem.'

He noticed the noise of the demonstration getting louder as he walked along, but as he was looking at his phone, Sandy had taken no notice of what the demonstration was about. At the court entrance, he glanced at the twenty or thirty people there who were making all the noise. One of their banners said, 'Dignity in dying'. Another said, 'A person should have the right to choose life or death'.

∞

After clearing security, Sandy hurried along to the old courts in the Old Bailey where court number one was situated. Outside the court, he found a very concerned-looking Hannah and Rich. 'I presume this demonstration,' Sandy said, gesticulating outside to the street, 'is about William and our case?'

'Oh yes,' Rich said, as the three of them went in to meet Ebony in court. Ebony had laid out in front of her two daily newspapers. The *Daily Mail* had the headline, 'Viscount Peveril takes his own life in France'. There were pictures of William Peveril and a picture of Chateau Peveril. The other newspaper was *The Times* and their headline was, 'Mercy killing in France'. The paper also had a picture of William Peveril, a different one from the *Daily Mail*, and a different picture of Chateau Peveril. The public were fascinated with the case and the characters involved – too interesting not to be – but not this, this story was wrong.

The journalist for both the articles was a freelance journalist. His name was Patrick Hallam. On seeing the name, Rich, uncharacteristically for him, cursed. Sandy looked across at Charles and Vaughan; they were enjoying the discomfort being shown by the prosecution team. Charles Holloway said, 'Trouble? Who knows if assisted suicide, if that is what is being alleged by those articles, is even an offence in France?'

Ebony, with a nod of her head, gesticulated for them all to go out of the court and away from the very annoying Charles Holloway. Once out of the court, Ebony said, 'I am afraid that Holloway and Slade are going to create problems for us with these articles.' Ebony then gave a series of quickfire actions she wanted the detectives to carry out. 'Rich and Sandy, can you find out if it is actually an offence in France? Also find out from James Peveril and Mrs Montague if William had ever mentioned taking his own life. Find out from his doctor if there was ever any mention of mental health issues.'

Sandy said, 'I have just seen the Chevaliers outside the court building. They could be seen and asked about William's mental health in the immediate time before he died.'

'There is one person who could also help with William's intentions and that is Monica,' Hannah said.

'Leave her to me, if and when I get her in the witness box,' a determined-looking Ebony said.

On seeing Saffron Dupont talking to Lofty and two other Operation Cornflower team members, Rich and Sandy went over to them. 'Saffy, do you know anything about what French law says about assisted suicide?'

Saffy scratched her head, looking like she was racking her brains; in fact, that was exactly what she was doing. 'I do remember a lot about this in the French newspapers. There have been moves to bring in a law that allows it in certain circumstances. I am not sure if it is now law, or it was law when Viscount Peveril died. I will immediately call the French Ministry of Justice.'

Rich said, 'Sandy, you go and talk to James and Arabella and I will talk to the Chevaliers with Lofty.' He looked at one of the other Operation Cornflower team members and asked him to search the HOLMES account for the records from William's family doctor, looking for suicide ideation or mental health issues. HOLMES was not named after Sherlock Holmes but a mnemonic of Home Office Large Major Enquiry System.

Ebony and Hannah had gone back into court to talk to the judge to see if he wanted to put off the assembly of a jury. Ebony wanted to go ahead with it to show the confidence they had in the prosecution case.

There was initially no sign of James or Arabella in the court building, but the Chevaliers and Suzanne had arrived and Rich went off with them to the café area. Rich took one of the other detectives and Lofty with him so they could talk to one each. Sandy called Arabella. 'Are you on your way to court?'

'No, we are not. James and I have been told that we are

not required there until this afternoon at the earliest and we won't be allowed to sit in court until after we have given evidence. After this, we will be present all of the time.'

'Have you seen any of the newspapers this morning? Sandy asked, presuming though that she had not, based on her positive response with him so far in the conversation.

'No. James just rang and told me not to answer the door or my phone. He said he was on his way straight home from his offices. I saw the call was from you so I knew that it would be all right to answer your call.'

'Call me as soon as James gets home, please.'

'I have just heard the door. Hang on.' Sandy listened while Arabella was going downstairs. 'James, it is Sandy on the phone. What is going on?'

'There are newspaper articles alleging Father wanted to take his own life.'

'What nonsense. Who would say those lies?'

In order to be part of the conversation between the brother and sister, Sandy shouted out, 'Arabella, put the phone on speaker.' On cue, the phone went on to its speaker.

James said, 'Sandy, how do we fight this obvious lie?'

'We can discuss that when you get to court later today. However, I need to know if your father ever mentioned to either of you any thoughts on taking his own life?'

'Not once,' they both replied in unison.

∞

He made his way back into the court and could see that the selection of the jury was in full flow. Sandy managed to get Hannah's attention and while she was waiting for a suitable opportunity to come and see him, he glanced to his left and could see Monica sitting in the dock. She was as far away from Henry as she could get. Their eyes met and she nodded at him.

When Hannah had made her way out of court, everyone had returned. Sandy told them what James Peveril and Arabella had said. Rich told them that the Chevaliers had never ever heard this said by his lordship, as they insisted on calling him. There was nothing on the family doctor record. Sandy knew this already as he had made an earlier enquiry with the doctor.

Saffy said, 'This took a lot of sorting out, but I think I am clear. There is currently no law in France that allows anyone to assist someone to take their own life or to ease their passing from this life to the next. The reason why the law is not completely clear is because a number of times only recently attempts have been made to change it.'

Hannah went back into court to relay the information to Ebony. After the jury had been selected and sworn in, the judge sent them off for an early lunch. The judge said, 'I am extremely concerned by the press reporting on this case this morning. Are you intending, Mrs Forbes-Hamilton, to add a charge to the indictment for each defendant of assisting a suicide?'

'Absolutely not,' Ebony replied. 'We have made immediate enquiries and there is not one shred of evidence to back this sad assertion.'

'Mr Slade, what is your view? It is not currently a line of defence that you have declared.'

Vaughan rose to his feet and said, 'Another charge is not appropriate and this is not what we are going to say happened.'

Charles was on his feet without being asked. 'My Lord, I am interested to know if it is legal in France to assist someone to take their own life by suicide. If it is, and that is what happened here, we would have no premise for a trial at all.'

Ebony shot a furious glance at Charles. There was now no doubt in everyone's minds that he had somehow organised the newspaper story. Justice Kane didn't just glance at him in fury but also said in fury, 'For goodness sake. Just answer the question, are you or are you not using assisted suicide as a line of the defence for Monica Peveril?'

'Maybe. I need to take further instructions from my client.'

Hannah rose to her feet. 'If it helps, your lordship, I can confirm that it is still currently an offence in France to assist someone to take their own life.'

Charles looked over his left shoulder and frowned at Hannah. He was trying to intimidate her and said, 'We are not then going to use this as a defence.'

Mr Justice Francis Kane QC was upset, angry and determined. This case had not started in the way he would want. 'Right, jury usher, tell the jury that I apologise but they are released today and do not need to return until tomorrow morning. They must not read newspapers or watch any news that mentions the case.' The usher went off to see the newly formed jury.

Justice Kane then addressed the press gathered at the back of the court. 'Are any of you from *The Times* or the *Daily Mail*?' Two journalists got sheepishly to their feet. Looking straight at them, he said, 'You can tell your managing editors that they are to be in this court at two o'clock this afternoon. I am issuing a summons for them to attend.'

He then looked down at the copies of the newspapers laid out in front of him, then said, 'Is Patrick Hallam here?' No one stood up. 'Mrs Forbes-Hamilton, tell your officers to get him here for two p.m. as well.' As soon as he had said this, he stormed out of the court.

Between them, Rich and Sandy tried to get someone in their media department that might have the details for Patrick Hallam. On looking out of the window down at the demonstration that had dwindled to ten people, Rich said, 'That's him there, standing to the side of them taking photographs.' Sandy looked down at a man in his fifties who was almost bald, with the hair he had left greying. He had on a short black bomber jacket. Rich pointed him out to Lofty and said, 'Him. Arrest him for attempting to pervert the course of justice.'

Within ten minutes, Lofty and a City of London police officer went up to the demonstration. They very professionally grabbed one arm each of Patrick Hallam and pulled him away before he had any chance to realise what was happening or to protest.

Chapter Thirty-One

At the allotted time of two p.m., stood at a bench behind two new barristers were the managing editors for the *Daily Mail* and *The Times* newspapers. Patrick Hallam was standing next to them; he had no one to represent him. His arrogant look from earlier hadn't changed. He had been released from custody with no further action to be taken at present. Rich's tactic had worked – Patrick Hallam was in court.

Charles, Vaughan and the two defendants were not required so were not present, but Ebony and Hannah were. James and Arabella were also in court; they had decided not to stay at home when they had been told they would not be required until the next day. They had no intention of missing this hearing as it affected, in their view, their father's end of life greatly. If it had been true that he had actually wanted to take his own life, they would have felt sad that he hadn't been able to share it with them, but it was just not true. The Chevaliers and Suzanne had headed off for, in their words, a long and relaxing French-style lunch.

As soon as Justice Kane entered the room and before he had even sat down, he looked beyond the barristers and went straight at the newspaper editors and Patrick Hallam. 'How dare you try and derail a criminal trial. I will put you all in contempt of court if you print another word of this and then award costs for the considerable expense of the criminal process to date against you.'

The barrister for *The Times* said, 'My Lord, I represent *The Times* newspaper. With the utmost of respect' – that means no respect, thought Sandy, who sat next to Rich and whispered what he thought to him – 'there was, and is, no order in place for this case in relation to reporting restrictions. Can I ask, if that is your intention, what reasons you are going to give for such an order?'

Really feisty, thought Sandy. The judge was equally feisty in reply. 'Are you questioning me? You might need to be aware that you personally could also be heading to be in contempt of my court.'

Ebony rose to her feet, 'Your lordship, I wonder if I can assist. The problem today is that the reporting is a total fabrication and that is what is causing the issue for us trying to prosecute the case on behalf of the Crown.'

'Can I ask, My Lord, what part of the story is a fabrication?' *The Times* barrister said. He was talking to the judge but looking at Ebony.

'This is not a case of assisted suicide but of murder – that is the fabrication. There is not one shred of evidence to support the claims in your newspapers. Where did you get your information from? Who is that person's source? No one. There is no source. A total headline-grabbing fabrication that could have derailed the whole criminal murder trial.'

Both of the newspaper editors and their barristers all turned and looked at Patrick Hallam, who had gone completely red and the arrogant manner was now totally gone. By his reaction it was clear to everyone that he had concocted the whole story to create maximum interest in his article. What they would never know was if Charles Holloway had played any part in contributing to the story or just capitalised on an opportunity to create doubt in the courtroom.

Justice Kane, in order to regain control, said, 'I am not giving an order outlining reporting restrictions. I don't think I need to. But let me, in the strongest terms, urge all media who are reporting on this case to fully comply with their obligations for trial reporting so as not to jeopardise justice. On a side note, you two newspapers need to check your sources more thoroughly.'

He then dismissed them and the court usher told them all that court was being adjourned until ten a.m. the next morning. Patrick Hallam almost ran out of court without a word to anyone. Rich said to Sandy, 'I hope we have heard the last of him for this court case.' Arabella wanted to know if she could sue the papers and Patrick Hallam, but James, backed up by Sandy, told her, 'Let's deal with one court case at a time.'

∞

The next morning at ten a.m. everyone was assembling ready for the first day of the court case to get started. The buzz of excitement and nervousness was felt by everyone.

Arabella, James and the Chevaliers were outside waiting their turn to give evidence. Sandy nodded at them but didn't have time to talk to them as he knew the case was about to begin.

As he entered the court, he saw that Monica had on a different expensive-looking dress from the previous day. Sandy also noticed sitting in the court was a woman who had been there the previous day. She looked very much like Monica, or maybe could be described better as a Monica type.

As she hadn't yet taken her seat behind Ebony, Sandy quickly walked up to Hannah and asked her, as Monica was now in custody for the period of the trial, how come she was wearing a different dress every day and did Hannah know who the woman was sat at the back of the court.

As usual, Hannah didn't miss a trick and smiling at him said, 'Good morning, Sandy, you are running late to court this morning. Monica's mother brings her a dress in every day. Ebony and I both think she will wear a different dress every day of the trial. What do you think? The court artist is going to love it and every paper will be buying the pictures.' They laughed together. As they were told to all rise as the judge was coming in, Hannah whispered to Sandy that the woman sat at the back of the court is the new Monica. She was Henry's latest girlfriend.

Sandy had no sooner got to his seat next to Rich when Ebony started with her opening speech. 'Members of the jury, I thank you for your service. This case is quite simple. It is about this man, Viscount William Harrison Peveril.' Hannah passed to the court usher twelve copies of the picture of William when he was the High Sheriff of Derbyshire. As she did this, Charles Holloway snorted, causing the judge to peer at him over his half-rimmed glasses. Ebony continued, 'He died as a result of having administered to him a single catastrophic dose of diamorphine, causing death in a matter of, at the most, a couple or so minutes. Who administered that dose?' She pointed at Monica and then Henry. 'Those two: Monica Constance Peveril, his widow, and her *lover*, Henry Fredrick Adams. They were locked in a sordid relationship whose future was best served without William on the scene.'

'I would ask you all when making your decision to consider, and only take account of, what you hear from the witness box, or when I, or my junior, Hannah Tobias, read to you an agreed statement, not what you might hear from others like the defence barristers, Vaughan Slade for Henry Adams or Charles Holloway for Monica Peveril. Let me, before I ask the first witness to come and give evidence, conjure up just one image for you. When William was lying dead on a slab in a morgue in Bordeaux, and his two children, who are our first witnesses, were sobbing at his side in total despair, grief and sorrow for the loss of a great, charismatic and generous man, these two' – she pointed again to Monica and Henry – 'were in a lovers tryst in a hotel suite in the Ritz Paris, lying in bed together, drinking champagne and spending well over five thousand euros.'

When Ebony paused to allow her words to be taken in by the jury and everyone present in the court, Sandy wanted to cheer. There was no other way to describe Ebony's speech as anything but stunning. Print that *The Times* and the *Daily Mail* as your headline in the morning, he wanted to say.

Ebony then asked the usher for Mrs Arabella Montague to be called to the witness box as the first witness in the case.

∞

As Arabella walked to the witness box, she looked every bit the CEO of a multinational, multimillion-pound business. Dressed in a navy pin stripe trouser suit, her hair looked immaculate and she had obviously been to the hairdresser the previous weekend.

After giving the oath and her full name, the CEO image fell apart and Arabella was now like a little girl mourning the loss of her father. Arabella managed to keep it together and was especially illuminated when Ebony said, 'None of us knew your father or anything about who your father, the victim, was. Can you in a few brief sentences describe him to the court – who he was, what he stood for, what he meant to his family?'

As Ebony said this, Charles snorted again. One thing he didn't like was a jury to get a feeling for a victim and then want to be on their side to gain justice for them. To be fair to him, he made no noise as Arabella went through her interesting, colourful and moving exposé of her father.

The next question for Arabella was the one that brought her back to being the grieving daughter. Ebony asked her to describe the last moment she saw her father alive and then the last time she spoke to him. There were a few tears and a couple of gulps of the water from the glass beside her as she gave the court her answer. She kept looking up at the public gallery, where her husband Monty had positioned himself on the front row. Sandy had mentioned to him that he would be better seen for reassurance by Arabella if he was up there rather than sat in the body of the court itself.

Ebony then said, 'How much is Peverils worth?'

'We had to have the company valued as part of Father's will, so I am sort of able to answer that question,' Arabella said.

'What do you mean, sort of?'

'In terms of assets and cash in the bank, after all outstanding debts had been paid off, over five hundred million pounds.'

There was a whistle and buzz around the court as she said this. Arabella then said, 'But the reason I said, sort of, is if we sold the company, we could probably ask for somewhere in the region of two billion pounds.' No noise this time in the court, just stunned silence.

Ebony had no further questions nor did Vaughan, but Charles, of course, did. 'Mrs Montague, I am sorry for the loss of your father.' Of course he wasn't in the slightest, thought Sandy. 'Was there a prenuptial agreement in place between your father and his wife Monica Peveril?'

'Yes.'

'So where, quite cleverly, my learned friend,' he said, glancing down at Ebony, 'has made out a possible motive of inheriting a great deal of money following the death of your father, for Lady Peveril, that is not true is it, as my client knew that she wouldn't inherit one penny of all of this money you just mentioned, would she?'

'I agree, the family business was excluded in the prenuptial agreement.'

Charles then said, 'You have always disliked Monica, haven't you, Mrs Montague?'

'That is not true.' Arabella glanced at Monica in the dock but she looked away quickly, firstly to her husband then back to Charles Holloway, and said, 'I have not had any relationship with Monica. I should have tried harder and for that I apologise.' Arabella again looked at Monica and her look lingered this time.

'It is this dislike of Monica that started this whole case. You went to your friend, DCI McFarlane, to get him to investigate and try to overturn the agreed and officially recorded cause of death for your father, which is one of heart attack.' Charles emphasised 'heart attack', looking directly at the jury as he did so.

'That is not true and had nothing to do with any relationship I may, or may not, have with Monica.'

Charles had no further questions; he thought he had made his point. Just as Charles was sitting down, he said quite loudly, certainly loud enough for the jury to hear, 'It had everything to do with it.'

Ebony visibly frowned at Charles as she rose for her re-examination. She said, 'What is Monica going to actually inherit in monetary terms?'

'I am not the executor of the will. My brother James is but I did see the figures last week. It has been finalised that Monica and my father's previous wife will each get a cash figure just short of four hundred thousand pounds.'

The buzz in the court came again, as to the majority of people this was an extremely large sum of money, but in reality, for the lifestyle Monica had, and craved, it was a drop in the ocean. Rich pointed out to Sandy that was until she snared the next viscount or even a duke who crossed her path!

Arabella was released from giving evidence. As soon as this had happened, the judge sent the jury out and said, 'Mr Holloway, I am concerned that you are almost alleging a conspiracy between Mrs Montague and DCI McFarlane. Is that what you are doing?'

Sandy suddenly felt on high alert, and butterflies started in his stomach and his mouth felt dry.

'Normally,' Charles said, rising to his feet, 'we have a crime and the police look for an offender. Not in this case, My Lord. In this case, Monica was the prey and DCI McFarlane and Mrs Montague were the hunters.'

Ebony went to respond but the judge gesticulated with

his hand that she remained sitting down. He said, 'Just be careful, Mr Holloway, that you don't overstep the mark. We would not be here if there was no evidence that a crime had occurred.'

Hannah looked round at Sandy and gave him a reassuring smile.

There was an agreed decision that James didn't need to give evidence and instead, Hannah read his statement to the jury.

Chapter Thirty-Two

The next witness to be called into court was Antoine Chevalier.

As Antoine Chevalier walked into court, Sandy saw that he was wearing the same green check three-piece suit he had had on when he had seen him yesterday. Today though, with the suit, he had on a yellow bow tie. Sandy thought it matched really well the colouring of his suit, no doubt picked out by Claudette, possibly with the help of Suzanne.

He gave the oath, saying, 'I swear by almighty God that I will tell the truth, the whole truth and nothing but the truth.' While he said this, he placed his right hand across his heart and held the bible high in his left hand. Sandy was convinced anytime soon he would burst into singing the French national anthem, La Marseillaise.

The court had appointed an official French interpreter but it didn't look like Antoine would need her. Saffy had also walked into court to support him. She was dressed very demurely, well, for her.

Ebony talked Antoine through his evidence and he seemed so pleased with his answers to her questions that he smiled, looking around at the jury. The only answer that troubled the prosecution team was when Ebony said, 'Monsieur Chevalier, is it possible that Viscount Peveril died of something other than a heart attack?'

'No, it was a heart attack. That is what I have told everyone.'

'We are telling this court that Viscount Peveril died of a fatal dose of morphine. Do you know what that is?'

'No,' Antoine said, realising that he may have now got an answer wrong.

It seemed to Ebony there was no point in continuing, so she sat down and Vaughan commenced his cross-examination. 'Monsieur Chevalier, do you recognise my client, Dr Henry Adams?'

'A doctor is he, how wonderful!'

'But do you recognise him in this court?'

Antoine Chevalier squinted around the court. The judge, looking at him quizzically, said, 'Monsieur Chevalier, do you by any chance need glasses?'

'Yes, your wonderful great lordship, but my wife Claudette tells me they do not suit me. I look really old in them.'

The judge, trying not to laugh, said, 'Have you by any chance got them with you? If so, could you put them on and answer Mr Slade's question?'

Monsieur Chevalier, in a very dramatic movement, took his glasses case out of his pocket and put them on. He almost jumped back when he saw how many people were in court. He had clearly only been able to see the judge and the front row of barristers, the QCs in the case and some of the jury to his right.

'No,' he said, taking his glasses back off again.

'Please can you put your glasses back on and look at the dock,' he pointed at the dock, so he knew where to look.

After looking at the dock and almost bowing to Monica, he said, 'No.'

Mr Holloway was next to cross-examine. 'You say William Peveril died of a heart attack. You are sure of this, aren't you?'

'Yes, very sure.'

'On the night he died, did William Peveril say his back was hurting him again badly?'

'Yes, but my lordship was capable of anything, including fighting any pain.'

Rich and Sandy looked at each other. This was new information. It was typical of Antoine, not wanting to say anything even slightly derogatory about his employers.

Ebony and Hannah were exchanging whispers but eventually Ebony said in re-examination, 'When you went in the room after the Viscount had died, did you see on the table near him, or anywhere near him, an injection syringe or tablet boxes?'

Antoine Chevalier shut his eyes as if picturing the room. He was doing what Sandy had told him to do, when taking his witness statement, too literally. The barristers and the judge all exchanged puzzled glances with each other, but eventually he opened his eyes and said, 'No, I saw nothing like that.'

Giving Justice Kane a long bow, he left the witness box. It appeared he felt he had given the performance of his life. Sandy and Rich nodded to him as he left the court.

After a short discussion, the evidence of Claudette was agreed, so there was no need for her to give evidence. In terms of Suzanne, Charles Holloway was keen for her to give evidence, but in the end thought it probably best not to call her to give live evidence. Hannah read the two statements to the jury and slowed her speech considerably while reading the section when Suzanne said she had seen Henry waiting in the car for Monica when she registered the death.

∞

The next witness to be called was Dr Francois Aubrey. The doctor didn't speak very good English, so the official court interpreter was used. Ebony talked him through his evidence slowly and deliberately. She had wanted his evidence agreed but Charles Holloway wanted him to attend in person. What was he up to, she wondered. She was soon to find out when her questions for the doctor for his prosecution evidence was concluded.

Vaughan Slade said he had nothing he needed to ask. He really was a barrister who expended as little excess energy as possible. Charles Holloway, on the other hand, did everything he could to dominate the trial process. He was always busy; he was always doing. The jury had no choice but to listen to him.

Charles said to Francois, 'I presume you have seen in your long and illustrious career a number of people who have died from a heart attack?'

'*Oui*, yes.'

'Roughly how many, a hundred?'

'Must be, many hundreds, I would have thought.'

'You made an official record that in your considerable and vastly experienced opinion, William Peveril died of a heart attack. Isn't that right?'

'*Oui*, yes.' The doctor nodded while saying this and Charles sat down, having nothing else to ask. He had, quite frankly, nailed his point.

Ebony in re-examination asked, 'Could you see if someone had died through morphine toxicity?'

'*Non*. Toxicology would be required. It is a fine balance

to give someone morphine. Depending on their frailty, sometimes only a little is required to be fatal.'

The doctor left the witness box. A good witness for the defence.

There had been prior agreement for the Gerard brother and sister not to be called, nor the hotel receptionists, who would give evidence that Henry was in Saint-Émilion at the relevant times. Hannah read their statements to the jury. She had had quite a busy day. When she read the statement from the manager at the Ritz in Paris, Sandy could see that the jury were following her every word.

Justice Kane felt everybody had had enough for one day. He thanked the barristers for their agreements on the evidence as he felt at least two days or more of the trial, and therefore public money, had been saved.

Sandy was finding it hard being in the presence of Hannah and not having boyfriend–girlfriend interactions. He thought that all day they hadn't touched, held hands or kissed. He worried that spending a few weeks of having to be professional to each other would affect their relationship.

He went for dinner with Rich and Lofty. Hannah was not his biggest concern, but what Charles Holloway had insinuated. He had briefly spoken to Arabella who had been so upset after giving evidence that Monty had taken her home.

Rich and Lofty reassured Sandy that he had done nothing wrong and Derbyshire Police were leading the investigation, not him. Two things still troubled him as he wandered back to the flat, hoping his dad had gone home to Ely so he could have time alone. The first thing worrying him was that in terms of priorities, at the start of the investigation he had prioritised this investigation above others. He probably shouldn't have, and his boss Jane Watson had felt that he shouldn't have as well. The second thing was the unusual and unconventional meeting at the Eagle pub in Cambridge with his grandfathers. Rich had got them to sign confidentiality agreements and they only used them as a sounding board, so maybe he was, as Rich and Lofty kept telling him, worrying about nothing.

Court the next day was to start with the evidence of Nicholas Stroud – an exciting day to be sure and one he was looking forward to.

∞

Sandy was running late for court the next morning as he had to do some work at the offices of the FCDO. He had told Juliet and Clare about Mr Holloway alluding to a conspiracy between him and Arabella. Juliet couldn't stop laughing but said she would have to be roped in as part of the conspiracy too. Sandy felt a lot better after speaking to Juliet; her experience, pragmatism and support for him was a tonic. The only thing that worried him as he rushed to go into court was that so many prosecution witnesses were being stood down from giving live evidence. Unbeknown to him at that time was that both Juliet and Clare had also, that morning, been cancelled to give evidence, as their evidence had been accepted.

Dr Nicholas Stroud was just being called to the witness box as Sandy took his seat next to Rich. He had waved at Hannah, who had been turned around looking for him. Sandy was also pleased that Arabella and Monty were now in court sat next to James. The fashion show was continuing with Monica wearing a bright orange dress and lilac scarf.

Dr Stroud had just given the oath and introduced himself when the courtroom door burst open and in walked Arthur Ramsbottom, the senior coroner for the Peak District. He very noisily found a spare seat. Everyone looked around at him, including the judge, who Sandy saw was frowning at Arthur.

Ebony asked Nicholas to talk through his post-mortem and then after a while they got to the stage where Ebony said, 'Dr Stroud, when you overtly examined the heart, you were sure William Peveril hadn't died of a heart attack. Are you still quite sure of that now, having had a chance to read statements and chair a medical expert meeting?'

'I am not an expert in heart pathology.' This comment brought furious scribbling by Charles Holloway. 'However, I have seen thousands of hearts and I would say from my vast experience' – he looked straight at the jury while he was saying this – 'that his heart is not what killed him. Especially when we take into account the morphine toxicity findings, which were well beyond a fatal level. That is what, without a shadow of a doubt, killed William Peveril.'

Ebony had no more questions for Nicholas for his evidence in chief and he had delivered exactly what had been required of him. Unsurprisingly, Vaughan had no questions.

Charles Holloway rose to his feet. The two of them looked at each other like gladiators in a ring. The combatants were in place and the duel was about to begin. 'Dr Stroud, it is fair to say you missed seeing that William Peveril had the heart disease that killed him?'

Nicholas turned away from Charles, looked at the jury

and said, 'As you can imagine, macroscopically, William's heart did look like that of a seventy-three-year-old, but it is not until you look at it under a microscope you would see the true level of the heart disease.'

Charles then said in a strong and authoritative voice, 'You are not qualified to conduct pathology in France, are you?'

'I have all the qualifications to—'

Before he could finish his sentence, Charles interrupted him. 'Can you, or can you not, carry out forensic post-mortems in France?'

'If you are asking, am I accredited to do this by the French government, I am not.'

Looking straight at the jury, Charles said, 'This is a death that happened in France, which the French didn't feel necessary to have a post-mortem or prosecute.'

'Was that a question or were you just making a statement?' Nicholas said. He then looked first at Ebony and then the judge, who said, 'Yes, stick to asking questions, Mr Holloway.'

'Very sorry, My Lord.' He clearly wasn't. 'The defence in this case have not had their entitled and legal right to have their own post-mortem. William's body was returned to his grave with undue haste.'

Arthur Ramsbottom rose to his feet, making a great noise and causing everyone to look around at him again. He shouted out loudly and assertively at Charles, 'I decide who has a post-mortem.'

Before the plainly upset, irritated and increasingly cross judge could say anything, Nicholas intervened, 'My Lord, that is Mr Arthur Ramsbottom, the senior coroner for the Peak District where Viscount Peveril's body was buried when he was returned to England.'

Justice Kane looked down at Arthur, who had sat down again, and realising he had overstepped the mark, he mouthed, 'Sorry,' to the judge. 'Mr Ramsbottom, this is my court, not yours. You will have your chance to preside over an inquest, if required, for Viscount Peveril, but please respect the court here. No more outbursts. Continue, Mr Holloway.'

But before Holloway could say anything, Nicholas said, 'You are legally and technically wrong on your comment relating to second post-mortems. The Chief Coroner's Guidance in 2019 reverses the presumption you are making in favour of a second post-mortem for suspected homicide cases. I provided everything that the defence forensic pathologists needed to review my work. They, as you know, agreed with my examination.' Dr Stroud had often, during this response, looked at the jury. He was a star at giving evidence and Rich and Sandy were in awe of his command of the witness box.

Charles had no more questions. Who had won the duel? Only time would tell.

Chapter Thirty-Three

Dr Stroud put his arm around Arthur Ramsbottom and the two of them headed off for, no doubt, a long and leisurely lunch.

As they left the courtroom, Vaughan Slade rose to his feet and said, 'My Lord, I have a legal issue to discuss with you and my colleagues, without the jury being present please.' Sandy and Rich were shocked by this intervention as they hadn't ever known Vaughan to intervene at a trial before.

Justice Kane seemed equally shocked and said, 'Will we need the afternoon to discuss a resolution to the legal issue, or will we be able to call any more witnesses today?'

'Possibly not. The Crown will need to take a position on the issue.'

Justice Kane released the jury, not just for lunch but for a long weekend, telling them not to speak or read anything about the trial. It transpired that a couple of the barristers had professional difficulties on the Friday. Hannah was one of them as she had the sentencing hearing for her arsonist in York.

Lofty went out to tell the two or three medical experts, who were waiting outside the court ready to give evidence, that they were no longer required today and needed to come back on Monday. Sandy and Rich felt that they should have gone with him because they knew these experts were very important and incredibly busy people and they were going to be livid about this turn of events.

However, Rich and Sandy needed to be present in court to hear the legal argument. Hannah looked around at Sandy and shrugged, telling him she was unaware of what this was about.

'As we know,' Vaughan said, once the jury had fully left the court, 'the Crown, in this case, have used the Offences Against the Person Act of 1861 to prosecute this offence, which was committed by a British citizen while abroad in France. They could equally have used article forty-four of the Istanbul Convention to do so as well.' Where was he heading with this, Sandy wanted to know.

Vaughan seemed to be enjoying his moment and was emphasising his Welsh accent. He stopped to have a sip of his water, pulled up his gown over his shoulders and then said, with dramatic effect, 'Neither the Offences Against the Person Act, nor the UK governments present commitment to the Istanbul convention, allow Dr Henry Adams to be prosecuted for the drug offence as currently specified in the indictment.' There were audible gasps from Sandy and Rich, but equally, Ebony, Hannah and the senior CPS lawyers who had missed it. Henry had a huge grin on his face but Monica showed not a flicker of emotion, as cold and unfeeling as ever.

'Very well,' the judge said, nodding in admiration at Vaughan for his clever legal footwork. 'Mrs Forbes-Hamilton, let me know the Crown's position in relation to this matter at one thirty.' He rose and left the court.

The prosecution team crammed themselves into the first room they could find. It would suffice as a place to meet. Ebony, removing her wig while she sat down, said, 'How sly, but very clever of Vaughan. He is right. I can't believe we missed it. Now, we can recover this, I hope, if we think Henry could have possibly supplied the tablets and injection here in England.'

Rich looked to Sandy to answer, who, with a shake of his head, said, 'I don't think so. Monica had already gone to France when the records in the Harley Street practice show he prescribed and dispensed the morphine. It must have happened in France.'

Unable to hide her disappointment, Ebony said, 'Any ideas, or should we throw the towel in for this count on the indictment?'

'There must be other offences committed by how he prescribed and dispensed the drugs, for example, forgery?' Sandy said, not wanting to concede anything.

'That will be for a different trial, maybe another day,' Ebony said, getting to her feet. The conversation was over. 'Grab yourselves some lunch and I will see you all back in court shortly.' Hannah went off with Ebony before Sandy had a chance to speak to her.

∞

As a dejected Rich and Sandy came back into court, after having had a walk outside with Lofty, they could see Ebony and the other QCs on the front bench in deep, and what appeared to be, quite aggressive conversation.

When Justice Kane came back into court, Ebony rose to her feet and said, 'My Lord, the Crown would like to withdraw the supplying drugs charge.'

'Very well,' the judge said.

Vaughan said, 'My Lord, our preferred option is that you instruct the jury on Monday morning to find the defendant not guilty of the charge.'

Sandy was extremely worried about this as he felt psychologically the jury might then be pulled along a 'not guilty' line of thinking.

'The Crown does not support that proposition. Mr Slade's legal argument was the indictment was wrongly framed, rather than we can't prove the defendant did it.'

'Yes, I agree,' Justice Kane said. 'Anything else I can help you with?'

Charles Holloway was on his feet in a flash. 'As the supply of the morphine has been dismissed, can we now lose all of those witnesses who are going to talk about it?'

'Decide and agree that among yourselves. My view is that you could potentially read some of the evidence rather than call all of the witnesses.'

Following this pronouncement by the judge, Ebony, Vaughan and Charles, along with their juniors, entered into an animated conversation, going through their files of the remaining prosecution witnesses.

Rich and Sandy went and waited outside and wandered around looking up at the incredible dome, murals and paintings.

They looked together at the painting denoting justice and hoped that that was what was happening in court number one at the Old Bailey for William Harrison Peveril and his family.

When Ebony came out of court, Rich asked if they could speak to her. They all crammed themselves back into the room they had been in before. Sandy said, 'Rich and I' – Rich nodded in agreement – 'are really concerned that you, and the other barristers, are coming to agreements about not using witnesses that we felt helped to construct, build and establish our case.'

Although Sandy was looking at and talking to Ebony, he was conscious of Hannah in the room. He glanced at her to find that she was expressionless.

Ebony said very calmly, looking at Sandy, 'I get your and DCI Singh's point, but we will, in cases like these, feel we are winning on some days when we are probably not, and losing on some days when we are probably winning. I am convinced though that the grains of sand being added all of the time to the scales of justice will, by the end of the trial, ensure these scales of justice are able to be fully served by the evidence in the case.'

Sandy and Rich thanked her, having made their point, and went to leave the room. As Sandy was leaving, Hannah said, 'I will call you when I get to my room in York later.'

'Yes, please,' Sandy said, but sadly their voices lacked warmth and were still portraying the professional roles they were both performing in the Adams and Peveril trial.

On the Friday, Sandy had to work in the FCDO offices in order to get caught up on his paperwork. He seemed to be one of only two or three of the consulate investigation team working in the office that day and as a result, the offices were extremely quiet.

He was just in the process of packing his things away in his backpack to head home to Ely for the weekend when he received a call from Hannah, who said, 'Sentencing just finished. Guess what he got sentenced to?'

'Ten years.'

'No. Four life sentences with a minimum of ten years.'

'Isn't that what I just said?' They both laughed together. Gosh, that felt good, thought Sandy, laughing and being back to normal with Hannah.

'He could, if he doesn't behave in prison, or if the parole board feel he is unsafe to be released, be in prison a lot longer than ten years,' Hannah replied, when she had stopped laughing. She was on a real high. 'I am taking the investigation team out for lunch then getting the train to my dad's. I will ring you tomorrow either before or after you play rugby.'

Sandy wished he too were going for lunch with Hannah. He had to make do with a Cornish pasty from a stall at King's Cross station as he caught the train to Ely via Cambridge.

∞

On the Monday, Sandy wasn't able to attend court, as Jane Watson and Phil Harris were not in the office and he was left in charge. As he was heading back to his flat in the city that evening, he got a call from Rich.

'Hi, Sandy, you didn't miss much in court today. Hannah Tobias spent most of the day reading statements.'

'No live witnesses then?'

'Yes, one of our clinical cardiologists gave evidence, they came across well. He stuck to his opinion that the cardiac disease was treatable and didn't seem from his examination to be imminently fatal.'

'What did Charles Holloway say in cross-examination?'

'Well, when our expert tried to mention the fatal dose of morphine, Charles shut him up straight away and warned him about straying into something that was not his area of expertise. He was looking at the jury all the time while he said this. The toxicologist, who gave evidence next, came across well in explaining the levels of morphine toxicity.

No cross-examination for her.'

'Did you get a chance to see the jury's faces when we withdrew the charge for supplying the morphine?' Sandy asked.

'Yes, I thought they all looked a bit surprised, which might be a good thing.'

Sandy declined dinner with Rich, which he felt bad about as Lofty wasn't in London until later in the week. There were though other members of the Operation Cornflower team there, as were Bob and Pete, one of whom was going to give evidence the next day, probably in the afternoon, by which time Sandy would hopefully be back in court.

As Sandy walked into court, he saw that Bob was walking ahead of him, heading into the witness box. As if sensing him, Hannah, who was on her feet, wig and gown on, turned and looked at Sandy. She deliberately made direct eye contact and gave him a smile that would have melted anyone's heart, so much so that as he sat down next to Rich, he got a very sharp elbow to the ribs and another smile, this time from his friend and colleague, Rich Singh.

Bob looked like he had had a haircut and his suit, if it wasn't new, was one that he reserved for appearances in court.

The off-putting part about him giving evidence was that Hannah read the questions and Bob gave the reply. The interview record for Henry went smoothly back and forth between them. The next interview with Henry, before he was charged, was in relation to him being asked about the prescribing and dispensing of the morphine and him making a no comment response. This also received very little interest by the defence barristers. Unsurprisingly, again there were no questions in cross-examination from Vaughan.

However, as soon as Hannah started going through the interview of Monica, the court was in uproar and there were tears of laughter. Even the judge and jury were laughing. Sandy looked across at Monica and could see her smiling. The only person not laughing was Charles Holloway. He was looking round at his junior and the instructing solicitor, who had actually been in the interview, and was frowning and gesticulating wildly at him.

Hannah even ad-libbed at the part of the interview when Monica had mentioned the clothes that Bob and Pete had been wearing in the interview. Hannah said, 'You look really smart today.'

'This is the suit I got married in, for the second time, three years ago,' Bob said. He then looked directly at Henry and said, 'And I have given up smoking.'

They hadn't got to this part yet in the interview but everyone laughed, which made Charles utter really loudly so that the whole of the court could hear him, 'Really!'

Justice Kane had also decided the time had come to intervene. 'I know that this interview is amusing but I am not able to fully concentrate on the questions and answers with the noise in the court, and I am sure the jury feel the same. Please can everyone try to keep as quiet as they can. Miss Tobias, please continue.'

There was still stifled laughter through the rest of Bob's evidence and there was no cross-examination from Charles, who wanted to get this debacle for his client over and done with as quickly as possible. He could be heard saying to the instructing solicitor, 'Whatever were you thinking about, letting her carry on like that in the interview?' If he could have got away with it, he would have sworn at him profusely.

Chapter Thirty-Four

The next witness to be called was the DMI for the phone evidence. Sandy had missed the DMI in the morning, who covered Henry's computer and the record of the prescribing and dispensing of the morphine tablets and the diamorphine injection.

The DMI presented his evidence very effectively; he dealt with it in sections. Messages first, nothing of significance other than establishing when the contact between Monica and Henry began and its intensity. Calls came next. Ebony asked, 'The phone call between Lady Peveril and Dr Adams on the evening that Viscount Peveril died, what time was that?'

'Originally, we thought the first call that evening was an hour after he had died, but we had failed to take into account the time difference between England and France.'

'So, did it happen before Monsieur Chevalier had made the call to the French doctor who declared death?'

'Yes, that's right. I have that time recorded five minutes or so later.'

'How long was the call between Lady Peveril and Dr Adams?'

The DMI looked down at his papers and then said, 'Fifty-five seconds?'

'Not long enough then for asking advice on CPR or anything else medical?'

The DMI grinned; he knew what Ebony was alluding to.

'I couldn't possibly say, as I am no expert nor have any idea what was said, but I wouldn't have thought so.'

Finally, the DMI went through the cell site analysis for each phone and showed a map to the jury, where they were when Henry arrived in France, and at the time William died. Ebony had no more questions for the DMI's evidence in chief.

Vaughan said, 'On the night that William Peveril died, the cell site data for Dr Adams shows he couldn't have been at Chateau Peveril, but was in, or very close to, his hotel room in Saint-Émilion, doesn't it?'

Before the DMI could reply, Justice Kane intervened and said, 'Of course it doesn't, Mr Slade, I rarely keep that infernal device with me!' This brought laughter from everyone in the court. 'It makes you so accessible, somebody always wants something from you, or for you to do something you don't really want to do.' He went on. 'What I am saying is, it shows where Dr Adams's phone was at that time, not him.'

Vaughan took his phone out of his pocket. 'I understand your thoughts entirely, My Lord, but I have mine with me.' He showed the jury. He looked at Ebony and she nodded. 'The prosecution barrister has hers with her and you officer, is yours with you?'

The officer tapped his pocket and said, 'Yes.'

Rich, Sandy and no doubt everyone in the court were doing the same. Having made his point, Vaughan sat down. Charles had no questions.

The judge decided that there had been enough excitement for the day, and after saying, 'Anyone walking into court this afternoon and hearing all the laughter would be surprised that we are dealing with a murder trial,' he looked straight at Arabella and James and said, 'I apologise, but there is no disrespect meant in anyway.'

Arabella and James lifted their hand to the judge to say it was all absolutely fine. They then all rose in court as he left.

Sandy had a quick ten minutes with Hannah before going out to meet Arabella, Monty and James to see how they were coping.

∞

Sandy couldn't be there the next day but planned to be there on the Thursday when it looked like it would be the start of the defence case.

When Sandy arrived in court on the Thursday, it was almost lunchtime. As he walked into the courtroom, he almost had to turn around again as he heard the judge telling everyone to be back in court for one thirty p.m. The next witness to take the witness stand would be Henry Adams.

Rich and Hannah went for lunch with Sandy to the café in the Old Bailey.

As they settled down with their sandwiches and drinks, Rich said, 'Two of the witnesses you took statements from, relating to Henry prescribing them morphine, gave evidence this morning. They told the court what a wonderful doctor Henry is and how well he treated them, including prescribing and dispensing morphine for their pain appropriately.'

'Shame I missed them. I thought they were prosecution witnesses,' Sandy said, taking a big bite of his tuna sandwich.

While Sandy was finishing his mouthful, Hannah said, 'We decided not to use them. The defence were a bit lazy, rather than find other patients they just used who we had found and taken statements from – a bit dangerous if you ask me.'

Rich said, 'The other witness this morning was from the Care Quality Commission, who carry out inspections of health and social care establishments. Although Dr Adams ran a private practice, so didn't need to do this, he had invited them in to carry out an inspection and to give him a quality assurance record. They said his practice was excellent.'

'How long ago was that though?' Sandy asked.

'Only nine months ago was the last visit,' Rich said.

'OK, who was the last witness this morning then?'

Hannah, after a final sip of her coffee, said, 'A manager from the medication regulator who annually inspects Dr Adams's dispensing register. They said he keeps immaculate records and has never once had a problem.'

One thing that Hannah and Rich mentioned, which had worried Sandy, was that there had been a judge-initiated legal discussion before the defence case had started, about offering the jury a manslaughter verdict as an alternative to help them when they had to make a decision on a verdict in the trial.

They were back in court in good time for the evidence of Henry Adams. After exchanging a few words with Arabella and Monty, Sandy went and took his seat.

As Henry walked to the witness box, Sandy glanced around the courtroom but couldn't see the woman that the Operation Cornflower team had called the new Monica. Rich informed him that he thought she had stopped coming yesterday. She had moved from nodding at them, to smiling at them, to saying hello to them. They thought that this might be a good sign, that someone like her was possibly seeing Henry as guilty.

Vaughan took Henry through his evidence, asking about his career as a doctor and his private practice. Then they went through his relationship with Monica. At the end of his explanation to the court, Henry said, 'It is over. We finished after our first police interviews and we haven't spoken since.'

To be fair to Henry, Rich and Sandy hadn't seen Monica or him exchange even a look at each other, let alone a word, bearing in mind they were only sat twelve feet from each other.

Vaughan then asked, 'On the night that William Peveril died, where were you?'

'In my hotel room in Saint-Émilion. I had seen Monica earlier in the afternoon but not that evening.'

'So, you were not anywhere near Chateau Peveril at the time of death?' Vaughan looked straight at the jury while he said this.

'No,' Henry said, mirroring what Vaughan had done and said this directly to the jury.

'How did you find out about the death?'

'Monica rang me to say he had just died. I told her to get a local doctor to declare death.'

'When you were arrested, it might seem to the jury that you are a violent man. Why did you react like you did when the police officers entered your consulting room?'

'I didn't know at first, I was being arrested. I thought I was being robbed.'

Vaughan handed over to Ebony for her cross-examination. After looking back and having a quick word with Hannah, she took a sip of her water, stood, then pulled her gown over her shoulders. Ebony looked excited; the cut and thrust of cross-examination was like manna from heaven for a barrister, especially one as gifted in the art as she was.

'What do you know about the prenuptial agreement that Monica and William had?'

Henry seemed taken back by this as a first question, in fact as a question at all. 'Nothing,' he said, then added quickly, 'Why would I?'

'Let's be clear, Dr Adams,' Ebony said, 'I ask the questions and you give the answers. I believe you were present at a charity event and overheard someone offer William over fifty million euros for the winery part of Chateau Peveril, is that right?'

Rich and Sandy exchanged glances at each other. Ebony was chancing her arm here as they had no evidence that he would have definitely heard the offer being made.

Again, Henry was taken aback by the question. Whatever questions his barristers had practised with him, these were not any of them. 'He turned the offer down straight away.'

Bingo! Ebony had nailed that Henry was aware that William was worth a lot – a tremendous lot – of money.

'Monica is not the first married woman you have had an affair with, is she?'

'No, she is not. Unfortunately, I am at an age where the women I meet are all married. Mostly unhappily though.'

After shuffling through her papers, Ebony said, 'One of those affairs ended in a very high-profile messy divorce for the woman involved, and her husband implicated you, which was reported widely in the newspapers, wasn't it?'

'Yes, not an experience I would want to repeat.'

'Bingo,' Rich said to Sandy – another good answer for the prosecution.

'The witnesses this morning, in relation to how you handle medication, were very impressive.'

'Impeccable,' Henry said, while looking very proud indeed.

'However, what they established to the court was, probably, the opposite of what you were trying to achieve.'

Henry again was taken aback by the statement and gave a confused look at Vaughan, seeking reassurance.

'I can see you are confused, Dr Adams. Try to look at me as I am asking the questions, and not Mr Slade, and direct your replies to the members of the jury,' Ebony instructed, clearly trying to rattle Henry. 'The witnesses established that you are meticulous with your medication record-keeping. That is why it is the opposite position to take for your defence. The last two morphine medications you prescribed, you did not record them correctly, as to who they were being dispensed to, did you? My colleague, Miss Tobias, read their statements to the jury and the two people you recorded as prescribing and dispensing the drugs to, never received them, did they?'

'I made a mistake. They must have gone to someone else.'

'Exactly my point.' Then looking at the jury, Ebony said, 'Thank you for confirming your fraudulent medical record-keeping to us. We know who we think that medication was intended for.'

Ebony paused again, letting her words resonate around the court. After shuffling through her notes again, she said,

'When Monica rang you that evening, why didn't you, as a highly trained medic, tell her to urgently perform CPR?'

'She said he was dead, so I didn't think it necessary.'

'People don't just die, do they. Your response seems the most bizarre response. And I quote you here, you told Monica to "call the local doctor to declare death".'

Henry did not reply as it appeared Ebony was not asking him a question.

There was no re-examination so Henry left the witness box to return to the dock followed by a prison officer. Vaughan told the judge that he had finished the defence case for Dr Henry Adams.

∞

The next morning was the turn of the defence case for Viscountess Monica Constance Peveril. There had been no indication from Charles Holloway whether she would be giving evidence or not. Ebony and Hannah were well prepared for it if she did though. Charles felt, while in discussions with the judge, that his defence should be completed by the end of the day.

The first witness to be called was the professor of clinical cardiology from the University of Oxford. After spending an incredible amount of time going through his qualifications and experience, Charles said, 'Professor, I don't intend to keep you too long. The question is simple: in your extremely knowledgeable and experienced opinion, did William Peveril die of a heart attack?'

'The question might be simple, but I am afraid the answer is not so simple. William Peveril had moderate heart disease. Common in a person, in particular a man of his age. Yes, he could have undoubtedly died from a heart attack.'

Charles had no more questions. That was extremely short and brief. His objective of putting this thought into the minds of the jury had worked.

Ebony rose to cross-examine the professor. 'You have seen the statement from the prosecution clinical cardiologist and we in this court have heard directly from him, and he thinks, based on the holistic medical evidence, that this was not the cause of death.'

Before Ebony could finish the point that she was building up to, the professor intervened. 'He is very good. I should know because I trained him, I mentor him and I am the one he comes to for advice and to peer review his work in complex cases. Yes, he is a good man.' This response brought a little bit of laughter from around the court.

'What I was going to finish by saying,' Ebony continued, with a smile on her face, 'was that William had a fatal dose of morphine in his body at the time he died. That is why he died. Don't you agree with your protégé?' Again, some laughter was heard around the court.

'I am not going to give you an answer to that question. I will not step outside my area of expertise, that is dangerous and too many medical experts do that. It is not helpful to anyone. Was William Peveril's heart disease so bad that depending on the stress put on his heart, would that have been enough to kill him? The answer to that question is, in my opinion, yes.'

The next witness was Lieutenant Marius Legard from the French Gendarmerie Nationale. Sandy and Rich exchanged glances at each other. 'Did you know he was coming to give evidence for the defence?' Rich whispered. They could see that Ebony and Hannah were equally off guard about his attendance.

'I received a text message from him a couple of days ago telling me he was coming to London and could we meet up after the court case. I replied yes but heard no more.'

After giving the oath and introducing himself, Marius, dressed in uniform and carrying his hat, looked at Charles for the first question.

'The official French record relating to the death of William Peveril is that he died of a cardiac arrest, is that right?'

'Yes, that's right.'

'The French police and the Ministry of Justice in France deemed this to be a correct diagnosis and have conducted no criminal investigation into the death. Is that right?'

'Almost right. We did assist the English investigation but did not, and have not, carried out one of our own.'

No more questions from Charles. Short and sweet, he had made the point he wanted to make.

Ebony asked in cross-examination, 'If your bosses in the Gendarmerie agreed and the investigating magistrate agreed, would you have carried out an investigation though?'

Charles wanted to stand and make a point about this question, no doubt saying it was hypothetical, but before he could, Marius said, 'Of course I would have investigated, hence I supported DCI McFarlane in every way possible with his investigation.' As he said this, he looked straight at Sandy.

Ebony had no more questions and Charles thought it best not to pursue it any further. What a long way to come for just a few minutes in court, thought Sandy.

The next witness to be called was Monica Peveril.

Chapter Thirty-Five

As Monica walked from the dock to the witness box, people looking at her would think that this was a model walking on a catwalk in London, New York or Paris, rather than in court number one of the Old Bailey as a defendant in a murder trial, being followed by a prison officer. True to the thoughts of Ebony and Hannah, Monica had worn a different designer dress to court every day. Today, in some respects, was no different. She was though, for the first time, not wearing a colourful dress but was dressed all in sombre black, including a little black jacket to go over the top of her dress.

After saying the oath and telling the court her full name and before Charles could even ask his first question, Monica started crying, softly at first and then sobbing. Charles looked at the judge for him to support his witness somehow. Justice Kane was not moved by the crying demonstration.

Sandy looked across at Arabella, Monty and James. They were all shaking their heads in disbelief. Monica conjured up a bright white handkerchief from a sleeve of her jacket, wiped her eyes and brought herself back under control.

Charles decided to proceed and asked her how she had met William and about their relationship. Monica slowly and deliberately went through her and William's story. She only occasionally stopped to have a short cry.

Charles said, 'Your husband's children never accepted you did they, and in fact they hate you?'

'They had all placed their mother, William's first wife, on a pedestal and she was irreplaceable, certainly not by me. I wouldn't say they hated me though, not even disliked me. We just had no relationship.'

Charles asked about how the relationship with Henry began and how it had developed. Then he asked about William's bad back and the pain he was in.

'I had got him some medication and his back was getting better. Then when we went for a walk in the vineyards after lunch on the day he died. He seemed to aggravate it when he slipped on a slope. After we had had dinner, he took some more medication and died of a *heart attack*,' Monica said.

'As you know, the jury has heard your interview with the police officers. Why did you act like that in the interview?' So arrogant and condescending to detectives you felt were beneath you, Sandy thought.

Monica looked round to her right at the jury. This has been scripted, thought Sandy. No doubt Charles the great director of courtroom drama had prepared Monica well. After shedding another tear, producing the white handkerchief, Monica said in a quiet, timid voice, 'I was so scared of those detectives, in fact the whole situation I was in. It was the only way I could try and take some control back. I admit it, I was terrified.'

'One last question, Lady Peveril. Did you murder your husband?'

'No, I did not.'

Charles sat down and Ebony lifted her sheath of papers onto her box. 'Did you love your husband?'

This question made Monica hesitate for a moment before answering. The easiest and best answer for the jury was, of course, yes, but Monica said, 'Love William? No, I don't think I did. Respect him, admire him, fond of him, yes, but love… not so sure what that means.'

'Did you love Henry Adams?'

'Desire him, yes. Excited by him, yes. Love him, no. In fact, I hate him now.' Monica looked straight at an expressionless Henry when she said this and when she mentioned hate, with such venom, it brought a gasp of surprise from around the court.

'Was Henry your first lover since you had been married to William?'

'No, I am afraid to admit it, he wasn't. But the only one during the last year!'

'Let's go straight to the comments you have made relating to William's last day. You say he was having medication. Where did this come from?'

Monica hesitated and glanced at Henry. Sandy looked at the jury and hoped they had noticed the glance. He wasn't convinced. 'I picked the drugs up in Saint-Émilion.' Yes, thought Sandy, from Henry Adams's hotel bedroom.

'Where in Saint-Émilion? We have scoured the village to find out where it could have been, but to no avail.'

'I don't know. Does it matter? The drugs were helping to ease the pain. Isn't that all that matters?'

'The whole court and everyone involved in this case is desperate to know.' Ebony took a sip of her water and pulled her gown over her shoulders. 'What happened after you and William went into your bedroom suite after dinner? Only the two of you were there. One of the two of you is dead, only you remain. Tell us what happened.'

The court had gone eerily quiet. Everyone was intently looking at Monica, who hesitated, looked to Charles for reassurance and said, 'His back really was hurting him again.' She hesitated again. 'He took some medication and died almost instantly.'

'You gave him the morphine, didn't you?'

Monica didn't answer. Justice Kane looked down at her and said, 'Lady Peveril, you must answer the question.'

'He died of a heart attack,' Monica shouted.

'You killed him so that you could be with your lover and inherit the money.'

'The money would not keep me for very long in the manner that William did.'

Ebony didn't want to be seen as bullying Monica, who had started her sobbing again, so said she had no more questions. The encounter between the two of them was more of a stalemate than a checkmate.

There were no more witnesses for the defence and the judge wished everyone a good weekend, with closing speeches starting on the Monday. This was going to be another weekend when Hannah and Sandy were not going to be together as on the Sunday, she was going to spend it with Ebony working on their closing speech. To compensate, Sandy was going to take his Morgan Roadster for a long drive on the Sunday.

∞

The first thing that Sandy did on getting to court on the Monday was wish Ebony the best of luck with her closing speech. Hannah grabbed his hand and lingered, holding it as if she were desperate for personal connection with him.

This was a move not missed by Ebony, who smiled knowingly at them both.

There was no sign of Rich as Ebony took to her feet. Apparently, he had a family crisis as one of his children was ill.

'Members of the jury.' Ebony said, smiling at them and totally enrapturing them, drawing them into her conversation. She was just like a schoolteacher with her small pupils all sitting around her in the classroom at the end of the school day while reading them a story. 'You have now heard all the evidence, and both I and the judge have reminded you on a number of occasions that the evidence is what you heard from the live witnesses or when Miss Tobias read an agreed statement to you.' Ebony nodded at the jury and they all nodded back at her.

'I am sure there are a number of things troubling you, and one of them is that of motive. The prosecution do not have to prove motive. It is not an essential element of the law. A motiveless murder is still murder if there is an intention to kill or seriously harm. Let me remind you that we have talked about love being a motive, greed for the money being a motive, Dr Adams not wanting to be cited in a messy divorce being a motive. However, what we have established is the means to commit murder, and that has totally been revealed in this case and is so overwhelming that the balance of the scales of justice does not need motive to tip it over for the defendants to be guilty.'

Ebony paused, needing the jury to take in her remarks. She looked around the court for a moment and then, taking another sip of her water, said, 'That means to murder is, of course, morphine. We, the prosecution, say, supplied by Henry Adams. How otherwise could Monica have got her hands on it? A drug that Henry knew only too well is dangerous beyond belief. The balance between giving the right amount to provide pain relief is too fine even sometimes for an experienced physician to manage. The intention to use morphine was as dangerous as a gun as a weapon for murder.'

Ebony paused and even the judge was nodding at her. Ebony Forbes-Hamilton was a master of the art of oratory, using her soft Scottish accent to its most powerful best. She continued. 'Occam's razor is a principle from as far back as the thirteenth century by a philosopher called William of Ockham. His principle gives precedence to simplicity. When there are two competing theories, the simpler explanation is to be preferred. The defence in this case will try and confuse you by multiplying the issues beyond necessity. That is not needed in this case. Keep your thinking to what is the simplest explanation. There is no dispute that William Peveril died of morphine toxicity. The heart attack is a red herring. Do not be taken in by it. The people that put that fatal dose of morphine into him' – she turned and pointed at the defendants in the dock – 'were those two, Monica Peveril and Henry Adams. They are guilty of murdering him.' Ebony then sat down.

Sandy wanted to clap and on looking around at Arabella, Monty, James and his wife Janice, who was in court today with him, they equally felt the same.

∞

The judge ordered a recess for a few moments and Sandy managed to speak to Rich on the phone to make sure he and his family were OK. It turned out that Rich's son had fallen off his bicycle and had broken his arm. Rich was in hospital with him when he took the call from Sandy. He explained how hard it was being a father, husband and detective all at the same time. This was one of those occasions when being a father and husband came first for a change. He was going to be in court the next day though.

The closing speech from Vaughan Slade on behalf of Henry Adams was brief. He was the king of brevity. Vaughan used one or two words where others would use a hundred. He never once mentioned morphine. He never once mentioned cardiac arrest or heart attack. He only mentioned William Peveril once. Sandy, after he finished, wondered what he had actually said, other than Henry was a wonderful doctor and was not present when William died.

The way that Charles Holloway rose to his feet left no one in any doubt that this was going to be the opposite of Vaughan's speech and they were in for a long session. Every time Charles made a point, he multiplied the point three- or four-fold. Ebony's point on Occam's razor had been totally lost on him. Sandy started after a while counting how many times, he said the words 'heart attack' or 'cardiac arrest': fourteen times he thought that Charles had said William died of a heart attack and eight times he mentioned cardiac arrest. Funnily enough, he didn't mention morphine at all.

Justice Kane told the jury and the court that his plan was to complete as much of his summing up as possible during the rest of the day. He would then conclude the next morning before sending the jury out to consider their verdict. When he mentioned this, Sandy felt the butterflies in his stomach start again.

Justice Kane, quite slowly, deliberately and

methodically read his notes from each day, of which was, as it turned out, a short trial. He covered each witness and what they had said. After he had covered all of the evidence, he turned to the law that the jury needed to think about in order to convict the defendants of murder. He said, 'The crime of murder is committed where a person is of sound mind (not medically mad), unlawfully kills (not self-defence or other justified killing, such as in war) any human being under the queen's peace (not in wartime), with intent to kill them or cause them grievous bodily harm. In this case, all you need to consider is whether Lady Peveril and Dr Adams intended to kill, or seriously harm, William Peveril.'

The next thing the judge said made Sandy worried. He knew that a discussion had taken place in court when he was not present, but he didn't agree with the judge mentioning it at this time. He wanted the jury to just focus on murder.

'As you know, we had a discussion before the defence case started about manslaughter as an alternative verdict, that could be returned in this case rather than murder. The Criminal Law Act 1967 provides that, in a case of murder, a person found not guilty may be found guilty of manslaughter. Although it may have been preferable to include these alternative offences on the indictment, that was not the case as the prosecution case was focussed on murder, and the defence case was that the defendants were not involved in an unlawful killing and would not offer a plea of guilty to manslaughter. I, as the trial judge, feel it is necessary to bring these alternatives, which we discussed earlier in the trial, to your attention. It is now pertinent to do so.'

Sandy looked around the court, firstly at the jury, who were listening intently to everything the judge said and not losing interest as he was talking about complex legal matters. That was good, he thought.

The judge continued by saying more about the law, this time about manslaughter. 'Where an unlawful killing is done without an intention to kill, or to cause grievous bodily harm, the defendants can be found guilty of manslaughter, not murder. Apart from the absence of intent, all other elements of the offence are the same as for murder. One of the types of involuntary manslaughter is that which is caused by the defendant's gross negligence, and another caused by his unlawful or dangerous act. You might think in this case that the use of morphine is both grossly negligent and dangerous. Another key element in this case is, have the prosecution established that the unlawful act, the administration of the morphine, was a cause of the death, and not a heart attack?'

Sandy had a sinking feeling that the judge had now moved on from giving the jury, and therefore Monica and Henry, a get-out from murder; he was now giving them a get-out from manslaughter. He was pleased when the judge stopped talking and told the jury to go home and have a good night's sleep and be ready in the morning to consider their verdicts.

Realising he was missing the calming and brotherly presence of his colleague Rich, he avoided going to talk to Hannah and Ebony but instead, Sandy went quickly out of the courtroom to see if the Peveril family were OK. Then he knew the person he needed to call was his Grandad Tom.

Chapter Thirty-Six

The next morning, Rich had still not arrived at court. He was, though, on his way with the head of media for the Derbyshire Police. On the train to London they were putting the finishing touches to the press statement that Rich would make after the court case. There were two versions: one, if found not guilty, and the other, if there were guilty verdicts.

The judge spent hardly any time finishing his summing up and giving the jury his final instructions. He then sent them out to consider their verdict.

The morning dragged by slowly and Sandy was glad when Rich arrived. He was even more pleased to see that he had brought Lofty with him. He hadn't seen him for a few days. Hannah and Ebony, as was the case with the rest of the barristers, had gone back to their robing room to work on cases they had coming up and start work on new cases. Hannah had told Sandy on the phone last night that she was in demand, and the clerk at her chambers was able to pass the requests for her services that she couldn't accommodate to other barristers in her chambers.

Arabella, Monty, James and Janice wanted to go back to Eaton Square but knew it was too far away to be back in court in time if there was a word that the jury had reached a verdict. Instead, they had gone out to a nearby café within which they had managed to almost set up a section as an office-type area. Both Arabella and James were busy getting through their backlog of emails and calls.

Lunchtime came and went, as did the afternoon. The judge, as the afternoon was almost over, sent the jury home for the night. There was a sombre mood over dinner with Rich, Sandy and Lofty not discussing the case. The highlight for Sandy was that Hannah had come to dinner that evening for the first time since the court case had started. Sandy didn't even mention her stopping over at the flat when she left slightly early to catch her train.

The judge the next morning asked the jury if they were close to making a unanimous decision. He was told they were not. He told them he wanted them to try really hard to all agree but if they couldn't before lunch, he would consider discussing with them a majority verdict.

Lunchtime arrived and the judge invited the jury back into court. He told them that he would now allow them to make a majority decision and to go out and consider this. The forewoman of the jury stood up and said, 'We have already reached a majority decision.'

Justice Kane scanned the court and could see that the Peveril family was present. There was an incredible buzz of anticipation filtering around the court. Hannah turned and looked at Sandy and smiled. Sandy tried hard not to hold Rich's hand, he felt that nervous.

The court clerk asked the defendants to stand, then said, 'On the count of murder against Monica Peveril, how do you find the defendant?'

'Not guilty,' the foreman said.

Sandy was stunned. He had a sick feeling developing in his stomach. He looked straight at Arabella but she seemed accepting of the verdict and just nodded at him. They hardly heard the same count put to the forewoman for

Henry Adams but knew before she said anything that it would be 'not guilty', which it was.

The judge said, 'What was the majority split?'

'Ten to two, your lordship.'

Arabella and the rest of the family started to get up to leave the court but then sat down when the clerk asked if they had reached a verdict on the alternative charge. The forewoman said, 'Yes, and this was unanimous.'

Rich looked at Sandy and whispered to him, 'That only makes sense if it is what I think the verdict is going to be.' He didn't have to wait long.

'On the count of manslaughter for the defendant Monica Peveril, how do you find the defendant, guilty or not guilty?'

'Guilty, and as I said, this was unanimous.'

'On the count of manslaughter against the defendant Henry Adams?'

'Guilty. This was the decision of us all.'

The Peveril family seemed to be over the moon with the verdicts and were smiling and hugging each other. Sandy could see that the tears had started to flow for Arabella.

Ebony leant back and grabbed Hannah's hand tightly, smiling intently at her. Rich was really pleased. Even though he thought he wouldn't be, Sandy was actually extremely pleased. His conversation with his Grandad Tom had resolved everything for him. Tom had told him that a detective's job was to put the case together with every inch of skill, guile and effort, but when it got to court, it was the job of the lawyers, the judge and jury to determine the result, not the detective. Manslaughter was homicide. It was an unlawful killing and an incredible result if that was the end result. Gosh, Sandy loved his grandparents.

The defendants in the dock, Monica and Henry, sat there emotionless. It would appear that as soon as the judge spoke about manslaughter as an alternative, their lawyers had been preparing them for this as an outcome.

∞

The judge ordered a recess until two p.m. He thanked the defence and probation service for having their reports on each of the defendants ready and he would read them over the lunch recess. He said he wished to start with the victim impact statement.

As they couldn't find a room large enough, the barristers, the detectives and the Peveril family all stood in a huddle at the far end of the court building, almost at the back end of the great dome in the Old Bailey. The setting had an incredible historical feel to it.

Ebony took centre stage. 'I do believe, without Monica telling us exactly what happened in that room that evening and what her intention was, that manslaughter is an acceptable verdict. I do hope,' she said, looking around at the family, 'that you feel that we have achieved justice for your father.'

Arabella was the first to speak. 'We really do, thank you. This has not been pleasant for us, which seems crazy for me to say this, as I was the one that started it all.' She looked directly at Sandy and said, 'Thank you.'

After a lot of hugs all round, where Sandy and Hannah waited to hug each other last, everyone went off for a quick lunch. Rich sat down with Sandy and went through his media statement.

Viscount James Peveril walked slowly and deliberately

into the witness box. He was always going to be the one that represented the family to give their victim impact statement. Although he was a lawyer, a politician and a viscount, in that moment he was a son who had lost his father.

'I will try not to make this a eulogy because that is not what it is supposed to be, but if I slip into talking like this, I am sorry, but I am just my father's boy. This is our family's victim impact statement. William Harrison Peveril was taken too soon, taken from his family before his time. He was unlawfully killed and taken from us.' James stood upright in the witness box, looking mostly at the judge as he spoke, but also at times glancing around the court to get everyone to feel they were in this moment with him.

'I remember the words of the song Cats in the Cradle. These words resonated with us and no doubt a lot of families throughout the land. When Arabella and I were very young, we used to ask him those words: "When you coming home, Dad?" To which he would reply, "I don't know when." We would say, "We will get together then, Dad, we will have a good time then." Obviously, this was then reversed as Arabella and I grew up and went off to university. I am sure we let him down when our mother was ill and then sadly died so young. We were too busy with our own lives to realise that our father, the charismatic, confident and wonderful man he was, was now a broken man. If we had realised this, maybe we could have helped him not to descend into two disastrous marriages, from one of which the wife took his life unlawfully.' James, as he said this, looked straight at Monica. She kept his gaze and never blinked or broke it.

'I know that my father loved Arabella and I deeply. He

always felt Monty was the perfect husband for her. He felt their pain when they were not able to have children. He was so proud of everything she did, not just her incredible business acumen but just the person she is.' A sob was heard in court coming from Arabella; her promise to hold it together had been broken.

James undeterred continued. 'My father loved his three grandchildren incredibly, a feeling that they knew and reciprocated. He was loved, not just in Derbyshire where he had been the High Sheriff twice, but throughout the country. As for me, I will miss him every day and every moment when I suddenly think of him. I have this lunchtime resigned from my role as an MP with immediate effect. The chair of my parliamentary constituency is distraught and Sir Kier Starmer, the leader of the party, has, with his regret, accepted my resignation. I will miss this role incredibly but I intend to continue my father's legacy and become the chair and president of all of his charities and make them my life's work. Dad, you were taken too soon from us, your life was cruelly and unlawfully shortened, but who you were will live on through me, Arabella and your grandchildren. I love you.'

∞

It was amazing how little Charles Holloway had to say in mitigation for Monica. In fact, it was quite sad that Monica had no one that made a personal reference for her.

Vaughan Slade on the other hand told them he had over one hundred personal references and would just highlight a few key ones. He had never spoken so much in one go for the whole of the trial.

The clerk instructed both of the defendants to stand. Justice Kane had strong words with them about how reckless and dangerous they had been with another human being's life.

'I do not know which of you I think is the most culpable. I have struggled with this for different reasons, that one of you must be more culpable than the other. I therefore think it appropriate to sentence both of you to ten years' imprisonment. Take them down.'

As Monica and Henry went down the stairs to the cells, they showed no emotion and made no comment. Justice Kane turned to the jury and thanked them for their service. He thanked the Peveril family for the dignity they had shown throughout the trial. He commended the key Operation Cornflower team, which included Sandy, Juliet, Rich and Lofty.

They all went outside the court to watch and listen to Rich, and then James, give their statements to the large number of press and media that were waiting outside the court.

An upstairs room of a pub in Fleet Street was where the team assembled next. Ebony had organised and was paying for a meal and drinks for them. The CPS lawyer, Ebony and Hannah were present and all sat at one end. Rich, Lofty, Sandy, Juliet and Clare made up the remaining members of the group.

The atmosphere at dinner was more celebratory than victorious. There had been extraordinarily little banter or laughter until Juliet stood and said, 'A toast for absent friends.' She raised her glass. 'To Saffron Dupont, our quirky, clever and loyal friend.' They all said, 'To Saffron.'

Rich toasted a couple of the other members of the

Operation Cornflower team who weren't present. Ebony stood and said, 'To Antoine Chevalier, who was the first person in all my years as a barrister that I have heard sing the oath when they gave evidence.' This brought lots of laughter around the table and shouts and someone raised a toast to Claudette and Suzanne Valadon.

Sandy rose and said, 'I toast my grandfathers, John and Tom.' There were mostly confused looks around the table but Rich and Hannah both said, 'To John and Tom.'

This happy mood continued with Nicholas Stroud and Arthur Ramsbottom being mentioned next. Juliet produced a couple of copies of the magazine of the *Daily Mail's* Saturday edition, which had a six-page spread of the court artist's pictures of Monica and her different designer dresses. Monica's mother had also been interviewed and told the journalist where each dress had come from. There was no doubting what Monica was angling to do when she was released from prison in too short a time in the future. The laughter in the room reached a crescendo when someone mentioned the Bob and Pete interview with Monica.

As everyone started to filter away and leave, Hannah went and sat next to Sandy. She took both his hands in hers and said, 'I know when I said no to staying over in the flat with you for the trial that you probably felt quite hurt.' Sandy went to speak but Hannah stopped him. 'OK, you were at least very confused that I said no. I just knew how it would be working together in court and that conflict might arise from time to time. I think we should avoid working together in the future and not be work colleagues but two people in a personal relationship.' Sandy smiled at her understanding exactly what she meant.

Hannah continued by saying, 'I just want to say that whatever you want from our relationship, I am in, I am all in.'

Before Sandy could reply, his phone started buzzing. It was Arabella Montague. Instead of saying what Hannah hoped he would say, Sandy said, 'It's Arabella, I really should take this call to make sure they are all OK.'

Hannah nodded and Sandy said, 'Arabella, what is it? Are you all OK?'

'My neighbour Vivienne Jones has fallen overboard from a yacht just off the coast of Barbados. She is missing and her husband Adam has just rang me from a police station in Bridgetown asking if you can help?'

Author's Note

I spent over thirty years as a police officer and the majority of these years were as a detective. I served as a detective in every rank, finally spending my last six years as the detective chief superintendent (head of the detective branch) of the Cambridgeshire Constabulary. As a detective, I led over a hundred major crime cases, a number of which were homicides or suspicious deaths. I absolutely loved this opportunity. The rank I enjoyed most though was the rank that Alexander McFarlane holds, that of a DCI. I am best known for my work as a detective around the UK for my role, over many years, as the national policing lead for the investigation of child death, as well as for my role as the senior investigator at the deposition site for the recovery and forensic investigation into the deaths of Holly Wells and Jessica Chapman, two ten-year-old girls from Soham, who were murdered by Ian Huntley.

In October 2019, my wife Debbie and I had a chance encounter in a remote hilltop village in the Atlas Mountains (Morocco) with a couple from Melbourne – Professor Anne Buist and her partner Graeme Simsion. They are both authors and were working on a romantic comedy novel together. Graeme authored the bestselling novel *The Rosie Project*. When I told him I had a detective crime novel in mind, he proceeded to give me a fifteen-minute masterclass on how to author a novel. Coincidently, both Professor

Buist and I were to be keynote speakers at a conference two weeks later in Melbourne, relating to children who had been murdered by a parent. This chance meeting cemented my thoughts to author the novel I had been talking about for years.

This didn't occur, however, until the first lockdown arrived due to the COVID-19 pandemic. Even though I was still busy with my safeguarding work and writing a number of reviews, I decided to write a first draft of a novel during this period. That novel, *Greed is a Powerful Motive*, and the second one, *Missing but not Lost* have been published by my brilliant publisher Cranthorpe Millner.

A lot of people will think that the inspiration for this story came from the case of Harold Shipman and they would of course be right, but not completely right as another key inspiration was the case of Dr John Bodkin Adams. A number of years ago, when visiting Hardwick Hall in Derbyshire (Hardwick Hall is, in my mind, my fictional Peveril Hall), I mistakenly read that in 1950, Edward Cavendish, the 10th Duke of Devonshire, had died unexpectedly after he had been visited by a GP called John Bodkin Adams. The mistake was that I thought I'd read that this had happened in the south of France. So, while plotting this story, my creative mind settled on Saint-Émilion near Bordeaux in France. However, it was the south coast of England in Eastbourne that he had actually died, not France. My mind was set though and I kept with Chateau Peveril and Saint-Émilion.

All of the characters in the novel are fictional. I have, though, used a number of themes from the original cases: the place where William Peveril was buried was in the same churchyard as the Duke of Devonshire in Edensor, Derbyshire; the method of death was the same one, morphine toxicity; I used the name Henry for my doctor (people with this first name are sometimes called Harry and of course Harry is short for Harold); I used the same middle name, Fredrick, as is Harold Shipman's middle name; and, of course, I used the surname of Adams for my doctor. The Shipman case started with a 'gut feeling', as did my story.

I look forward to continuing DCI Alexander (Sandy) McFarlane's story in the future with his investigation into the movie star who has gone overboard off the coast of Barbados.

Acknowledgements

To my wife Debbie, who is and has always been my greatest supporter in all that I do. Debbie was the first to read this novel and then painstakingly helped me to carry out a first edit for every page of it. For this and everything, I am truly grateful.

To all my family: my mother Florence; my children Daniel, Rebecca and Matthew; and my father-in-law Sydney Barton and sister-in-law Ruth Chaplain-Barton for reading and commenting on the story.

Also, to my close friends who have taken the time to read the novel and to give me feedback. Thank you to Judi Richardson, Lorri and John Kendall (my Canadian family), Joanne Procter, Andrew Harrison (my writing and sourdough buddy), David Marshall (my work buddy), Angela and Mark Craig (my friends, but also my daughter's mother- and father-in-law), James Bambridge, Jane Ashton, Glenys Johnston, Mike Richardson, Mark Birch and Wendi Ogle-Welbourn.

I would also like to thank Dr Nat Cary (Forensic Pathologist), Sonya Bayliss and Nick Casey for their knowledge and experience in assisting me with my research into exhumations and subsequent post-mortems. Thank you also to Tim Cowley, owner of Rustic Vines, for his tour and advice in relation to the chateaux, wine (lots of tastings!), and scenery around Saint-Émilion, France.